Where did he go...?

Annja peered around the edge of the reef and the shadow was gone.

It really was almost as if the unknown figure had disappeared right off the coral reef.

What were the chances that he'd been taken by a shark? She shook her head. No, there'd be some sort of evidence of an attack. His oxygen tanks would be lying on the ocean floor. His weight belt would have been shredded.

Annja's mouth went dry and she glanced down at her oxygen gauge.

It was running close to empty.

She needed to get back to the boat. But in the next instant, she knew where the shadow had vanished to.

He'd resurfaced.

The boat engine roared overhead, its sound muffled through the water, but Annja glanced up and saw the white foam as the boat suddenly shot back the way they had come out.

Leaving Annja all alone in the dark ocean.

11066725

Titles in this series:

ROGUE Angel

Alex Archer

THE ORACLE'S
MESSAGE

A GOLD EAGLE BOOK FROM

WORLDWIDE®

TORONTO • NEW YORK • LONDON
AMSTERDAM • PARIS • SYDNEY • HAMBURG
STOCKHOLM • ATHENS • TOKYO • MILAN
MADRID • WARSAW • BUDAPEST • AUCKLAND

Recycling programs
for this product may
not exist in your area.

First edition September 2011

ISBN-13: 978-0-373-62151-4

THE ORACLE'S MESSAGE

Special thanks and acknowledgment to
Jon Merz for his contribution to this work.

Printed in U.S.A.

The
LEGEND

...THE ENGLISH COMMANDER TOOK
JOAN'S SWORD AND RAISED IT HIGH.
The broadsword, plain and unadorned,
gleamed in the firelight. He put the tip against
the ground and his foot at the center of the blade.
The broadsword shattered, fragments falling
into the mud. The crowd surged forward,
peasant and soldier, and snatched the shards
from the trampled mud. The commander tossed
the hilt deep into the crowd.
Smoke almost obscured Joan, but she continued
praying till the end, until finally the flames climbed
her body and she sagged against the restraints.

Joan of Arc died that fateful day in France,
but her legend and sword are reborn....

1

The turquoise waters of the South China Sea swirled into the flow of the Mindoro Strait and the Sulu Sea to the south, bobbing the small catamaran over gentle swells. The motion was almost hypnotizing to a very tired but very relaxed Annja Creed as she steered toward the GPS coordinates she'd punched in for a little-visited coral reef off the northeastern part of Palawan in the Philippines.

She'd fled New York City two days earlier, amid a stretch of work that had left her positively drained and eager for any excuse to leave town. Sharing a bottle of Santa Margherita pinot grigio with her good friend Bart McGilley, she'd remembered that she'd wanted to go diving in the Philippines for a long time. On her last trip there, the terrorist group Abu Sayyaf had cut that dream short by taking her hostage and Annja had seen a lot more of the tropical rain-forest jungles of the south than she ever wanted to see again.

In the wake of her experience, she'd found out that the government had rounded up a lot of the Abu Sayyaf followers and most experts considered the group fairly neutralized.

Annja knew there was a chance they'd regroup, but for the time being, they were content to lie low.

And that seemed like enough of an opening for Annja.

The twenty-two-hour flight from New York with a brief layover in Osaka, Japan, had left her even more tired, but the thought of some alone time and diving at the little-known coral reef inspired her.

She'd flown from Manila to the southwest island of Palawan, jutting out into the South China Sea. She and her fellow tourists had landed on a small dusty airstrip that looked like it might have been used for smuggling, transferred to a jeepney—one of the gaudily decorated World War II U.S. Army jeeps that had been converted into buses—and bounced their way through a stretch of jungle down to a river.

On the river, a small boat snaked along the tributary until they emerged into a bay. Once there, they transferred to a larger boat that skimmed its way across the waves toward the island of Apulit. As they'd neared the shore, Annja heard music and saw the resort workers coming down to the beach strumming guitars and bearing trays of fruity drinks.

One sip told Annja that Club Noah was going to be an absolute delight. The tiny resort consisted of just forty cabanas perched on stilts over the gently lapping waves of the little U-shaped bay.

Annja spent her first few hours ditching the last remnants of her overly stressed world by having a few more of the incredibly refreshing and intoxicating fruity welcome drinks and by taking a long nap in a beach hammock. The breeze blowing in from the beach rocked the hammock and Annja had passed out. After a quiet evening exploring the beach and resort she retired to her cabana for a good night's sleep.

When she awoke the next morning, she polished off a large breakfast and then made plans to rent a small boat and diving gear. The dive master had not wanted her to go off alone, but Annja had insisted and eventually handed him a hundred-dollar bill that convinced him.

She knew that diving alone wasn't very safety conscious, but she'd done it enough times that she no longer felt worried about the possibility of something happening that she couldn't resolve. She'd faced down danger enough times to know her own abilities. By 10:00 a.m. she was happily sailing out to the dive spot alone and on her own terms.

She was roughly two miles offshore, and the tiny island sitting far off in the distance seemed a lot farther away than she'd expected it, too. Briefly, she reconsidered whether she should have brought the dive master along. But then she shrugged it off and set about readying herself for the dive.

Annja let the small anchor over the side and attached the dive flag to it so anyone coming near would know there were divers in the water. The last thing she wanted was a large boat steaming over her as she explored the area.

Annja stripped off the clothes she'd worn on the way out. The sun overhead blazed down and she felt the first beads of sweat starting to form along her hairline. It would be good to get into the water.

She strapped the weight belt around her waist and checked to make sure it was secure. A quick look at the oxygen tank gauge assured her that it hadn't leaked since she'd checked it onshore. She slid into the gear and tightened the straps around her shoulders. The open-circuit gear was the most commonly used around the world and Annja had no problems checking to make sure the oxygen flow was good.

She slid a pair of flippers on her feet and put her face mask into the water, smearing the inside of the glass before settling the mask on her face. She checked the straps around her head and sucked in, testing the seal.

The catamaran bobbed in place and Annja sat on the edge of the far side of the boat, away from the anchor. Looking around, she could see a boat in the distance, but it was too far away to be of any concern to her.

Other than that, she was alone.

Here we go, she thought.

And with that, she leaned back and pitched over into the water.

She'd decided not to wear a diving suit, opting instead for just her one-piece bathing suit. She figured the water wouldn't be too cold, and she was right. As the sea enveloped her, she felt its cooling effect on her body. But it was still at least seventy-five degrees, if not closer to eighty. She suspected there would be cooler currents and warmer currents, given the proximity of the island to three different bodies of water.

She blew out and tested all her seals. All good. She descended slowly. In this area, the water depth was only about fifty feet.

Immediately, she saw schools of brilliantly colored fish dart away from her. Pilot fish swam closer and in the distance she spotted clown fish zipping through the water.

About twenty feet below her, Annja made out a brilliant array of bright pink coral. Her eyes widened when she saw the lush life swirling around the structure. A moray eel seemed to sense her approach and ducked back inside after opening its mouth and showing her a wide array of needle-sharp teeth.

I wouldn't want to get a hand caught on any of those, she thought.

She allowed the weight belt to pull her down, only occasionally kicking her flippers. The tug of the current moved her gradually to the side and Annja had to right herself to keep on the level heading she wanted.

Unlike a lot of coral reefs, the one Annja now approached was classified as a small table reef, meaning it was mostly isolated and didn't have a lagoon nearby. As she descended farther, Annja could see the incredible biodiversity present. Starfish littered one side of the reef, while saddleback butterfly fish with their distinctive black markings on their backs wove and dodged nearby.

A school of triggerfish passed close by, each one seeming to inspect Annja as if she was some unknown intruder.

Annja spotted more clown fish and marveled at the brilliant orange of their scales.

A dark shape passed in the periphery of her vision and Annja's heart beat faster for a moment until she turned.

She spotted a grouper.

Annja considered them to be an ugly fish, the way they floated through the darker waters, with their mouths opening and closing and their dead eyes locked on to whatever they happened to be swimming toward.

If she hadn't known better, she might have felt a twinge of fear. But groupers, for all their horrid appearance, presented no threat. And Annja had a sharp diver's knife strapped low on her right leg, just in case.

She almost laughed. And if that didn't work, she thought, she could simply bring her sword out. She felt sure that would take care of pretty much any threat the sea could throw at her.

Her breathing had settled down nicely, her inhalations coming slow and steady as she felt the last of her cares slip away for the moment. This was what she'd wanted for so long and to think that she was finally there, drinking it all in. Annja had left the rest of the world above and behind her.

She felt great.

She drifted deeper and could see the powder-white sand on the floor of the ocean where it met the edge of the coral reef. As she suspected, the water was a little cooler there, and she moved back toward the warmer waters, aware that she'd have to make sure she didn't stay too long. She knew she'd risk hypothermia if her core temperature came down too much.

This dive was about reconnaissance, anyway. She had just wanted to get out and find the reef, take note of some of its features and then prepare to come back over the next few days for more investigative work. Documenting this reef and its life would make for a fun project and it would totally take her mind off the work she'd left back in New York City.

She blew out a stream of bubbles that floated skyward. She glanced up and saw the bright sunlight filtering down toward where she bobbed close by the edge of the coral.

A school of powder-blue surgeonfish seemed to be buzzing close by a section of coral and Annja could see they were dining on the algae that had encrusted one portion of the reef.

The levels of life here were simply amazing. Annja could see how coral reefs accounted for so many of the ocean's species cohabitating in close proximity to one another. The reefs themselves supplied a level of food that brought small fish. And the small fish attracted larger fish that dined on them.

And so it went up the food chain.

Right to the apex predators.

Annja steered herself left and saw the sharp spikes of a crimson-colored crown of thorns starfish atop an outcropping of coral. The notoriously voracious starfish dined on the coral and Annja wondered how long it would take to reduce the outcropping until it was level with the rest of the reef.

She heard the faint sound of a motor and glanced up toward the water's surface. Perhaps the boat she'd spotted in the distance earlier had moved closer. She thought she spotted a dark shape closer to the surface, but dismissed it as a shadow.

It was probably caused by a cloud, she thought.

She turned her attention back to the reef.

Long spindly tendrils of sea grass waved to and fro as the current moved it about. Annja spotted smaller clown fish threading their way through the stalks, no doubt trying to use it to hide themselves from predators.

I wish I'd brought my camera, she thought then. The images in front of her face were truly incredible.

Still, there'd be time enough for that. She had a week at the Club Noah resort before she'd be forced to return to the hustle and bustle of her daily existence.

That was seven days away, though. And she didn't want to spend her time thinking of what the return to her world would do to her outlook on life.

No, she was here now and that was what was most important.

She turned back toward where she'd been watching the clown fish. But the little guys were gone.

She drew closer to the sea grass and peered inside.

She spotted a clown fish huddled farther back, closer to the wall of coral that was behind it.

Annja frowned. Is it me that's got him spooked?

The answer to her question came a moment later as a jackfish shot past her face mask, through the sea grass and gobbled up the poor clown fish. Annja saw the blur of movement, but had hardly enough time to register the effect.

One second, the clown fish was there; the next, it was simply gone.

The jackfish didn't hang around, either.

Life on the reef, she thought. Everyone's got to eat.

Annja looked around again. She realized the motor noise had stopped, but she didn't see any other anchors leading down to the bottom. Just hers. So there was no one else in the area.

She felt a sense of unease she couldn't explain. She checked her oxygen gauge and saw she still had plenty left.

A moment later she felt herself torpedoed from behind and thrust into the sharp coral face itself.

2

The impact of the blow from behind sent Annja into the coral face-first. Her mask came loose and slipped off.

Annja slammed her eyes shut and took a breath.

What the hell hit me?

She flailed about in the water, feeling around for her mask. Calm down, she told herself, it's here somewhere. She felt to the right and found the mask.

Bringing it over her head, she started purging the water from it by sucking in air through her regulator and then blowing out through her nose, hoping she could get the water level down so she could at least open her eyes.

She sensed the movement around her and fought to keep herself from panicking; her heart thundered in her chest as she kept purging the mask.

And then she felt the water level drop below her lids and she risked opening her eyes.

A dark maw of razor-sharp teeth filled her view.

Annja jerked herself to the side as the giant body shot past her. In her periphery, she saw the dark vertical stripes and now her pulse raced.

A tiger shark.

They called them the garbage cans of the deep. Annja's brain ran down the laundry list of facts she knew about them. *Galeocerdo cuvier* in Latin, they were one of the most dangerous sharks in the ocean, second only to the great white. They were predators, and dozens of human deaths had been attributed to them over the years. They were well known in the South Pacific and the waters of the Philippines, although Annja hadn't thought there'd be much chance of one being here near the reef.

That would account for the lack of other sharks around the reef, though, she thought. Normally, there'd be other species—especially reef sharks, blacktips and others more at home near the coral.

This guy must have frightened them off.

And now, getting some distance from her pursuer, Annja could see why. The shark was massive, at least fourteen feet running from the tip of its blunt snout to the notch in its tail.

She took another breath and kept blowing out through her nose, clearing more of the water from her mask. She'd need her eyesight in order to get out of this scrape unscathed.

The tiger shark swam in lazy circles around the reef, but always kept Annja in his vision.

She ran her hand down her right leg and freed the knife from its sheath. The serrated edge could cut into the tough shark hide without much problem. But in order to do that, Annja would have to get close.

Really close.

She took another few breaths and then watched as the shark suddenly turned and shot away from the reef, its dark striped form vanishing as it gained distance from the reef.

Was it gone?

Annja frowned. She'd heard about this particular tactic

before. The tiger shark would sometimes leave, hoping to entice its target into the open only to return and attack more violently than before.

I've got time, Annja thought. And I won't fall for that move.

She kept her back to the coral and the knife up in front of her. After two minutes of bobbing in the water, she was forced to confront the idea that maybe the shark had grown bored and left.

Annja looked around the reef. Some of the smaller fish had returned. But the jacks and grouper were nowhere to be seen. And there were no turtles anywhere close by, either.

A dark shape shot past her and she knew the tiger shark was back. It had gone overhead, close, and Annja had ducked down to avoid it.

It turned itself around and she marveled at how perfectly streamlined its body was. It looked like a banking fighter jet as it came in closer again. Its eyes never left her, but Annja had found a reasonable spot from which she could defend herself, if necessary.

If you're going to attack me, she thought, you'll have to commit and come in.

That would give her the opening she'd need to take it on.

But fourteen feet worth of apex predator wasn't an even match, she decided. The tiger shark could cut her in half without much effort.

Suddenly the knife looked pitifully small in her hand.

Annja sensed the attack instead of seeing it. The shark shot straight at her, coming in hard and fast, seemingly unconcerned about the coral.

Or the knife.

Annja shot up and brought the knife down, embedding it on the top of the shark's snout. It jerked once, wrenched the knife free from Annja's hand and then swam away, a thin tendril of blood trailing behind.

Annja sucked in air and tried to still her hammering heart.

She glanced down and more worry seeped into her as her oxygen gauge showed that she'd have to surface soon.

That would mean leaving the relative protection of the reef.

Overhead, her boat looked far away.

And small.

Annja looked around, but the shark had vanished again. I hope that knife hurts like hell, she thought.

The level on her gauge continued to drop.

Annja was going to have to make a run for it.

I'm not doing this alone, she thought.

She summoned the mystical sword she'd somehow inherited from Joan of Arc, and the gleaming blade was snug in her hands, right where she wanted it to be.

She looked around but couldn't see the tiger shark anywhere.

It was time to go but the problem was that on the ascent she'd have to rise no faster than her air bubbles. To rush it, she'd be risking the bends—when her body couldn't get rid of the nitrogen in her blood. That could be as fatal as being attacked by the shark. She was only in about fifty feet of water, but she still had to maintain proper protocol.

That meant she'd be exposed for what would feel like an awfully long time.

But the level of oxygen she had was dwindling and she'd have to go for it, regardless of the risk from the shark.

Another quick glance and Annja kicked off, her fins churning behind her as she rose from the coral reef.

Instantly, she felt the presence of the shark, as if it'd been waiting behind the coral for her to show herself.

It came fast as Annja drifted higher.

She could see the rows of teeth in its mouth as it came toward her like a missile. Annja brought the sword up in front of her and swiped it through the water. It felt like she was moving in slow motion, though, cutting through the liquid of the ocean.

Still, it sliced into the tiger's snout before the shark suddenly backed away and shot back down toward the reef.

Annja turned her eyes up and judged she was perhaps halfway to the surface. Her bubbles rose faster than she did, but only just. Annja didn't want to remain underwater any longer than necessary.

The grim expression of the dive master lurked in her memory. She could hear his scolding now, telling her how foolish she'd been to go diving alone. Annja frowned. Maybe it had been foolish, but maybe she'd needed to do it.

She looked back just in time to see the tiger shark lurking near the seafloor. Annja's diving knife still poked out of the top of its snout. Annja wondered if the shark would spend the rest of its days with that blade permanently planted there.

She kicked some more and cut the distance to the surface. Her heart was thundering and Annja tasted stale air.

Her tank was almost empty.

She glanced back and scarcely had time to bring the sword up as the shark rammed into her again.

Her regulator was knocked free and Annja had only a second to grab the last gulp of air before the hose was ripped away by the rush of movement.

Annja tried to put it back in her mouth but the hose was torn open. A slow stream of bubbles was being released from the tank on her back.

So much for that, she thought.

Annja shrugged one side of her straps free and then the other.

The tank fell down toward the reef, trailing the last bits of air behind it.

Annja jerked around and saw that the tiger shark was level with her at a distance of maybe fifty feet.

She brought the sword up in front of her.

The tiger shark's eyes seemed to register the threat but cared little about it. Annja was on the menu and it meant to finish this.

It glided at her so smoothly that Annja barely registered the movement, so streamlined was the shark's body that it caused no disturbance in the water. All that did register was the fact that the shark suddenly seemed to grow in size.

Time slowed.

Annja marveled at the magnificence of the creature coming to try to kill her. The teeth so perfectly suited for cracking sea-turtle shells were also perfect for shredding human skin and bone.

And then it seemed to gather more speed.

Annja readied herself and felt her body take over. She cut up, stabbing right at the tiger shark, and plunged the sword straight into the shark's nose. She knew that all sharks had sophisticated electrical sensory systems in their snouts, and she hoped by attacking it so savagely the shark would virtually short-circuit.

The effect was instantaneous. The shark seemed to stand straight up on its tail in the water and then jerked back, freeing itself from Annja's sword. A dark flow of blood spilled into the water, clouding Annja's vision.

And then the shark turned and shot away, trailing blood behind it.

Annja looked overhead and saw she was only eight feet below the surface. She kicked, surfaced and gasped air into her starved lungs.

Her boat bobbed on a swell a few yards away and she clawed through the surf toward it, willing the sword away to the otherwhere with the power of her mind.

As she reached the catamaran, she felt herself rise up as something struck the boat from below.

The shark hadn't fled, after all.

Damn, Annja thought.

Disregarding the boat, she ducked back under the surface and saw the tiger shark, grievously wounded, circling around, preparing for another attack.

Annja summoned her sword and waited.

The shark had a look that told her it would attack her until one of them was dead.

There would be no quarter.

Annja steeled herself and the shark came at her, moving with an almost supernatural level of speed through the water.

Annja bent backward as the shark's jaws snapped close by her head. She saw its belly pass over her face and plunged the sword as far as it would go into the underside of the massive beast.

The blade cut deep, scoring a line across the belly. Entrails slipped out while blood spewed into the ocean around her, turning everything dark and cloudy.

Annja imagined that she heard a deep rumbling gasp from the shark and then it simply turned over and slipped away from her.

Dead.

She watched it sink down to the ocean floor. Instead of Annja being its dinner tonight, the tiger shark would be dinner for the smaller fish around the reef.

Annja nodded grimly. There was no joy in killing the magnificent beast, but she'd had no choice.

She turned toward the surface and broke through, again taking a deep breath of air. She turned toward her boat, but misjudged the distance. In the choppy water she was thrust forward and knocked her head on part of the catamaran.

She saw stars and felt blackness rushing for her.

Her final thought before she slipped under the waves was that at least she'd killed the tiger shark.

Somehow, death by drowning seemed better than being eaten by a shark.

3

She heard voices. That was enough to tell her she wasn't underwater.

But was she dead?

"Miss?"

She opened an eye and found a tanned, handsome face staring into her own. Judging by the scar on his cheek, he'd seen some sort of fighting at one point in his life. But there was an eagerness in his expression that told her he was very concerned.

She tried to speak but coughed instead. A bottle of water found its way to her lips and she took a greedy gulp, coughing some more and letting the better part of it dribble all over her face.

"Easy, easy." His voice was strong and soothing.

Annja smiled. "I guess I'm not dead, after all."

"Almost. But not quite."

Annja propped herself up on one elbow and saw she was in a boat, one much larger than her catamaran. "What happened to my boat?"

"It sunk."

Annja frowned and then remembered that the tiger shark had rammed the pitifully small catamaran. And when she'd surfaced after killing the shark, she must have hit her head against a piece of it. She felt her head and found the large bruise. She winced at the touch as pain sliced through her body.

"You'll need to get that looked at, I suspect."

Annja touched the spot again. The skin was bloated, swollen, and felt a little mushy to the touch. But she thought it was probably nothing worse than a bad knock. "I'll be all right."

"For a moment, you weren't."

She looked into his eyes and then smiled. "My name's Annja."

"Hans."

"You're German?" She could hear the accent now.

"I am."

Annja sat up and saw another couple of men sitting in the boat looking at her with a mixture of amusement and concern. "I'm on your boat, I take it?"

Hans nodded. "We saw the commotion in the water, saw your diving flag and wondered if you might be in some sort of danger."

Annja shrugged. "Tiger shark."

Hans started. "A tiger shark? You're sure?"

"I know those stripes, Hans. Trust me."

"How did you get away?"

Annja shook her head. "I didn't. I killed him instead."

That brought a low murmur from the other men on the boat. Hans smiled. "How large was the shark?"

"Probably fourteen feet. Give or take a few inches."

"And you killed it? With what?"

Annja almost said something about the sword but caught herself. "I had a diver's knife with me."

"That must have been some knife," Hans said.

"I stabbed the shark in the head with it over and over until it died."

"You're quite a remarkable woman, Annja."

"I don't feel so remarkable right now." Annja groaned. The bobbing of the boat, which wouldn't have bothered her if she'd been uninjured, now made her intensely nauseous.

Hans moved out of the way just in time as Annja rushed forward and vomited into the sea. After heaving a few more times, she leaned back and wiped her mouth. "Got any more of that water?"

Hans handed her the bottle and held up his hand. "Perhaps you shouldn't drink it quite so fast this time."

Annja nodded. "Yeah, that would be good idea." She swirled the water around in her mouth and then spat it out along with the taste of bile. She took another sip and tried to hand the bottle back to Hans.

But the German only held up his hand. "That's fine. You can keep that bottle. We have more."

Annja smiled. "Not into sharing with the damsel in distress?"

Hans shrugged. "Well, ordinarily, I would not mind. But seeing as you have just, uh, purged…"

"Yeah," Annja said. "I don't blame you."

Hans leaned closer. "Where is the person who was diving with you?"

Annja shook her head. "It was just me."

"You? Alone?"

"Yeah."

Hans whistled. "You are either incredibly brave or rather foolish."

Annja eyed him. "Probably a little of both. But I'm an expert diver. I didn't see anything wrong with going it alone."

Hans shook his head. "Anything can happen under the

waves. As you found out. I hate to think what would have happened to you if we hadn't been in the area."

"I would have died," Annja said.

Hans looked at her. But seeing nothing in Annja's face that betrayed a sense of weakness, he merely sighed. "I think that would have been a shame."

"I agree," Annja said. She glanced around the boat. Oxygen tanks, regulators and fins were stacked neatly nearby. "You guys going diving, too?"

"We were."

"Were?"

"Well, before we found you. Our diving plans will now take on a secondary importance until we determine you are safe."

"I'm safe."

Hans pointed at her head. "I would rather have a medical doctor make that decision, Annja."

Annja frowned. "I know my limitations, Hans. I'll be all right."

"Still." Hans smiled. "You are on my boat right now. And I shall make the decisions. Now, you're free to stay aboard, accept my hospitality and the ride back to the resort. You're staying at Club Noah, I presume?"

"I am."

"Excellent. In that case, we can take you right into the medical facility. I know the doctor there quite well."

Annja sighed. "I don't have a choice here, do I?"

"Not unless you'd like to jump overboard and swim back."

Hans had a smile on his face, but Annja saw there was no way he was going to budge on his decision. She shrugged. "What the hell." At least he seemed to genuinely be concerned about her. That was a nice change.

Hans said something quickly and quietly to another man on board and the engine churned beneath their feet. Instantly, the boat swung around and zipped back toward the resort.

Despite her nausea, Annja found the sea spray and breeze a welcoming relief. She might have a concussion, she decided. And if that was the case, she did need to get checked out.

Hans pointed ahead of them and Annja saw the resort looming. The ship's engine downshifted and the boat slowed as they neared the shore. Hans said something else in German to the driver, who guided the boat up toward the dock close to the medical facility.

Annja groaned as she saw the dive master coming down the dock. As he noticed the boat approaching, he squinted, saw Annja and then frowned.

"Great," Annja said. "Here comes the 'I told you so.'"

Hans stepped out on the dock and helped Annja ashore. She turned and watched the dive master striding toward her, his tanned bald head gleaming.

"What happened, Miss Creed?"

"I had a run-in with a tiger shark."

That brought him up short. "Tiger shark? In these waters?"

Annja frowned. "They're all over the place around these parts. Nothing unusual about that."

But the dive master shook his head. "We don't usually see them around here. For some reason they tend to avoid the area. Most of our sharks are blacktip and reef."

"Well, you don't have to worry about the tiger shark anymore," Annja said. "I killed him."

"You did?"

Hans laughed. "I was just as amazed as you, my friend."

The dive master seemed to remember what he'd come to do and pointed a finger at Annja. "I told you not to go diving alone, didn't I? You could have been killed out there and no one would have known it."

"I would have known," Annja said. She nodded contritely. "But yes, you did warn me and I ignored your advice. I'm sorry. It was wrong and don't think that I'll be doing it again. I'm not in a rush to repeat that particular mistake."

The dive master seemed marginally mollified. "Well… good."

Hans put a hand under Annja's elbow. "We need to get her to the doctor, however. Annja knocked her head on a piece of her catamaran—"

"What happened to the boat?" the dive master asked.

"The tiger shark rammed it. It's gone," Annja said.

"Good Lord."

Annja grinned. "Think of how *I* felt."

"You said you killed him?"

"Yes."

The dive master turned and walked away. "Well, at least that's done."

Annja glanced at Hans. "I think he was more concerned about the boat than he was about me."

"I think you're right."

Annja took a deep breath and felt her legs go wobbly. "Whoa."

Hans caught her arm. "Easy, Annja. We need to get you inside. You can't stay out here in this blazing sunlight. It isn't good for your condition."

He guided her up the ramp toward the main path and then steered her into the doctor's office.

A dark-skinned Filipino rushed over as soon as he heard them enter. "What happened?"

Annja winced as her head throbbed. "Hit my head on a part of the boat."

Hans took over and told the doctor what had happened. The man introduced himself as Dr. Tiko. He grabbed a penlight and peered into Annja's eyes for a few seconds. Annja winced as the light pierced her brain. "Damn."

Dr. Tiko stepped back. "A mild concussion, I think. Not too serious, although right now she probably doesn't feel all that well," he said to Hans. He glanced at Annja. "Do you, Miss Creed?"

"No, I don't feel very well at all."

Dr. Tiko gestured for Hans to help him and they got Annja up onto one of the beds in the facility. Dr. Tiko covered her with the sheet and then checked Annja's blood pressure and pulse. "You need to rest. I'll stay here and keep an eye on you."

"I don't want to rest," Annja said. "I just need a few minutes to get myself back together."

But Hans put a firm hand on her shoulder and kept her from getting up. "Annja, I will have to insist that you stay here and let Dr. Tiko take care of you."

"Last I checked, we're not on your boat anymore."

"No, we're not."

"Then I don't have to do what you say," Annja said.

Hans shrugged. "That's true. I would prefer it if you stayed here, though. After all, it would be a shame to see any lasting harm come to you."

Annja sighed. "Well, okay, since you put it like that."

Hans looked at Dr. Tiko. "You'll stay here with her?"

"As long as it takes to make sure she's okay."

"All right, then." Hans looked at Annja. "I'll come back later to check on you, if that's acceptable to you."

"It's acceptable."

Hans smiled. "Good."

"You're going back out there, aren't you?"

Hans nodded. "We didn't get a chance to complete our dive when we ran into you."

"Thank you for bringing me back here and not listening to me being stubborn."

Hans smiled again. "My pleasure. Now rest, Annja. I will see you later. And then we can talk further."

Annja watched him go and, in another minute, she felt the blackness swallow her up whole.

4

Annja awoke several hours later, feeling only a dull throb where once her head had thundered. Dr. Tiko sat quietly at his desk, typing onto a computer and only noticed Annja was awake when she moved and the sheet fell away.

Annja was still in her bathing suit and felt dry, sun baked and in desperate need of a shower. Dr. Tiko came over with a glass of water.

"How are you feeling?"

"Much better."

He eyed her. "Really?"

Annja smiled. "Why is it that no one seems to believe what I tell them around here?"

Dr. Tiko shrugged. "I don't know, Miss Creed. It could be because you made a rather silly mistake earlier that could have easily killed you."

Annja held up her hand. "All right, I admitted my mistake. I don't need to be treated like a teenager." She took a sip of the water Dr. Tiko offered and marveled at how much easier it went down now.

"That's good stuff."

Dr. Tiko nodded. "Well, I'm pleased to see you're feeling better. I've watched you while you were asleep and took your vitals at varying points throughout. I suspect you'll have a bit of a headache for a while, but nothing too serious."

"So I can go?"

He smiled. "I suspect you'd like to get changed. Maybe have a bite to eat?"

Annja hadn't thought about food, but Dr. Tiko's suggestion made her stomach rumble and she nodded with a grin. "Now that you mention it, I'm famished."

Dr. Tiko stepped back. "All right, I can discharge you. But if your headache worsens, I want you to promise that you'll come right back here and see me. If I'm not here, just call the main desk and they'll page me. I live here at the resort, so it's no trouble whatsoever."

"Thank you."

Annja stepped down, momentarily concerned that she might still feel wobbly, but her legs felt much stronger now. She stepped out of the doctor's office and saw that evening had settled in. Out on the sea, the sun was already gone, leaving behind only a blaze of reds and pinks as sunset turned into an inky darkness.

Annja walked the smooth paved path back to her cabana and stepped inside. She'd left the window open and a strong breeze blew in, chilling her.

First order of business, she thought, a hot shower.

It felt wonderful ditching the bathing suit and even better feeling the water sweep away the dried salt crystals that had clung to her skin. She'd gotten a bit of sun, but nothing like a burn, which would have made the day all the more painful.

As she conditioned her hair, she took a moment to luxuriate in the scent of the lavender and rose petals, feeling a renewed sense of hunger.

At last, she stepped out of the shower, wrapped herself in a towel and walked out of the bathroom.

Under her door, someone had slipped a piece of paper. Annja squatted down, not trusting her head to suddenly bend over. She picked it up.

"Please join us for dinner. Hans."

Annja smiled. There was only one place to get a meal at Club Noah and that was at the main administration building at the curve of the U that laid out the resort. The building, while not large, housed offices and various amenities. As well, it led to the large pavilion where the meals were served for resort guests. A massive thatched roof kept the pavilion sheltered, but it was open on three sides, inviting the ocean breezes to give diners the feeling of being almost one with nature.

She stepped into a white tropical gauzy cotton dress after applying just a hint of makeup. Annja never went overboard, but she figured a little bit tonight couldn't hurt. She wanted everyone to realize she was fine and healthy. And there was the fact that Hans was rather a handsome man. No sense showing up looking like she'd just suffered a concussion.

Ten minutes later, she stepped out of her cabana and locked the door, sliding the key into her clutch. She walked down the path toward the pavilion. Night at Club Noah was as magical a time as any. The torches lighting the pathway cast long flickering shadows and the sea breezes kept the mosquitoes at bay.

She passed a set of stairs carved into the side of the mountain that towered over the resort. At the top, on one side was a tribute to the Virgin Mary and on the other was an open-air bar where resort guests could grab a late-night cocktail. Unfortunately, as Annja had discovered, the mosquitoes loved to hang out there and the resort staff didn't seem to have any idea how to keep them away.

Annja passed several resort workers who said hello to

her and asked how she was feeling. Club Noah was small enough that every staff member knew who was staying at the resort at any given time. Annja loved the personalized sense of care that she found here. A friend of hers had recommended this place and she could see why he had.

As she approached the pavilion, Annja could hear the sounds of diners and the clink of glasses and silverware. She stepped into the pavilion and looked around.

"Annja."

She turned and found herself looking at Hans, who had swapped his diving gear for a lightweight shirt and linen pants. He wore sandals and looked like he'd only recently shaved. She could smell the brace of aftershave on him and found she quite liked it.

"Hi."

"You're feeling better?"

Annja touched the side of her head. "A little bit of a headache, but it's nothing I can't handle."

Hans smiled. "I'd say there appears to be very little that you cannot handle. I'm quite impressed with you."

"Thank you." Annja glanced around and saw the buffet table laid out with a suckling pig the Filipinos called *lechón.* On other platters were a wide array of fresh seafood, noodles, fresh carved beef and chicken and much more.

Hans noticed her staring and smiled. "I take it your appetite has returned?"

"In spades," Annja said.

"Allow me to help you," Hans said. He escorted her to the buffet table and handed her a plate, then got one for himself. "Are you familiar with the *lechón?*"

Annja nodded. "I've had it once before."

Hans grinned. "Then you may as well have never had it before. They do an amazing pig roast here. Look at the way the skin simply falls away from the moist meat. It's incredible."

Annja pointed. "You'd better put that on my plate, then, or I may dive in right here."

He laughed and heaped a serving on her plate before helping himself to some.

When they'd finished at the buffet table, Hans nodded toward a longer table where four men sat around it eating. "Please join us."

"Are you sure? I don't want to intrude."

"And who else would you eat with?"

She smiled. "Well, I haven't really met anyone else here yet."

"Exactly. So it's settled, then."

Annja smiled, but found herself warming up to Hans despite his somewhat overbearing attitude. She guessed he might be somewhat protective of her since he'd rescued her earlier. May as well go along with it for now, she reasoned. If it got to be too much later, she could educate him on how she could take care of herself.

Hans led her to the table and Annja noticed there were two unoccupied chairs. Hans put his plate down by one and then held Annja's chair out so she could sit down.

She glanced at him as she did so. "You are aware that chivalry is an endangered species, right?"

"Endangered, perhaps, but not yet extinct."

Annja looked across the table and saw the faces of the other men who had been on the boat earlier. "Nice to see you all again."

They smiled and asked if she was feeling better. But one man, older than anyone else, remained silent until at last Hans cleared his throat.

"Annja, I would very much like to introduce you to the head of our little group here, Joachim Spier."

Annja leveled her gaze on the older man, who regarded her with warm blue eyes and a thin smile. "Herr Spier."

He stood and held out his hand. Annja shook it and found

it was surprisingly strong. "It is my sincere pleasure to make your acquaintance, Annja Creed. When Hans told me about you earlier, I could scarcely believe our luck."

Annja glanced at Hans. "Luck?"

Spier smiled broadly as he sat down. "Imagine, the great Annja Creed—famed archaeologist and pursuer of history's monsters. What would the chances be of us both being at this glorious resort at the same time?"

Annja smiled. "Apparently better than either of us would have dared to think."

"Indeed," Spier said, nodding. "Indeed." He leaned back. "But please, do not let me interrupt you. Hans has told me of your tremendous ordeals of earlier today and you must certainly be hungry. When you have dined some, then perhaps we can all discuss…things."

Annja didn't need any more coaxing and took advantage of Spier's pause to enjoy the food before her. As Hans had suggested, the *lechón* was even more delicious than she remembered it being. The crispy pigskin concealed a delightfully moist meat underneath, buffered by an almost gelatinous thin layer of fat that made each mouthful even better than the last.

She helped herself to a lot of water and then grudgingly accepted a small glass of white wine when Hans offered. "Not too much, I don't want to have to pay another visit to Dr. Tiko tonight."

That brought a round of laughter from the table and Annja found herself enjoying the company of the German men more and more. They all talked animatedly in heavily accented English about diving in the area. Annja appreciated the fact that they refrained from switching back to German—mostly, she assumed, for her benefit.

Finally, she set her silverware down and lifted her glass of wine to her lips. The cold liquid tasted incredible and she leaned forward. "Thank you for giving me some time, Herr Spier. I was pretty hungry."

Spier nodded. "I can see that. It's a good sign given your earlier state, I should think. Nothing like a hearty appetite to set one on the road back to full strength." He lifted his glass and nodded in Annja's direction. "To your health."

"Cheers."

The men all laughed and toasted one another and then drank again. When Annja set her glass back down, she felt Hans eyeing her. She turned and smiled at him.

Spier spoke up. "Perhaps now that we have all dined, we might speak of other things than just the wonderful nature of the meals they serve here, eh?"

"Absolutely," Annja said.

"What brings you to Club Noah?" Spier asked.

Annja shrugged. "A much-needed rest. I'm burned out. I've been crisscrossing the world for years and haven't taken nearly enough time for myself lately. My workload in New York was getting to be too much, so I decided on a whim to simply drop everything and come here."

Spier nodded. "You are a woman of action."

"Some have said that, yes."

"Excellent. I respect that immensely. And if it were only based on your reputation and from what I have observed watching that television show that you are on, I would have surmised much the same."

"Thank you."

Spier waved his hand. "It is not worthless praise, by any means. And there is never shame in being proud of your accomplishments, of which you have a great many."

"Well, I'm pleased you think so."

"I know so," Spier said. "You've done much for the world of archaeology and history. You ought to be commended for the service you've given to mankind."

"I'm hardly worthy of that," Annja said. Too much praise made her uncomfortable.

Spier noted her discomfort and smiled. "Suffice it to say that we are extremely happy to have you in our presence here, Annja. Very happy indeed."

"And what brings you all to the Philippines?" Annja asked. "Just a vacation, perhaps?"

Spier lowered his voice and shook his head. "We have come here for a much more grand purpose than mere relaxation."

"Really?"

He drew closer to Annja. She could see the depth of his eyes and found herself almost hypnotized by them as he drew her into his conspiratorial attitude. "We seek a treasure rumored to be in this very area."

Annja perked up. "Treasure?"

"They call it the Pearl of Palawan."

5

A balmy ocean breeze blew across the pavilion as Spier regarded Annja. "Have you ever heard of the Pearl of Palawan?"

Annja shook her head, listening to the crashing waves on the beach. "I have not. But to be honest with you, I'm not very interested in treasure. From what I've experienced, things of such value have a way of destroying people."

Spier smiled. "But imagine what good this could do if it were recovered. We could educate people about the origins of it."

Annja frowned. "And just what are its origins?"

Spier ordered himself a glass of peppermint schnapps and waited until it arrived. He sipped it once and then leaned back in his chair. Clearly, Annja thought, he was a captivating storyteller used to commanding attention.

"Years and years ago," Spier began, "the Pearl of Palawan—a solid black pearl of such opulence and size that it made men weep in desire to possess it—first appeared in the annals of Filipino history."

"I'm not as familiar with this country's history as perhaps I should be," Annja said. "But I know some."

"So you know of the Moros."

Annja winced, remembering her last trip to the Philippines. "I know a little bit about them."

"They were the first to document the pearl. But legend has it that it has existed for even longer than the period of greatness of the Moros empire. According to several documents I have unearthed, the pearl dates back many thousands of years, back to a time when fact and fiction were often entwined with each other."

"And what do the legends say?" Annja asked.

"They say that those who possess the pearl have at their disposal an object that can grant the owner incredible vitality and power."

"Is that so?"

"Indeed."

Annja leaned forward as Spier helped himself to more schnapps. "Pardon me for saying so, Herr Spier, but you seem to already possess a great deal of vitality. And I'm fairly adept at knowing when I'm in the presence of a powerful person. You fit that bill easily."

Spier smiled. "Thank you, my dear. I appreciate the sentiment, but I assure you the pearl's powers would dwarf my own."

Annja leaned back. "Do you know where the pearl is supposed to come from?"

Spier chuckled. "I must confess I'm a bit reluctant to tell you. I sense that you view the legend of the pearl with a bit more skepticism than I expected."

"Forgive me if I am being rude," Annja said. "It's just that over the years I've found a lot of supposedly powerful legends have turned out to be nothing but fantasy, usually perpetrated by someone seeking to manipulate events for their own well-being."

Spier said nothing for a moment but then looked at her. "But tell me something. You've probably found that just as many things live up to their legends...don't they?"

Annja smiled. "Well, you've got me there. I have indeed."

Spier nodded. "And that's why you should keep an open mind about this, as well."

"Tell me more."

"I have heard," Spier said, "that the pearl was reportedly created by an ancient civilization long since lost to the earth. These people inhabited a wide swath of land in the Pacific that was subsequently destroyed by volcanoes and earthquakes. They brought the pearl into being for the express purpose of using its power to rule their kingdom."

"And what happened?"

"It ended up destroying them."

Annja nodded. "Another powerful lesson, I suppose."

"It would seem," Spier said. "But one never knows exactly what may have transpired to destroy their civilization." He grabbed at his glass and downed the remainder of the schnapps. "The pearl next shows up in the Moros history as belonging to a certain Queen Esmeralda. It was a gift given to her by one of her subjects who was enamored of the woman. Driven to prove his love and worth, he reportedly dove into the sea, swam underwater for seven days and, on the seventh day, emerged from the surf bearing the pearl."

"Well, that would, of course, be impossible," Annja said.

"Unless he grew gills," Spier said with a laugh. "And I certainly don't think he really did that. But the story is interesting."

"Did he get his woman?" Annja asked.

Spier shrugged. "Actually, the queen, upon receiving the pearl, is said to have undergone some sort of transformation. Instead of rewarding her suitor, she had him executed."

"Tough love," Annja said.

"Indeed." Spier sighed. "But the pearl did not stay in possession of Queen Esmeralda for very long. It seems that bad luck was destined for the Moros as the Spanish soon started visiting the Philippines."

Annja nodded. "I've read something of their conquests here."

"Then you know they battled the Moros and had a tough time of it in the thick jungles."

"Yes."

"But not being ones to give up, such as they were, the Spaniards eventually succeeded in wresting control of the region from the Moros. And Queen Esmeralda was taken hostage by the invaders."

"I assume she was meant to be a slave?"

"Perhaps, or a bride for some lucky Spaniard," Spier said. "Whatever the case, she bought back her freedom."

"With the pearl?"

"Of course. When the leader of the Spanish heard her pleas for freedom and learned how she intended to buy her way out of captivity, he could scarcely conceal his greed at the thought of possessing the pearl."

"She gave it to him?"

"Queen Esmeralda ordered her subjects to bring the pearl to the Spanish. In exchange, she was to be freed." Spier smiled. "But in a cruel ironic twist, Esmeralda herself was betrayed by the Spanish and, instead of freeing her, they refused to let her go. After all, they now had the pearl and the queen."

"Nasty business," Annja said.

Spier continued. "Esmeralda was distraught and managed to free herself from the chains that held her belowdecks. She made her way to the top of the main mast and threw herself overboard. But before she did, she cursed the entire Spanish flotilla. Then she dove into the sea, never to be seen again."

"So the pearl made its way to Spain?"

Spier shook his head. "No, as soon as Esmeralda dove into

the sea, the ocean grew violent. Dark clouds surged over-head while the waves pounded the fleet on all sides. As the sun vanished, the fleet was thrown into chaos. Two of the ships ran into each other, others were dashed on an unseen reef that tore their hulls wide open. As thunder and lightning crashed across the sky, the entire fleet was destroyed in the space of only a few minutes."

"Incredible," Annja said.

"When the clouds parted, the sea was like glass. There was no trace of the Spanish fleet. No survivors bobbed in the water on pieces of wreckage. It was almost as if they had never even been there at all."

"But surely their ships would have come to rest underwater."

Spier shrugged. "There have never been any found that could be attributed to the story."

"So, it would seem that the story itself is rather suspect," Annja said. "After all, reports of shipwrecks would mean the potential for something salvageable underwater."

"Only if you knew exactly where the ships were supposed to have gone aground. Otherwise, how could you possibly say?"

Annja smiled. "And you think you know where they are?"

Spier grinned. "I might have an idea."

"So what happened to the pearl, then? It was lost, too?"

"Legend has it that it returned to its proper owner—the very civilization that created it in the first place."

"The civilization that no longer existed. Supposedly."

"Yes."

Annja sighed. "That's an awful lot of supposed history right there, Herr Spier. I hope you'll forgive me if I don't fall for it hook, line and sinker."

He chuckled. "I would have been disappointed in you if you had, Annja. I know you are a woman of facts, yet you are also a woman who can't help but be intrigued by legends and myths."

"I'm a romantic at heart," Annja said. "What can I say?"

Spier eyed her. "Say that you'll come diving with us. Say that you'll help us find the pearl."

"You're serious about going after it?"

"Absolutely."

"And the warning signs in your story? They don't bother you at all?"

"What—that whoever possesses the pearl seems to come to an unfortunate end?"

"Yes."

Spier spread his arms and laughed some more. "My dear, I am eighty years old. In some ways, I feel as though I were as young and strapping as Hans here. But I am not. Eighty is much closer to the grave than it is to the womb. And so, if the legends are true, then I will not go reluctantly should my time come to pass sooner than I expect. And even if it does, I should pass from this world to the next knowing that I had a hand in retrieving a truly wondrous relic." He pointed his empty glass at Annja. "What could be better than that?"

Annja smiled. As much as she hated to admit it, Spier had intrigued her with his tale. And while she was supposed to be here enjoying her rest and relaxation, she'd already found she missed the excitement of exploration. The visit to the reef today had shown that she always needed a sense of some sort of adventure in her life. Wasn't that why she'd gone against the dive master's advice and went diving alone?

Spier watched her. "I may have only just met you, Annja, but I know people. And after eighty years on this planet, I think I have the ability to see some people better than they perhaps know themselves. You and I are alike in many ways. You have the thirst for adventure flowing deep within your very soul. And as much as you might want to fight against it from time to time, you know full well it will never relinquish its hold upon you or your heart."

Annja grinned. "Not until I'm dead, I suppose."

Spier nodded. "Exactly."

"And what will you do with the pearl if you are actually able to locate it?" Annja asked.

"It's my hope that we would present it to the world together," Spier said. "That others might learn much from it. How it was made, what properties it possesses."

"I'm interested in knowing how this ancient civilization was able to make a pearl at all, considering that we weren't able to manufacture artificial pearls, per se, until quite recently."

"Perhaps that old civilization was a lot more advanced than we would give them credit for," Spier said. "Or perhaps they had access to a species of giant oysters that gave them such objects on a routine basis. Who can tell?"

Annja smiled. "Well, I suppose we won't know for sure unless we manage to find it."

"That's the spirit."

"How big is the pearl supposed to be?"

"Roughly the size of a child's ball. Perhaps ten inches across."

Annja sat back. "That would be massive for a pearl."

"Absolutely."

"And that would mean that if it came from an oyster, it would also have to have been huge."

"Beyond measure almost," Spier said.

Annja nodded. "Okay."

Spier leaned forward. "Really?"

Annja smiled at him and then looked at Hans, who had remained silent throughout the story. "Well, it just so happens that I don't have all that much going on aside from recovering from a mild concussion. So maybe a little excursion would be a good thing for me."

"I assure you it will be," Spier said. "The search for the pearl will prove to be a fantastic adventure, I'm certain of it."

"Maybe we'll even find it," Annja said with a laugh.

Spier called for another round of drinks and then winked at Annja. "I'm almost positive that we will. Now that you have joined our expedition."

6

Spier and the rest of the men excused themselves after they'd had another round of drinks. Annja nursed her glass of wine as Hans stayed behind, as well. Part of her was happy about that, but part of her suspected something else might be going on. Just before Spier had left the table, he'd exchanged a knowing look with Hans.

Annja was comfortable with the decision she'd made to join the expedition, but she wanted to make sure that Hans didn't have any misconceptions about the nature of their relationship.

They waited in comfortable silence until the pavilion had pretty much cleared out. One of the resort's boats was taking a big group over to a neighboring island where they had a nightclub. Annja had no interest in going.

"Joachim is very pleased that you've decided to accompany us on this expedition," Hans said.

Annja looked him over. He was smiling at her and seemed brimming with confidence. "How did you get that scar?" she asked.

He touched his face self-consciously. Annja grinned. "I didn't mean to imply that it's horrible or anything. I was just curious."

Hans smiled. "Doesn't the discussion of scars and how we got them usually take place after we've slept together? Isn't that what people like us do in the afterglow of orgasm?"

"People like us?" Annja sputtered, surprised by the man's blunt statement. "And what is that supposed to mean?"

"You can't deny it, Annja. I knew it from the moment I looked at you. You're a warrior."

Annja raised an eyebrow. "So does that mean you're one, too?"

"I was," he said. "Once."

Hans got a faraway look in his eyes and Annja frowned. She knew what it was like to have dark memories. Sometimes the demons that you'd killed stayed away for a while. But sometimes they came back.

"Military?" she guessed.

Hans nodded. "I was a paratrooper. In Afghanistan. Working with the coalition forces at the time. Such as they were."

"I didn't think Germany had much of an official presence over there."

Hans sighed. "We had a few units. Some of whom disgraced themselves. Public opinion caused the chancellor to resign. Germany pulled out most of its units. But you know that doesn't stop the shadow governments that work despite the best interests of the people they're elected to supposedly protect." He finished off the remainder of his drink and slapped the glass back down on the table. "An arrangement was reached with the United States. Germany would supply a small unit of commandos—specialists trained in mountain warfare—for long-range reconnaissance patrols. Our task, as it was set forth, was to locate high-value Taliban targets."

"So you were special operations."

Hans nodded. "Don't hold it against me, all right?"

Annja smiled. "I won't."

Hans looked out at the frothy black sea. "We were dispatched to a high mountain pass in the Helmand province. Do you know it?"

"In the southwestern part of the country, isn't it? But I thought it was mostly desert."

"Helmand is the main source of opium in the country. It produces more than the entire country of Burma. Intelligence suggested that the Taliban was funneling fighters mixed in with opium shipments. But rather than venture south through the desert toward the Balochistan area of Pakistan, they instead chose to journey north toward the Helmand River."

"You were ordered to intercept them?"

Hans nodded. "We set up our observation post atop one of the higher mountains in Nawzad. We were able to use small unmanned vehicles to keep track of all the entry points in the region." He shook his head. "It was exhausting work, sitting in that mountain range. The sun scorched us mercilessly. We had to maintain strict secrecy the entire time. The locals were all friendly to the Taliban and would have given any of us away if they had known we were there."

"How did you manage to stay concealed for so long?"

Hans grinned. "Well, that's what we were trained to do. My unit was sent out to live on the mountains all over the world. We went in with just enough supplies—mostly ammunition, medical and communications gear. We took some rations, but otherwise we were to live off the environment. It was a very special group of men I had volunteered to serve with. Any one of us would gladly have died for the others."

"What happened?"

Hans paused a moment before continuing. "On the third night we were there, we got a message that one of the drones had visual contact with a drug convoy approaching our area.

"It was night, so we had a tough time trying to pick them out among the rocks down near the river, but we also had night-vision equipment. Once we switched on, we could see them clearly. One or two pickup trucks, a whole host of mules laden with large boxes of opium packed tightly for transport. And they had close to one hundred fighters with them."

Annja leaned forward. "How many of you?"

"Four."

"Those aren't good odds any way you cut it."

Hans shrugged. "We called in close air support. We had laser painters—do you know what those are?"

"It shoots an invisible laser at a target that fighters and bombers can use to guide their ordnance, right?"

Hans looked at her a second before grinning. "You seem remarkably well-versed in military terminology, Annja."

"You're not the first soldier I've met, Hans."

"I'll bet."

"So, anyway…"

Hans grinned. "We directed a squadron of planes down on them and they turned the entire river basin into scorched earth. When the dust and debris cleared, the only things left behind were the smoldering hunks of what had been the pickup trucks. Everything else had been utterly destroyed."

Annja nodded. "So, mission successful. Good stuff."

"Ordinarily, on a mission like that, we would have been immediately extracted and moved to a different area. That's just to protect the unit, you understand."

"Sure. Why leave you there when the locals would have known that there must have been a unit operating in the area."

"Exactly." Hans sighed. "It amazes me that it seems so logical to you, and yet to my own government it was not what they did."

"They didn't pull you out?"

"No. They left us there. The first strike had proven so successful, they wanted us to stay in place to make sure the Taliban didn't try to come through the region again."

"But—"

Hans held up his hand. "I know, I know. It defies all proper sense of logic and intelligence. But bureaucrats are not warriors for good reason. They'd be dead within minutes if they ever stepped onto a battlefield."

"That must not have gone over well with the other members of your team."

Hans frowned. "To be honest with you, Annja, it was the first time I'd ever considered the notion of disobeying a direct order. We talked it over, though, and in the end decided we had the benefit of being a small and highly mobile unit. We knew the region and felt comfortable with the idea that if we were discovered, we could exfiltrate to the extraction site and get pulled out by helicopter."

Annja felt a strong breeze blow over and, despite its balminess, felt a shiver run through her body.

"The Taliban were, of course, furious that one of their convoys had been so utterly decimated. The cost to them in terms of monetary value—along with the cost in human life—must have been quite extraordinary."

"They wanted your unit."

Hans nodded. "They knew, like you said, that there had to be someone operating in the area. I found out later that they had put a bounty on our heads. The equivalent of fifty thousand dollars for our capture or death. To your local Afghani, that much money was like being promised the keys to a kingdom."

"They turned those mountains into a war zone."

Hans nodded and kept talking. "The first indication we had that our lives were about to get really terrible was when our sentries signaled us that we had the enemy approaching. But they didn't just come at us from one direction. We could have easily handled that." He frowned. "They swarmed all over that mountain, creeping up through unseen crevasses we didn't even know about. They stalked down old goat trails.

Over boulders. And when they attacked, it felt like hell itself had been unleashed upon us. Bullets flew everywhere, ricocheting off rocks, splintering whatever stubby trees happened to be in the area. The sound of gunfire never wavered. We scrambled and fought back as much as we could, but they were relentless."

Annja's heart beat hard against her chest. "How did you ever get out of there?"

"Somehow we made our way back to our extraction site. But when the first helicopter came in to pick us up, the Taliban launched a Stinger missile—you know, the ones your CIA gave to the mujahideen to fight the Soviets way back when? Anyway, the helicopter exploded, killing everyone on board before we could even get close to it."

"My God…"

"We asked for another rescue mission. But we were denied, told it was too hot a landing zone for them to try again. We were directed to an alternate landing zone for rescue."

"Did you go there?"

"Not before one of our team was killed by a grenade. He threw himself on it to protect the rest of us. We would have all been killed otherwise."

Annja bit her lip. "Brave man."

Hans nodded. "He was indeed." He glanced away. "The secondary LZ was two miles to the east. It may as well have been a thousand. They attacked us every step of the way. Another member of my team took a bullet to his shoulder and we had to tend to his wounds. While we did, another shot took him right between his eyes. His head exploded all over me and my friend, Tomas."

"Jesus," Annja said.

"I hope he was with him," Hans said. "But it certainly felt as though God had deserted us on that day. The Taliban kept up the attacks as we traversed the boulders and ravines, making our way to the secondary site."

Annja shook her head. "No wonder you've got scars."

Hans ran a hand over the scar on his face. "If only they were all as superficial as this one." He paused and then looked at Annja. "It took us the better part of a day to reach the secondary landing zone. By that time, night had fallen, so we felt good about our chances of a pickup. After all, darkness would help the rescue chopper avoid detection to some extent."

"Did they come for you?"

"They didn't want to. But we screamed at them on the radio until they relented. We were down to just the two of us by then. Tomas and I pledged that neither of us would let ourselves be captured. We'd heard enough of what to expect from Taliban torturers if they should have ever caught up with us. We'd each save a bullet for taking our own lives if it came to that.

"For a while, everything went quiet as we lay nestled between two boulders. The stars came out on that cold night, blinking as they did against the backdrop of night. It was eerily quiet and almost beautiful. Tomas and I lay back-to-back ready to fight and die if need be.

"But when we heard the chop of rotor blades, the entire mountainside opened up again. It was as if they knew exactly where Tomas and I were hiding because every bullet and mortar shell seemed to be locked onto our very position. Somehow they never managed to land a direct strike, though, and we stayed safe, right up until it was time to leave and run for the chopper."

Annja was leaning forward, closer to Hans now. Hans seemed to be breathing faster, almost as if he was reliving the event.

"We saw the chopper touch down and we ran out from the boulders. We'd ditched all our gear so we could move faster. I ran like I'd never run before. Bullets whizzed past us. Dirt kicked up in our faces. Explosions everywhere. I had to run zigzag to keep from being hit. We were so close to getting out and then I was falling into the back of the chopper.

"I turned and saw Tomas on the ramp coming in. He smiled at me. I grinned back. We'd made it. And then a single bullet burst through his chest. He died right there on the back ramp of the chopper as we lifted away. He fell to his knees and died, that smile still on his face."

Hans was silent.

Annja took a deep breath. "I'm so sorry," she whispered.

Hans cleared his throat and clenched his jaw. "The scar came from a bullet that caught me across my face, but never entered the side of my head. Just a flesh wound, in other words."

"You were incredibly lucky."

Hans eyed her. "Was I? I sometimes wonder if perhaps my friends who died were the lucky ones. We never should have been left out there. We never should have been abandoned like that. Three good men died because of political idiocy."

There wasn't much Annja could say to that.

Hans stood. "You'll have to forgive me, Annja, but I think I'm going to get some sleep now. I'll see you down at the dock tomorrow morning. Joachim likes to get started early."

And then he turned and left the pavilion.

Annja watched him go and frowned. This day hadn't ended how she'd thought it would. That was for sure.

7

By the time Annja got down to the dock by the dive master's hut the next morning, Spier, Hans and the rest of the team were already there. Hans, for all the horror he'd relived with Annja the night before, looked happy and fresh from a good night's sleep. He smiled as she came down the walkway and took her by the elbow to guide her off to one side.

"I want to apologize for my conduct last night."

Annja smiled. "Your conduct? It's not like you made an unwanted pass at me, Hans."

He shrugged. "I haven't talked about Afghanistan with many people. It is a time in my life when I faced death and lost the people I felt closest to. As such, the memories tend to run together and come out in a jumbled mess of sadness, anger and confusion."

Annja laid a hand on his arm. "It's okay. Really. I don't think anyone would have come through something like that unscathed in some fashion. And, if anything, it's my fault for being so nosy about your scar and how you got it. I certainly wasn't expecting the story you told me."

Hans smirked. "No, I suppose you weren't."

"But that's beside the point," Annja said. "I'm glad you shared it. It helps me understand who you are."

Hans grinned slyly. "And why would you want to know something like that?"

Annja thought about responding but instead looked over his shoulder. "Are you going to introduce me to the rest of the team?"

"Didn't I do that last night?"

Annja shook her head. "Actually, no. By the time I sat down and Joachim started talking, there wasn't much time to talk to anyone else."

"Mein Gott," Hans said. "How rude of us." He dragged Annja over to where the rest of the team were preparing their gear. "Annja, allow me to introduce Gottlieb, Mueller and Heinkel. You already know Joachim."

Each of the three other divers nodded and smiled at Annja in turn. Like Hans, they were all exceptionally athletic, muscular and had strong jawlines. She wondered if they were all ex-military like Hans.

She supposed they probably were.

Joachim smiled at her. "Did you have a good night's sleep?"

"Very."

"Excellent. So, no lingering effects from the concussion?"

Annja shook her head. It was true. She felt perfectly fine today. "I don't think so, no."

"Well, that's good to hear," a voice said behind her.

Annja turned and saw Dr. Tiko. She grinned at him. "No doubt thanks in large part to your excellent care, doctor."

"Don't believe a thing she says," the dive master said coming down the walkway.

Annja sighed. "I thought I already apologized to you yesterday."

"You did, but I still don't trust you."

Dr. Tiko came over to Annja. "You're certain your head isn't hurting you at all?"

"I'm fine."

Dr. Tiko frowned. "Even still, I'd much prefer it if you didn't go diving today. There's a chance you could still be suffering from your concussion."

Annja shook her head. "I'm not missing this chance to go exploring, doctor. And besides, you told me it was a mild concussion."

"Even a mild concussion can prove troublesome if it's not treated properly and the patient hasn't had enough rest and recuperation."

Annja smiled. "Doctor, I assure you that this is not the first time I've had a concussion. I know what to expect."

"You've had them before?"

"A few."

"How? More boating accidents?"

Annja frowned. "Something like that." She didn't think it would be a good idea to mention falling down the sides of mountains, armed assailants, ice shelves and the like.

"Then that's even more reason for you to stay here and rest today. The cumulative effect of repeated concussion can cause lasting brain damage."

Annja laughed. "I'm pretty sure that's already taken effect." I have to be crazy to do the things I do, she thought.

Dr. Tiko looked at her like she was quite insane. "Miss Creed, I may have to insist that you stay behind from this expedition."

"Dr. Tiko." Spier came walking over with a broad smile on his face. "I don't think that's really necessary and neither do you."

"Don't tell me my business, Mr. Spier."

Spier put a hand on his chest. "I wouldn't dream of doing anything of the sort. But it's just that this expedition is very important, and all the more so now that the illustrious Annja

Creed has deigned to join our merry band. After all, it's not every day the resort of Club Noah has such a celebrity as this staying on its grounds."

Dr. Tiko's eyes narrowed. "Celebrity?"

Spier gestured to Annja. "Surely you haven't failed to notice that this is the one and only Annja Creed, famed archaeologist and host of the ever-amusing and educational television program *Chasing History's Monsters?*"

Dr. Tiko's eyes narrowed. "I don't watch television."

Spier chuckled. "Well, you will simply have to take my word for it, then, won't you? Annja is a brilliant researcher whose knowledge will be of vital importance to my research in this area."

"Your research into the underwater formations that haven't been charted yet?"

"Exactly."

Annja smiled at Dr. Tiko. "I'm really feeling quite all right, doctor. If I wasn't, there's no way I'd be this stubborn."

The dive master snorted to himself. "I find that doubtful. She'd be stubborn in any condition."

Spier looked at the dive master. "I think we're all set from here on out, sir. Thank you for your assistance."

Realizing he was being dismissed, the dive master harrumphed once, spun on his heels and stalked away.

Dr. Tiko wasn't so easily convinced. "Perhaps I should come with you. I can remain on the boat and make sure that Annja is well when we get there and when she resurfaces again."

Spier looked pained. "That would be a marvelous idea, doctor, but I'm afraid of what might befall the other resort guests if you were not around to help them should they require medical attention. After all, how would it look if the resort's only doctor abandoned everyone else just to look after one of the more beautiful guests here?"

Dr. Tiko nodded. "Perhaps you're right."

Spier smiled. "Besides, all of my men have medical training. I'm sure we can stabilize Annja should she require any care while we're out diving. And then we'd be right back in to see you as soon as possible, anyway."

Dr. Tiko paused and then reluctantly nodded his head slowly. "All right. This goes against my better judgment, but I'll agree to it. If anything happens out there, get her back to me as soon as possible."

"We won't hesitate," Spier said.

"In that case," Dr. Tiko said, "have a good dive."

"Thank you."

Annja watched Dr. Tiko walk away and then glanced at Spier. "Thanks for intervening like that."

"Think nothing of it. I meant what I said. Your participation in this dive is most welcome and to think of you staying here alone onshore would be painful, to say the least."

Hans nodded at the twenty-foot sloop they were stowing gear on. "We should get aboard before the doctor changes his mind."

Spier chuckled. "Or at least decides he wants a bigger payoff."

Annja stopped. "You paid him off?"

Spier smiled. "Just a few dollars to brighten his day. Last night after dinner I went to have a talk with him. Just to make sure he saw things our way."

"Then what was that all about?"

Spier smiled broadly. "Why, keeping up appearances, of course."

Hans helped Annja get aboard. "Joachim knew the dive master would be raising a commotion this morning. And if it looked like Dr. Tiko had given in too easily, then he might lose his job. So they acted out a little melodrama for the sake of the other staff workers."

Annja laughed despite herself. "All of this just for me? You guys are making me feel a little more important than I think is warranted." Still, she was pleased by the fact they valued her participation so much.

"I consider it money well spent," Spier said, climbing aboard behind her. "Dr. Tiko is a good man, and a good doctor. It's always wise to keep such people on friendly terms. One never knows when they'll prove especially useful given the right situation."

Mueller was the last man aboard, releasing the ropes that held the sloop to the dock. Heinkel gunned the engine and they reversed and then shot out toward the bay.

The early sun felt hot on Annja's skin, but the cool splashes of water kept her from sweating too much. The sloop, designed for fast movement, seemed to jump the waves as they zipped away from Club Noah toward the area where Annja had been diving the day before.

"I wonder if we'll see more tiger sharks," she said aloud.

Hans looked at her. "If we do, we'll be sure to point them in your direction since you seem so adept at killing them."

Annja frowned. "I didn't want to kill it, but it left me no alternative."

"We're not judging you, Annja," Spier said. "I think we're all quite a bit in awe of you actually. It's not every day that you meet a woman who is able to kill a fourteen-foot tiger shark."

"I suppose not," Annja said. Good thing they don't know what I used to kill the damned thing, she thought.

They made good time, and within twenty minutes they'd arrived at more or less the same location as the day before. Gottlieb got them all squared away with gear, and Hans helped Annja into her rig. She tested the regulator, found she had good oxygen flow and then prepared her mask.

Spier spoke quietly in German to his team, who had huddled a bit closer to one another, effectively meaning Annja couldn't hear them.

"Excuse me?"

Spier glanced at her. "Forgive me, Annja. I don't mean to exclude you."

"Secrets, Joachim?"

"Hardly," Spier said. "We always have a small prayer before we go diving. It's nothing secretive at all, just more of a personal tradition that we enjoy doing. We like to think it keeps us safe."

"Has it so far?"

Spier nodded. "Yes."

"Well, then, that's a good thing," Annja said. She glanced at Hans. "Maybe I could have used something like that yesterday, huh?"

Hans grinned. "I don't think you needed any prayers, Annja. You seemed quite capable on your own without divine intervention."

"I needed you guys, though."

Hans shrugged. "We were just passing through. Anyone else in the same situation would have done the same thing."

"You're being modest."

Spier cleared his throat. "I hate to break up this little gathering, but we're wasting time. I don't want to lose the day. The weather report says we could get some rain this afternoon, which means our window for proper exploration is a small one."

"Sorry," Annja said. "You're right. We should get going."

Spier nodded. "If you get into trouble, look for Hans. He'll be close by your side today."

Well, that's not a bad thing at all, Annja thought. She glanced at Hans, who gave her the thumbs-up and a smile around his mouthpiece before falling backward over the side of the sloop.

Annja heard the splashes as, one by one, the team dropped over the side of the boat and vanished into the sea below.

She took one final look around.
Here we go again, she thought.
She dropped back into the ocean.

8

Annja felt the bright blue waters of the sea envelop her once again as she turned over and got her bearing. She saw Spier and the rest of his team ahead of her, but off to her right side floated Hans, watching her protectively.

She gave him the thumbs-up sign and he nodded, pointed and they descended together.

A world of bubbles rose from the team as they dove deeper toward the coral reef. Annja found that she had a small feeling of uneasiness in her stomach, but quickly decided it was due to her fear that there might be another tiger shark lingering in the area.

She needn't have worried. She could already see that the activity around the reef was far greater than it had been yesterday. She spotted a few blacktip sharks meandering around the reef, snatching up smaller fish when the opportunities presented themselves.

Hans eyed her as she looked at the sharks, but unlike yesterday, they were only six-footers. Hardly the massive size of the tiger shark. And while they'd need to be mindful, she knew that the blacktips posed little threat.

Still, she glanced down and reassured herself that she'd replaced the diving knife she'd lost yesterday. The new knife sat snug in its sheath alongside her right calf.

All of the other divers were similarly outfitted. And unlike yesterday, being in a group gave everyone a much better level of protection.

Why did I go diving by myself yesterday? she wondered. It was really reckless of me.

Hans pointed ahead at the coral reef and Annja saw a moray eel poking its head out of the crevice in the formation. She nodded back at Hans and they continued on.

Spier seemed only marginally interested in the reef life itself. He never paused and Annja could see the strength of his leg muscles as they slowly powered him deeper into the depths. For an eighty-year-old man, Spier had remarkable strength and he seemed to have an endless supply of it.

Annja might have wondered what his diet was if she hadn't seen him devour a ton of fish, beef and pork last night. He seemed to eat whatever he pleased and not suffer for it. But then again, he was also extremely active for his age. Maybe his metabolism had something to do with his extraordinary health.

Spier led them along, past the part of the coral reef where she'd met the shark. Annja was surprised. I thought we'd start with exploring this part of the reef, she thought.

She glanced at Hans, but he didn't seem to notice.

Annja poked him and he turned. Annja gave him an inquisitive look but he only winked and then pointed for Annja to follow Spier's lead.

What was going on here?

Annja kicked her legs, pleased that her head hadn't started aching once she'd descended. The last thing she wanted was to prove Dr. Tiko right by coming back ashore with a worse headache than how she'd shown up yesterday.

But she felt good. Powerful.

She smiled, tasted the salt water and spat it out around her mouthpiece.

Hans swam ahead of her and Annja churned her legs to catch up. They had gone past a school of surgeonfish and Annja spotted a sea turtle lingering nearby, its hooked beak giving it the appearance of an odd-shaped nose.

Annja felt a lot better seeing it. If the sea turtle was around, the chances of spotting another tiger shark seemed even more remote. Tiger sharks loved to eat sea turtles and their teeth were especially suited for cracking the shells to get to the rich meat inside.

Spier led them farther along the reef and then hovered in the depth of the water. He turned and gestured for Annja to come closer. Annja kicked and moved over to where he floated.

Spier pointed at the area of the reef Annja hadn't had the chance to explore yesterday. She swam down and looked at the conical-shaped coral.

The formation was very strange.

From her past diving trips, Annja knew that shapes like that didn't appear naturally.

But if it wasn't natural, then what was it?

She looked at Spier and gave him a quizzical look. He nodded and pointed to another area. Annja glanced around. Heinkel and Mueller had already branched off from the team and were exploring on the other side of the reef. She looked at Hans and he pointed in the same direction that Spier had.

So we're going to split up, Annja thought. All right, then.

She swam over to Hans and they glided along the base of the reef, careful to avoid any dark holes that might conceal more moray eels. A reef shark swam lazily by, barely even glancing at them.

Hans looked at Annja as if to make sure she was okay being that close to a shark. She gave him a thumbs-up and he nodded. They continued swimming.

Finally, Hans had them stop near the edge of the reef. Looking up, Annja could see their boat some distance above. They'd gone down and then moved perhaps a half mile farther away, running the length of the reef.

From where she floated, Annja could make out the dropoff where the reef gave way to much deeper, darker water.

Were they on the edge of some sort of atoll? She frowned. Yesterday it hadn't seemed like the reef stretched on for such a distance, and yet here they were.

Hans started exploring the base of the reef and Annja followed. They poked and prodded the various outcroppings, but Annja couldn't see anything that resembled the conical outcropping Spier had shown her a few minutes before.

Maybe this was a dead end?

Annja sighed. The problem with diving was the communication was very scant. You had a few hand signals and that was it unless you had speaking masks.

But Hans seemed unconcerned with the lack of communication and kept his survey going. Annja floated above and behind him, looking where he looked but also keeping her eyes peeled for anything of interest.

Gradually they worked their way around toward the back of the reef. The water there was much warmer. Annja thought she spotted another conical outcropping and she swam right for it.

Hans had to kick to catch up, but he saw what she was eyeing and followed her lead.

Annja came to rest floating in front of an encrusted piece of coral that seemed strangely symmetrical. She looked across and saw that there was another outcropping and she decided they were almost like miniature towers.

She ran her fingers down the edges of the towers and

found small holes that appeared as though they'd been deliberately carved in the structure.

Annja's mind raced. Hadn't Spier said something about a long-lost civilization? Was this evidence that they existed? Or was this simply some sort of natural occurrence, as unlikely as that might have seemed?

She noticed Hans looking at the towers intently. When he glanced back at her, Annja gave him a shrug. I don't know what it is, she wanted to say.

Hans removed his diving knife and pried away some of the built-up barnacles, trying to get a better look at the structure.

Annja watched as the mollusks came away in his hand. And there, underneath the buildup, Annja thought she saw something smooth.

She ran her hand over the exposed patch and almost shouted. It was as smooth as marble.

In fact, she thought it might well be marble.

But how? How could marble have developed under the sea?

Had this supposed city of the lost civilization slipped into the ocean for some reason? Had an earthquake opened up the ground and tossed them into the seas?

Annja shook her head. Whatever this was, she needed more answers than she could find just floating in the ocean.

Hans was making notes with his grease pencil on an underwater clipboard. He's mapping the area, she decided. This must be along the lines of what Spier was searching for.

Interesting.

Hans looked up and nodded at her as if they'd managed to find something of importance. But Annja wasn't sure what they'd found. What she really wanted was to get to her computer and do some research.

Maybe she could talk to some locals and see what they knew about this supposed lost civilization.

There was probably nothing to it. But Spier certainly believed there was. Annja wondered if the story of the pearl might not hold some other purpose for Spier. He was eighty and seemed to be fighting his growing age with a tenacity that defied the aging process.

Did he think the pearl would help him stave off his inevitable death?

It was possible, she supposed. It wouldn't be the first time she'd run into crazy people who thought that immortality was worth whatever price you had to pay to try to achieve it.

Annja glanced at her oxygen gauge. They'd been underwater for almost forty minutes and would have to surface soon.

Hans seemed to read her mind and pointed back the way they'd come. Annja followed him. They left the warmer waters and Annja shivered slightly as she breached the cooler waters where the reef dropped off.

She glanced to her side, thinking about how close she'd come to being devoured by the tiger shark yesterday. Out there in the deep waters, they ruled the roost.

Hans pointed ahead and Annja saw the rest of the team had reassembled back at their entry point.

Time to surface.

Annja checked her depth gauge and saw she'd have to rise slowly. She'd gone deeper than she had yesterday and would need extra time to reduce the danger of the bends.

Mueller and Heinkel went up first. Annja watched them slowly rise toward the surface. Spier and Gottlieb went up next and then Hans and Annja started their ascent.

Annja watched her air bubbles.

Hans watched her as they rose together, his eyes locked on hers.

Annja tried to grin at him, but she tasted more salt water

and gave up trying. There'd be enough to talk about once they got back onto the boat.

Sunlight filtered down through the waves and Annja could feel its warmth even ten feet below the surface. A few small fish rose to investigate her, but then quickly scattered when Hans moved his hands in the water.

Annja kept her eyes always moving. She could taste the last third of her oxygen now. It was stale in her mouth.

Spier had timed his exploration perfectly.

Annja broke the surface a few minutes later and saw that dark, angry clouds blotted the horizon.

The sloop bobbed in the waves nearby. Mueller and Heinkel were already aboard, with Spier and Gottlieb closing in on the sloop.

Hans came up next to her. "You all right?"

"Absolutely."

Hans noticed the clouds. "Looks like things are going to go downhill from here, don't they?"

"Definitely going to rain. Hard."

Hans nodded. "So, it will be a good afternoon for a hearty lunch and then perhaps a nap."

"A nap?" Annja asked.

He winked. "I'm a growing boy. I need my rest."

She pushed him toward the sloop. "Let's get aboard."

She swam over to the sloop and Hans helped her climb up. Heinkel took her oxygen tank and weight belt. Gottlieb handed her a towel and Annja rubbed it over her hair.

Spier smiled at her. "So, Annja, what did you think of our first dive?"

"It was bigger than I imagined. I thought it was just like any other reef when I started to explore it yesterday."

Spier laughed. "Hardly. Although I'm not surprised you were drawn to it. It's intriguing, isn't it?"

"You could say that."

"So, are you convinced?"

"About what?"

"That the reef is, in fact, the remnants of a lost city."

9

"How can you be so sure?" Annja asked as the sloop whisked them back toward the Club Noah resort. "Those ruins might be something else entirely. There's no record of the civilization ever existing."

"But the pearl had to come from somewhere, didn't it?" Spier's eyes sparkled in the fading sunlight.

Annja glanced to the west and saw the clouds growing darker. They'd be lucky to get back to the dock before the sky opened up on them. Already, the waves they bounced over were churning white as the wind kicked up.

"We don't have the pearl yet," Annja said. "So, there's no way of knowing for sure where it might have come from."

Spier smiled as if he were humoring a child. "I think we'll be able to convince you more fully on our next dive."

Hans frowned. "That likely won't happen until tomorrow. Judging from the approaching storm, it's going to be quite unsettled for a while."

Spier shrugged. "We could always go night diving tonight once the storm clouds pass."

"A night dive?" Annja frowned. She hadn't gone night diving in a very long time. The risks of diving at night were always so much more than during the day. For one thing, visibility was almost nonexistent unless you had state-of-the-art lights.

"We'll be fine," Spier said, as if reading her thoughts. "We're all experienced night divers and Heinkel here has brought along the powerful lamps we'll need to set up on the reef."

"You think the dive master will let us take his boat and gear out for a night dive? He strikes me as rather easily upset," Annja said.

Hans laughed. "A few well-placed dollars should suffice."

"More bribery?"

Spier shrugged. "Why not? At least this way we know we'll be able to get what we came here for."

"And what *did* you come here for?" Annja asked. "I mean, I know you want the pearl and all, but for what purpose?"

"I thought I told you last night," Spier said. "I wish to have the scientific community take a look at it. Examine it. Discover the true nature of the pearl and what its powers might be."

"Maybe it's just a black stone," Annja said. "Without any powers whatsoever."

"That would be regrettable," Spier said. "To have traveled all this way only to find out such a thing. Tragic."

Annja felt a few raindrops hit her face and looked up. The sun had vanished, replaced by the boiling cloud mass above them. Dark streaks mixed with gray, swirling about like steam from some evil black-magic cauldron.

"I think we're about to get—"

Annja never finished her sentence because at that moment a crack of lightning flashed above them, followed by a rumble of thunder.

A deluge of rain flowed down over them in sheets of tepid

water. Mueller guided the sloop to the resort's dock and they scrambled ashore, grabbing their gear and making for the dive master's shack.

He seemed genuinely glad to see them and took all the equipment back. Spier smiled at him. "You'll refill those tanks right away, won't you?"

"Why would I do that?"

"Because we'll need them again later tonight."

"Later? This storm isn't going to let up anytime soon. You'd be foolish to go venturing out in this."

"We won't," Spier said. "But we will once it passes."

"That could be midnight."

"So it might be midnight." Spier held out his hand and, while the team looked away, Annja saw the dive master pocket the sheaf of bills Spier passed him.

Money certainly doesn't seem to be an issue for Spier, she thought. I wonder where he gets it all.

It occurred to her that she knew very little about Spier or his team. Aside from Hans.

She smiled. She knew a lot about him already.

"You all right, Annja?"

She looked up and saw Hans eyeing her. She smiled at him. "I'm fine. Just a bit tired, is all."

"What about lunch? You could do with a meal," Spier said. "I suspect we all could before indulging in a little siesta."

Annja hadn't thought about food, but the suggestion of it made her stomach rumble. "I could eat."

They ran from the dive master's shack to the main pavilion. Strong gale-force winds lashed at the pavilion but aside from the tables set near the open-air walls, the rest of the area stayed nice and dry. Annja supposed that they knew how bad the weather could get and the resort had been designed accordingly.

There was something rather cool about eating in the midst of a torrential downpour, anyway. She dined on some fresh crab-and-lobster-meat salad, drank some of the fresh mango juice and watched as Spier and his team compared notes on the morning's dive.

"You saw those conical outcroppings, Annja?" Spier asked after a few moments.

"I did."

"And yet you refuse to believe they indicate the existence of a lost civilization?"

She smiled. "Forgive me for saying so, Joachim, but a few conical outcroppings do not a lost civilization make."

"Well, they don't refute its existence, either."

"Granted, but I'd like to know a bit more about what we're supposed to be hunting for here."

"Like what?"

"Like what civilization this is supposed to be, exactly."

Spier paused and took a bite of his sandwich. "You've no doubt heard of Atlantis."

"Of course."

"The legend of a prehistoric earth inhabited by technologically advanced races, that sort of thing." Spier shrugged. "It's nothing new, of course. But the conventional thinking has always maintained that Atlantis must have been located in either the Mediterranean or the Atlantic."

"But you don't believe that?"

Spier wiped his mouth. "It's not that I don't believe it, it's just that I'm not interested in Atlantis."

"Okay."

"But I am interested in the other civilizations that were reported to have existed at the same time. Lemuria and Mu."

Annja frowned. "Most people think that they were one and the same."

Spier shook his head. "I don't think so. I think there were three centers of innovation on prehistoric earth—that is, the earth that existed prior to a massive cataclysm that wiped out the races and the evidence that they ever existed."

"So you think that Lemuria or Mu is the civilization the pearl comes from?"

"I'm fairly convinced of it."

"But what evidence do you have?"

Spier shrugged. "It's not evidence that I need in order to believe. I need faith first. If I am then able to locate evidence, then all will be well."

Annja sighed. She wasn't going to be able to argue with Spier about how utterly unscientific an approach that was. She'd met people like him before. They got an idea in their heads and there was no way of prying that idea loose unless you could shock them into seeing reality. With Spier, she wasn't sure she was going to be able to do that.

Not that there was any harm in his believing the pearl might come from a lost civilization. Annja was game enough to go along with the expedition for as long as it took. And there was something intriguing about the conical structures on the reef.

"I scraped away some of the growth and what was underneath was truly amazing," Hans said suddenly.

Annja had almost forgotten about that. "Marble," she heard herself saying. "It looked and felt like marble."

Hans nodded. "I agree."

Spier's smile widened. "Very interesting."

Annja looked at him. "I wouldn't say that necessarily supports your idea of the reef being evidence of a lost civilization, however."

"Yet marble does not occur naturally underwater," Spier said. "Surely you'd concede that point?"

"Of course."

"So, it must have gotten there somehow."

"Yes, but it could have been anything. An earthquake, a terrible storm."

"I don't think the Moros or other early Filipinos used

marble," Spier said. "I don't believe it's even indigenous to the local geography."

Annja frowned. She'd need to look that up. If it was true, then that might be another point in Spier's favor, but she wouldn't jump to conclusions before she had a chance to check things out for herself.

"I can look into it," she said.

Spier nodded. "That would be good, I think." He pushed back away from the table. "All in all, I think we had a fruitful dive today. And when we continue, I'm certain we'll find even more spectacular things."

Gottlieb spoke up. "Are we going back tonight?"

"Depends on the storm," Spier said. "If we can escape the weather, I should think a nighttime dive would prove most exciting." He glanced at Annja. "Are you interested in coming along?"

Annja smiled. "You'll still have me along?"

"Why wouldn't I?"

Annja shrugged. "I haven't exactly drunk the Kool-Aid, yet."

Spier's eyes narrowed as he processed the reference, and then he smiled. "Ah, yes, well, no worries. I don't like people who automatically believe everything they're told, anyway. I find your skepticism refreshing actually. It will help keep us all honest, I suspect."

Annja smiled. "Glad to help."

Spier nodded. "And of course you're welcome to join us. I would miss your presence if you were not with us."

"As would I," Hans said quietly.

She smiled at him. "All right, then. I may take the afternoon and see if I can pull anything up on my computer about some of the things we've discussed."

Spier shrugged. "As you wish. I doubt you'll find anything that would put us off our quest, however. My faith is, as is the faith of my team, very strong."

"I don't doubt it," Annja said. "But until such time as I have faith of my own, I'll stick to facts."

Spier smiled. "We'll see you later, then."

He walked out into the pouring rain and quickly disappeared from view. The rest of the team dissolved into smaller conversations in quiet German that Annja could barely make out.

Hans seemed happy to simply sit close by. "Still feeling well?"

Annja nodded. "Totally. No problems at all. Just a bit tired."

Hans smiled. "Nothing like an afternoon nap to restore your energy."

Annja winked. "I suppose that would depend on exactly what the nap entails, wouldn't it?"

Hans leaned back. "I am a true believer in the power of a siesta."

"And what about an afternoon delight?"

"Afternoon delight?"

Annja sighed. "Never mind. If I have to explain it, then it's already lost its appeal."

Hans narrowed his eyes, but after a moment he grinned. "Ah…I think I understand now."

"Do you?"

"I suppose there would be only one way to find out for sure."

Annja grinned. "A fact-finding mission?"

Hans shrugged. "Reconnaissance."

Annja nodded. "Recon works for me."

Hans smiled.

Annja stood and yawned. "Guess I'll grab a nap."

She walked out into the pouring rain.

Hans followed.

10

When Annja woke a few hours later, rain continued to pelt the cabana. She'd left the veranda open again, welcoming the gusting winds. She looked out from the bed and watched as the waves battled one another beneath the dark clouds.

A quick glance at her watch told her that it was after five in the evening. Presumably, dinner would be served soon in the main pavilion. But before she ate another meal, Annja wanted to do some research.

She eased herself out from under Hans's arm. He shifted, mumbling in his sleep. Annja looked down at him and smiled. He was handsome even with his eyes closed.

She took a quick shower and dressed, then eased out the door, running softly down the main path toward the administration building. She could have used her own computer, of course, but she wanted a little privacy, and since she had a guest with her, it seemed a better idea to do this without Hans looking over her shoulder.

She made it to the administration building without getting too wet. The rain seemed to be letting up some, but as soon as she thought that, another crash of thunder broke and the intensity of the rain kicked up another notch.

She stood in front of the main desk and looked at the smiling woman sitting there. "Do you have internet access here?"

"Of course. We have a bank of computers you can use."

Annja smiled. Even in the remotest places on earth you could still manage to access Google.

The woman led her to a small room tucked away off the main corridor close to the dining pavilion. Annja entered and found the room was cooled with a small air conditioner. She welcomed the cool, dry feeling of the room, and sat down behind the computer.

She spent the better part of the next two hours researching everything from lost civilizations to rumors of giant oysters. What she found didn't do much to refute Spier's theories, but neither did it support them.

Rumors of lost civilizations were as plentiful as ever, but there was little proof to suggest that any had ever actually existed. Every few years someone seemed to come out with a new theory on their existence and why expeditions should be launched to discover if they were, in fact, real. But no one ever seemed to come back with any proof.

Giant oysters, on the other hand, were real enough, and Annja found several newspaper accounts of oysters reportedly three times the size of a man's hand. Pacific oysters, especially, seemed to be something of a nuisance to mussels and some naturalists called the oyster a plague that was spreading throughout the world's oceans.

Of course, whether any oyster or giant clam could produce a pearl the size of the one Spier was seeking was another question entirely. Annja did find mention of another large pearl, the Pearl of Allah, which had been located by a diver right in Palawan itself back in 1934. It measured an astonishing nine inches across, but didn't resemble a stereotypical pearl at all. The Pearl of Allah was lumpy and misshapen. Of course, that didn't mean it was worthless. Recent estimates had placed its value at around forty-two million dollars.

Annja leaned back. Maybe there was something to Spier's story, after all. A giant pearl didn't seem to be out of the realm of possibility. Even if they weren't smooth and round and black like the one in Spier's story.

Interesting.

Annja did a little more digging, this time on Spier himself. What she found didn't do much to help build a story around him. From what she was able to dig up, Joachim Spier was a self-made man who had started building his fortune after he got involved with investing. Teaching himself to be a day trader, Spier made millions and then invested those proceeds further, exponentially increasing his net worth. It was rumored that he now possessed a net worth of roughly one billion dollars, making him one of Germany's wealthiest individuals.

Prior to becoming an investment guru, Spier had served in the German military after World War II, eventually earning his parachute wings as one of the famed parachute commandos. There wasn't much to Spier's service record and several sections had been blacked out.

After his discharge from the military, Spier lived in Munich and married his high-school sweetheart. Spier's wife died from cancer in the late 1970s. They never had children. Spier never remarried, but then became something of a recluse. He was generous in his charity work, though, especially to foundations devoted to prolonging life.

Annja sighed. Was Spier after some kind of fountain of youth?

But at eighty, why had he only started looking for the pearl now? If he was so concerned about his vitality, wouldn't he have started looking for it long ago?

On a whim, she started to type in Hans's name but then realized she didn't know his last name. She switched her query and typed in news about German involvement in the Afghanistan war. She found a few articles detailing the friendly fire incidents that had caused so much political strife back in Germany. But there was one site that listed the extensive number of German casualties in the war. It seems they hadn't all been pulled out, after all.

But she found nothing much about German special-operations units deployed to Afghanistan aside from several German media reports that claimed up to twelve members of a KSK unit, which Annja learned stood for *Kommando Spezialkräfte,* had been killed. Whether Hans's teammates were included in that number, she wasn't sure. But Annja had been around enough soldiers involved in special operations to know that what happened and what got reported were often at opposite points in their peculiar universe.

It was certainly reasonable to assume that Hans was telling her the truth about the failed operation. Certainly, other units had been bungled in their handling by higher-ups and bureaucrats before.

She switched off the computer and got up from the desk. She could have stayed in the cool room awhile longer. She was completely dry, but checking her watch, she also discovered she was ravenous.

Nothing like a lot of swimming to remind you how to eat, she thought.

Outside, the pavilion was largely subdued and the rain continued to fall steadily. Annja doubted that Spier would be able to get his night dive in tonight.

"And I thought I might have scared you off."

Annja jumped a little and turned. Hans stood there grinning at her. He looked freshly showered and shaved.

Annja blushed. "No. I just needed to check some things out."

He frowned. "You couldn't check them out in your room?"

"You were sleeping so soundly, I didn't want to disturb you."

Hans grinned. "I apparently overexerted myself this afternoon."

"Apparently."

"You hungry?"

Annja nodded. "Famished."

While they dined, other team members came in and sat with them. Annja watched the pounding surf and shook her head. "Feels like monsoon season around here today."

Gottlieb, who hadn't said much so far to Annja, nodded. "I hear from the weather report that this may continue into tomorrow morning."

Hans sighed. "Not much chance of a night dive, it would appear."

"Gut," Gottlieb said. "Then we can sleep in a little bit. I don't know about you, but I've been quite tired."

"I could do with an early night," Annja said. When no one said anything, she attacked her salad with renewed interest.

"So, Annja, did you manage to find some time to do research?"

The new voice belonged to Spier. He held a plate in front of him and sat down at their table. Annja noted he had a large pile of food again. She nodded at his meal and smiled. "I wish I could eat that much without putting on any weight."

Spier smiled. "It's all in how you keep yourself active."

Annja shook her head. "I don't know many eighty-year-old men who can eat like you do, Joachim."

He leaned closer. "I'd wager you don't know many eighty-year-olds that are anything like me."

"That's true. You're quite unique."

Spier laughed. "Ha, always a pleasure to be an oddity, I suppose." He bit into his steak. "So, tell me, what did you find out?"

"Nothing much on lost civilizations. Just that a lot of people I would probably label as crazy seem to believe in them."

"I'm crazy now?"

"No, you seem sane enough."

Hans chuckled. "That's only because you don't know him well yet."

Gottlieb joined in the laughter and Spier seemed to revel in it. "He's right, Annja. Once you get to know me, you'll see I'm just as crazy as any of those people on the internet."

Annja smiled. "Wonderful."

"But seriously, did you find anything of interest?"

Annja shrugged. "Did you know about the Pearl of Allah?"

Spier smiled. "Ah, so you did find out something."

"Nine inches across supposedly."

Spier nodded. "It is indeed."

"So finding a giant pearl isn't necessarily out of the question."

Spier leaned closer. "Did you read the description of the pearl?"

Annja nodded. "They said it was a misshapen mess. But it's still worth forty-two million dollars."

Spier sniffed. "Money. It always comes down to money. I wonder what sort of a world we would have if mankind had not invented the concept of such a thing."

"You wouldn't be worth almost a billion dollars, for starters," Annja said.

Spier nodded. "True. But the world might be a better place. One devoted to the furthering of mankind's intelligence."

"Is that why you want the pearl?"

Spier took another bite of his steak and shrugged. "I have many ideas for why I want to find the pearl. Perhaps this is my last great hurrah. I'm old. Soon, I will most certainly pass on from this mortal place and begin my next great adventure. But maybe I want one last mighty event before I do that."

Annja picked at her carrots. "The pearl we're looking for is supposedly round, right?"

"Yes. Round and as black as the very night itself." Spier pointed outside where the light was fading. "Or perhaps as dark as the weather here."

"No diving tonight, I guess," Annja said.

Spier sighed. "Alas, we are sometimes forced to accept Mother Nature's influence on our worldly desires."

They passed the remainder of the dinner talking about the pearl and what they expected to find out at the dive site. But as the hours passed and true night settled in, Annja found herself growing sleepy.

She could see that Hans was interested in spending more time with her, but Annja begged off.

"I think I'm going to call it a night," she told him when they were done with dinner.

"Was it something I did?"

Annja smiled. "You've got nothing to worry about in that department. I think if anything you wore me out, is all."

"See you tomorrow morning?"

"Absolutely."

Hans nodded. "Joachim wants to get started early again providing the weather decides to cooperate, of course."

"Call me if anything comes up."

"I will."

She watched Hans walk toward the other section of cabanas before turning and heading out through the rain. She smiled as she quickly grew soaked. The rain felt refreshing and she felt reenergized.

Annja passed her cabana and continued walking around the resort. No one was out on a night like this and every breeze blew more water over her.

She walked closer to the water's edge and then over to where the dive master's shack was situated.

Ahead of her, she thought she saw movement.

Annja squinted and then used her peripheral vision to scan the area.

Someone was moving in the shadows down by the dock.

Maybe it was Dr. Tiko keeping late hours at the medical clinic. Or maybe it was the dive master finishing up his work before calling it a day, she thought.

But a quick glance at both places showed Annja there were no lights on in either one.

And what's more, the figure ahead of her seemed to be trying to keep his movements concealed.

Annja squatted on the path and watched as he moved from the dive master's shack down to the dock and back again several times.

The realization came to her. Someone was planning to go diving tonight, regardless of the storm.

Without thinking about it, Annja moved down the path to get a better look.

11

The pounding rain concealed any noise Annja made as she stole her way down the path. She thought briefly about going back to get Hans, but then just as quickly disregarded the idea. She'd told him she was tired, after all, and if he thought she had blown him off in favor of a walk, then he might be hurt by it.

No, better to get a look at this herself.

She froze as the figure came back up the walkway and vanished again inside the dive shack. Annja watched as he dragged out what looked to be oxygen tanks and then stowed them aboard one of the resort sloops like the one she'd ridden on out to the dive site.

Who would be crazy enough to go diving in this weather? At night, no less? They'd need to be an expert navigator to get through the storm, and an even better diver if they hoped to find whatever they might have been looking for under the swirling waves.

The whole thing struck Annja as verging on suicidal.

Then again, anyone who had seen her go off on her own probably would have thought much the same thing.

Annja moved closer to the dock and paused behind a large tree. A crack of thunder made her wince. If the lightning flashed at the wrong time, she'd be visible to the shadowy figure in front of her.

But so would he.

He vanished into the dive shack and Annja made her way down to the boat. She was right. There were four oxygen tanks and multiple mouthpieces and regulators aboard. Masks and fins completed the gear.

She heard a noise behind her and had to sink down behind one of the pilings. The shadowy figure put down several bags and Annja saw what looked like high-powered lights going into the boat.

Was it possible that Spier was launching the dive, after all? She frowned. That didn't make sense. Spier didn't have any reason to keep the dive from Annja. Unless he wasn't being entirely forthright with his reasons for wanting to find the pearl.

Still, it didn't seem like something he would do. He'd invited her to dive in the first place. And then there was the matter of Hans. Would he go behind Annja's back to do this? She mused about it for a moment and then decided that he probably would not. There was something there between them, she felt, and she doubted that he would spoil their blossoming relationship by being covert like this.

Of course, he had been in special operations. Stuff like this was what they did all the time. Maybe to Hans and the rest of the team it didn't even seem duplicitous. Maybe they just thought of this as a normal night out.

But if that was the case, then where was everyone else?

The shadowy figure covered all the gear with a tarp and then vanished into the dive shack again. Annja took a breath and moved closer to the boat. She looked under the tarp and confirmed that there were lights there.

Whoever was in the dive shack was going for a little nocturnal exploration.

She heard the twig crack and whirled, seeing the shadow come down toward her. Annja had no time to hide and instead found herself sliding into the boat and concealing herself under the tarp.

Luckily, the waves in the tiny bay were already causing the boat to bob up and down. The shadow didn't notice the commotion.

He stepped onto the boat.

Annja heard the roar of the engine and her heart jumped in her chest. She heard the rope as it was tossed onto the tarp that covered her and then felt the boat ease away from the dock. In this weather, the noise of the engine wouldn't even penetrate the din. No one would know that the boat was gone.

And no one would miss Annja.

The boat bounced over the waves and Annja struggled to hold on to the sides of the boat without alerting the shadow. She could confront the person, of course, but she felt there had to be a good reason for why he was doing this in secret.

And she wanted to know why.

So she stayed put and let the motion of the boat move her about. The real task would be staying concealed when the shadow stopped the boat and prepared to dive.

That came sooner than she expected. A quick peek out from under the tarp revealed that the shadowy coastline in the distance appeared to put them in the same location that Annja had dived earlier with Spier and his team.

But what would bring someone else out here on a night like this?

The tarp shifted and Annja froze. She heard nothing that would indicate the identity of the shadow she shared the boat with, but judging from the motion of the boat, he was strapping on his diving gear.

A few moments later, Annja heard him go over the side.

She crept out from under the tarp. Rain still pelted her, and the cloudy sky overhead gave her very little ambient light to see anything.

She checked the equipment and found that one of the arc lights had gone over the side, as well.

As if on cue, a circle of light came from below the boat. Annja peered over the side and saw that the shadow had set up lights around the coral reef.

"What is he doing down there?"

She glanced back at the gear. There were enough oxygen tanks, she figured. Enough other gear, as well.

Before reason could prevail, Annja pulled her dress over her head and, in her bra and panties, started strapping into the diving gear. In a few minutes, she was ready.

Over the side she went.

The water embraced her and she slid into the dark liquid without being able to see anything except the light in front of her far down below.

There was a real danger, she knew, of running into another shark. They fed at night, and in the inky darkness of the sea she could easily be mistaken for food.

She sank deeper toward the light. That would be the safest place to be, she supposed.

At the bottom, she could see the shadowy figure working on another light rig. She didn't think he'd brought much over the side with him, but she saw that there was a lot more gear down here than she'd expected.

Maybe this was his second trip out to the site?

She didn't know. He could have been ferrying supplies out here all evening for all she knew. Another potential reason why this couldn't possibly be Spier or his men.

Annja drifted slowly farther down, trying to remain just

out of the light's ambient pool. If the shadow turned and saw her, the jig would be up, of course. And Annja wanted to know what he was doing down here.

A dark shape shot past her in the dark. She winced, feeling the burst of adrenaline and fear flood her system. She was exposed, she knew, but she had little choice until the shadow moved again.

When he did, he crossed over the top of the reef to the other side.

Annja sank lower and wound her way slowly around to where she could spy on the shadow without him seeing her behind the coral. He wore a dark wet suit that covered his entire body. The mask he wore obscured his face and Annja had no idea who she might be diving with.

She smiled. But at least she wasn't alone. The dive master would be so proud.

The shadow put another set of lights down near the base of the reef and flicked them on. Bright yellow light illuminated an area of the reef and the fish responded accordingly. Most of them backed into their tiny crevices, into the darkness.

But Annja saw that the larger fish crowded around the light as if to investigate this burning sun in their world. The shadow ignored them and immediately started focusing his attention on the various outcroppings nearby. With a silver-bladed knife, he pried into them.

Annja recognized the part of the reef as being where Hans had found the covered marble. But the shadow wasn't near that. Was he looking for it?

Annja frowned and checked around her. Something about floating in the dark sea made her feel as though a thousand eyes were upon her.

She smirked. Of course there were. All of the life on the reef would know she was there.

Well, everyone except for the shadow.

Another dark shape on the edge of her vision darted past her. Annja whirled, kicking up a disturbance in the sand, but by the time she'd turned, the shape was gone.

Another shark?

She swallowed and fought against the rising tide of fear. She should leave, of course. The boat was above her.

Somewhere.

Provided she didn't screw up too much, she would be able to find it again. But what then?

She peered around the edge of the reef and the shadow was gone.

Annja whirled around. Where did he go?

She crept around the edge of the reef, thinking he must have moved on to another section. She looked around trying to find his air bubble trail. If she could see that, then she could pinpoint his location without too much difficulty.

But she saw nothing.

It really was almost as if he had disappeared right off the coral reef.

Annja looked behind her into the depths but saw nothing there, either. He had to be around there some place, she thought.

But where?

She crept around to where she'd seen him last. She recognized where he'd scraped off a few barnacles, but the outcroppings yielded nothing that gave her a clue as to where he'd gone.

What were the chances that he'd been taken by a shark? She shook her head. No, there'd be some sort of evidence of an attack. His tanks would be lying on the ocean floor. His weight belt would have been shredded.

She frowned. Unless something even bigger than the fourteen-footer had simply taken him in its jaws and swam off.

Her stomach ached.

Annja's mouth went dry and she glanced down at her oxygen gauge.

It was running close to empty.

Her mind whirled. The tanks should have been filled if they were going to be used for diving.

Why hadn't this one been filled all the way?

She hadn't been down that long!

She needed to get back to the boat. But in the next instant, she knew where the shadow had vanished to.

He'd resurfaced.

The boat engine roared overhead, its sound muffled through the water, but Annja glanced up and saw the white foam as the boat suddenly shot back the way they had come out.

Leaving Annja all alone in the dark ocean.

She glanced back down at the comforting lights surrounding the reef. He'd left them on, which had to mean he was coming back, right? Why would he leave them on otherwise? It didn't make sense.

She had to get to the surface.

And that meant leaving the comfort of the light.

But Annja had no choice. She was already feeling the chill of the cooler water entering her body. She'd be hypothermic if that guy didn't bring the boat back soon.

She guessed they were about a mile offshore.

She could swim for it.

But in the storm it would be a tough slog.

First things first, she thought. Let's get to the surface. She watched the bubbles rise in front of her and made sure she ascended slower than they did.

Almost there.

She tasted the staleness of the air in her tank. It was almost gone.

The darkness around her seemed to expand and envelop her.

Annja fought for breath. She was twenty feet from the surface.

Fifteen.

Ten.

The darkness closed in as Annja took her last breath.

She broke the surface.

And then passed out, bobbing in the swells.

12

"I must say that I find your choice of lingerie particularly... compelling."

Annja blinked her eyes and found herself for the second time in as many days on another boat other than the one she'd arrived on. It was still night and she felt drops of rain on her skin.

But she was alive.

And that was what mattered most, she supposed. Even accepting the rather sarcastic voice that had greeted her upon her return to consciousness.

Worse, it was a voice she knew.

"Hello, Roux."

His face hovered closer. "So you do recognize me. Well, that's good at least. Means you didn't sustain any lasting brain damage when you blacked out."

Annja rubbed her head and sat up. Her sometime mentor, Roux, draped a thick woolen blanket around her shoulders. "Keep this around you—it'll warm you up some until I can get us back ashore."

"What are you doing here?" Annja's teeth chattered and her pulse raced. She took some deep breaths and willed herself to calm down.

"I'd ask the same thing of you," Roux said. "You should be in New York."

"I was. I got tired of being there."

"So you flew halfway around the world?" Roux smiled. "Your ability to surprise me is without limits."

"I'll take that as a compliment," she said, hugging the blanket tighter.

"Please do," Roux said. "I meant it as such." He pulled the engine cord and the tiny motor sprang to life. Roux sat down and, with one hand on the rudder, guided the boat toward the darkened coastline.

"Where are we going?"

"The trip back to Club Noah will take us too long. I'm afraid you might have hypothermia, so we need to get you some place warm as soon as possible."

"I'm fine," Annja said.

"No," Roux said. "You're not. Now stop being your usual stubborn self and let me help you at least."

"And why would you do that?"

Roux put a hand over his heart. "Is that any way to treat an old friend? Honestly, if I wasn't such a nice guy, I might take real offense at that statement."

"You're an old swindler," Annja said. "Stop pretending otherwise."

Roux shrugged. "Fair enough. But I'm still enough of a friend that I plucked you out of the water and saved your life."

"Thank you for that," Annja said. She pointed. "And what's with the wet suit? Were you diving?"

"That was the plan. Until you interrupted it by floating in the ocean in your underwear."

"Yeah, well, I didn't realize I was going to be going for a dive tonight."

"No? Then what brought you out here?"

"I saw someone back at the resort. I followed him."

Roux shook his head. "And why on earth would you do a thing like that? It was the middle of the night. And there was a storm raging. What possessed you to follow him?"

Annja shrugged. "My natural curiosity?"

"I know all about that natural curiosity of yours, Annja. And I also know it's gotten you into trouble more times than any of my other friends."

"You don't have any other friends, Roux."

Roux sighed. "More sharp-barbed commentary from the wounded exhibitionist. Honestly…"

The tiny boat bobbed over the swells and then Roux guided it into a small tree-lined cove. The waves grew less violent and he beached the little craft on the sandy shore. Stepping out, Roux held out his hand to Annja. "Is it all right to offer my hand to a young maiden like yourself?"

"It's a bit outdated," Annja said. But she accepted his help, anyway, and stepped onto the beach. "Where are we?"

"On the other side of the island. Your resort is over the mountain there. You're welcome to head back that way, although I think the bugs would eat you alive before you'd get close."

Roux busied himself with making a fire and, despite the deluge that had fallen, the older man managed to have a blazing fire going in a few short minutes.

He stepped back and admired his work. "There, that should warm you up nicely in no time. Plus, it'll keep the bugs away."

Annja moved closer to the flames and felt the heat surge through her body. Her teeth no longer chattered and she felt more alert. But she kept the blanket wrapped around her. No sense giving Roux any more of a peep show than necessary. Annja thanked her lucky stars that it hadn't been Garin Braden who'd found her. He would have had a hard time restraining himself.

Roux and Garin had become as much a part of her life as Joan of Arc's sword. The two men had followed the sword through time ever since Joan's death, and now that Annja possessed the sword they all tried to understand—and sometimes fight—the power that linked them.

"Whiskey?"

Annja looked up at the small thermos cup Roux had produced from somewhere. She took it with a nod. "Thanks."

Roux found a log and rolled it over to sit on. "So, you're here expressly for the purpose of relaxing? Is that it?"

"Relaxation has taken a backseat in my life, in case you hadn't noticed."

"Well, sure," Roux said. "What with you choosing to save the world all the time."

"I don't *choose* to do anything. I simply seem to be in bad situations that need correcting. More often than I'd ever want, for that matter."

"More problems accepting your destiny, I see," Roux said. "I do find it so amusing sometimes. Honestly, I do."

"Well, I'm thrilled I can provide you with endless amounts of fun."

Roux took the cup back and drained it before refilling it. "So the Philippines called out to you for rest and relaxation."

"There's a reef here I wanted to explore, as well," Annja said. "Apparently it hadn't been properly cataloged."

Roux took another sip of his drink and grinned. "And so, yesterday you arrived and promptly went diving by yourself."

"How do you know I was here yesterday?"

Roux spread his hands. "Annja, Annja…now really, after all this time that we've known each other. Are you really so surprised that I know where you are all the time?"

"You seemed surprised enough when you fished me out of the drink."

"That's because I assumed you were safely and soundly tucked away in your cabana with your new boyfriend. I didn't think I'd find you bobbing dead to the world on the swells out here, waiting for some shark to grab you. Again."

"You know about that, too?"

Roux shrugged. "I heard some things. How did the sword work underwater? Slice him right through, did it?"

"It did the job."

"Ah, yes, you wouldn't see the glory in killing such a fine beast, I suppose." Roux shook his head. "Shame, really. I wish I could have seen it."

"Well, next time a huge shark wants to have me for its lunch, I'll be sure to let you know first."

Roux nodded as if that was the most logical thing in the world. "Excellent. I'd appreciate that."

"I'm sure you would," Annja grumbled. The fire crackled and, despite everything that had happened, Annja felt sleepy. She leaned back against the tree and let her eyelids droop slightly. "Tell me why you're here, Roux."

"Maybe I'm on vacation, too."

"You're an awful liar," Annja said. "Didn't Garin ever tell you that?"

"More times than I care to remember. Such insolence from that spoiled lothario. I don't have to tell you that you're lucky I found you tonight instead of him. You wouldn't still have those white lacy things on if he had."

"I already considered that," Annja said. "Now stop trying to change the subject."

"Was I?"

"You were."

Roux let a few seconds pass while more of the wet wood crackled in the heat of the fire. Finally, he stood and helped himself to more whiskey. "Very well, since you seem to already be tuning in to the nature of this place, I suppose it's only fair to tell you what's going on."

"And what is that?"

"You've heard of the Pearl of Palawan already. I know that guy Spier has told you about its powers."

"He's really said nothing about the supposed powers it has," Annja said. "Right now, he just wants to find the damned thing."

"Let me guess," Roux said evenly. "You don't believe it exists, do you?"

Annja shrugged. "I don't know what to believe actually. You know I look at everything with a healthy dose of skepticism."

"True enough," Roux said. "But you are simultaneously emboldened by a sense of wonder. It's what makes you so utterly charming."

Annja frowned. Whenever Roux handed out compliments, something was definitely up. "Uh, thanks."

"You're welcome, my dear." Roux chuckled. "So, Spier is looking for the pearl that once belonged to the great Queen Esmeralda of the Moros."

"Was there really such a person?" Annja asked. "I couldn't find any reference to one today when I searched online."

Roux sniffed. "More reliance on technology." He shook his head. "If the world were to end tomorrow—"

"You'd probably be behind it," Annja said. "Yes, I know all about your hard-line stance on overreliance on technology. Of course, you're a hypocrite because I know you use the same technology to keep up with things that happen all over the world."

"It's more of a when-in-Rome situation, I assure you," Roux said. "I don't go in much for being at the mercy of machinery."

"Queen Esmeralda?"

Roux shrugged. "I'm sure there probably was a Queen

Esmeralda at some point long ago, but that's not really important anymore. She's such a passing figure in the legend, it's scarcely worth mentioning her name, to be honest."

"So what is important, then?"

"The real origin of the pearl, of course."

Annja looked at him. In the flickering firelight, Roux's features seemed to age and show his true lifeline of six hundred years. He'd seen an awful lot over the centuries. But sometimes it was hard figuring out where his knowledge ended and where his manipulation of facts began.

"Let me guess, you think it came from Lemuria or Mu, too?"

"Is that what Spier believes?"

"I think so."

"How interesting." Roux rubbed his chin thoughtfully and tossed another log on the fire. It blazed and hissed as the water evaporated, but then started to catch, tossing up plumes of smoke into the air.

Annja watched it drift skyward. The bugs were kept to a dull roar thanks to the heavy cloying smoke that surrounded them.

"Roux?"

"Sorry, Annja. I just get caught up thinking sometimes. Forgive an old man, would you?"

"Fine."

"Spier is certainly more resourceful than I've given him credit for thus far."

"Thus far?"

"Oh, certainly. I've known of his search for the pearl for some time now. I didn't think he'd get so close, though. Especially when I was also searching for it."

"Why?"

"Its powers, of course. The pearl is reputed to be incredibly powerful when possessed by one with the ability to tap into its true nature."

"And what sort of true nature would we be talking about here?"

Roux smiled. "The power to control the world, of course. Isn't that what all these ancient relics are supposed to do?"

"Some," Annja said. "Not all."

"Well, the ones worth going after all do." He chuckled. "And naturally, Spier wants the pearl for his own purposes."

"What purposes would those be?"

Roux shrugged. "I haven't quite figured that out yet."

"All right, then. Why do you want the pearl?"

Roux smiled at her. "You know I have an affinity for possessing items of antiquity such as the pearl."

"Yeah," Annja said. "I know."

"Well, I want the pearl most especially so. I've discovered something of its true nature, you see...."

13

"And what would its true nature be?" Annja asked. A log cracked in the fire, tossing sparks and embers onto the wet sand where they fizzled and grew dark.

Roux smiled. "Well, now that would be telling, wouldn't it? And honestly, I'm not certain that you should know just yet."

"Why not?"

"It's a loyalty issue," Roux said. "You have this annoying habit of running off to do good whenever you sense an injustice. Frankly, that's caused my personal agenda some problems over the past few years."

Annja frowned. "You were the one who told me to embrace my destiny. You were the one who told me to step up and accept the responsibility that the sword placed on me."

"Well, sure," Roux said. "But within reason, Annja. After all, we're in this together."

"We?"

"You, me, Garin." Roux shrugged. "Who else knows about the sword and what it can do?"

"A few people who have seen it in action over the years."

Roux looked horrified at the thought. "You should have killed them."

"Why on earth would I do a thing like that? They didn't deserve to be killed for simply seeing the sword."

Roux shook his head. "I don't think I would have left any witnesses behind. No sense giving people something to talk about."

Annja shook her head. "And what would they say? 'Oh, I saw this magical sword'? Please."

"They might," Roux said. "And what happens then? The next time they see you, they try to take it away."

"Yeah, good luck with that plan. No one has succeeded yet." Annja stared at the fire. Between the woolen blanket and the heat from the flames, she was warming up rapidly. "If it was possible to take the sword, don't you think someone would have done it already?"

"Maybe the time isn't right yet," Roux said quietly.

Annja glanced at him. She'd always suspected Roux had several agendas operating at any one time. She also suspected that he would have loved to possess the sword. He'd denied it, of course, but there was something about the way he looked at it from time to time that led Annja to believe it in her gut.

She shifted. "Well, if anyone wants it, they don't have to attack me. Maybe I'll just give it to them if they ask real nice."

Roux sighed. "You know that won't work, Annja. Based on my research, it might even destroy the sword."

"Destroy it how?"

"It might shatter again. Thousands of pieces that would have to be reacquired and pieced back together. I can't tell you how hard it was to find them all the last time that happened. I'd rather not do it again."

They were quiet for a minute. Annja cleared her throat

after inhaling a gust of smoke. "Tell me about the pearl, Roux."

"I said no."

"You said no, but I also know you. And you're dying to let me take a peek at the knowledge you have. So what is it? What is it about the pearl that makes you so excited?"

Roux tossed another soggy log into the flames and watched it for a moment. "You won't believe me, Annja."

"Try me."

Roux glanced at her. "Fine. The pearl isn't organic. It's man-made."

Annja shrugged. "So what? What's so incredible about that?"

"The pearl dates back to a time in earth's history when such a thing would have been supposedly impossible to create."

"Our understanding of history's been wrong before," Annja said. "How old is the pearl supposed to be?"

"Roughly twenty-five thousand years."

Annja gasped and looked at Roux. "That's impossible."

"See?" Roux shook his head. "Honestly, Annja, I don't know why I bother with you sometimes. After everything you've seen in connection to the sword and after all the experiences you've had, you still cling to this ridiculous notion that the world is as the world seems to be."

"My skepticism keeps me from becoming a loony," Annja said. "Anyone else would have flipped out if they'd suddenly found themselves with Joan of Arc's old sword. Me? I seem to handle it pretty well."

"Maybe you're Joan of Arc reincarnated," Roux said.

Annja waved her hand. "You know, I thought of that once. But, to be honest, I don't know what I believe. If I was Joan of Arc in another time, then I ought to have some of her memories locked away somewhere inside my head, right?"

"Only if you happen to believe the usual silliness that most New Agey types espouse."

"You don't think I'd have her memories?"

Roux shrugged. "I don't know for certain. What I do believe is that the process of reincarnation might prove so traumatic that the soul does its best to almost cocoon itself from the trauma. That would mean that memories, emotions and the like would only be released very, very gradually throughout the next life. In some circumstances—say, something like being burned at the stake—the soul might never release any indication of the former life."

Annja looked at the fire and tried to imagine what it would be like to have the flames lick their way through clothing and flesh, burning from the outside in while a crowd watched.

She shook her head. It was too awful to think about.

"It was a terrible sight to behold, Annja." Roux said this quietly above the winds that still rustled the nearby trees.

"Did she suffer for long?"

"I have no way of knowing exactly when she lost consciousness," Roux said. "So, I can't say."

Annja shook her head. "The people who did to that her…"

"They paid for their crimes—I'm certain of it," Roux said.

Annja looked at him. "How are you so certain?"

Roux shrugged. "Because I have to believe that any just and loving God would never allow one of His children to be killed in such a manner without repercussions to those who committed the grievous act."

"That's rather Old Testament."

"I happen to like the Old Testament, Annja. It's a lot more properly intimidating than the new huggable versions they perpetrate on the unknowing these days. Imagine if more people thought they'd be facing God's wrath when they faced Him, instead of a big welcome hug. People might actually check their ridiculous behavior from time to time. That would be a good thing indeed."

Annja sighed. The night was growing long and she needed some sleep. Hans was expecting her at the dock in the morning.

She looked up at Roux. "You were going diving tonight."

"Yes."

"So that was you back on the resort stealing oxygen tanks?"

"No. That was your dive master actually. I paid him a nice little bribe to bring all that gear out and set it up for me to use."

Annja frowned. "You might have a word with him about his inability to fill oxygen tanks all the way to capacity."

Roux smiled. "Well, he probably didn't think he'd have another person using them. You didn't happen to notice the label on the back of the tank you used, either, did you?"

"What label?"

"The one that said it wasn't to be used. I had him bring out two that were half-empty so I could use them for inflating several flotation devices if I found anything down there worth bringing to the surface."

"I must have missed that," Annja said.

"I'm not surprised, considering you were in the midst of a rainstorm." Roux stood and looked out at the ocean. "Although it certainly seems to be calming down now."

"Is this your way of telling me to skedaddle?"

Roux looked back at Annja. "You're not in much shape to go diving, Annja. You're not even dressed for it."

Annja grinned. "You've got a point there."

"I can take you back to the resort."

Annja nodded. "And then you're going to return to the dive site."

Roux shrugged. "I paid good money to get that gear out there. It would be a shame to see it being squandered like that."

"And what will you do if you find something?"

Roux cocked an eyebrow. "Why, what do you expect me to do?"

"I don't know…maybe share it with the world?"

Roux laughed. "And attract publicity? Good Lord, that's the very last thing I ever want."

"People deserve to see what you find, Roux."

"People," Roux said, "have tried their very best to destroy this planet time and time again. I don't believe they deserve anything except a serious slap across the face to wake their collective pathetic soul. I sometimes doubt mankind would know what to do with something good. Most likely they'd simply try to destroy it."

"Don't forget, Roux. You're part of mankind, too."

"A regrettable thing that," Roux said. "And if it helps, I don't actually consider myself part of the human race any longer."

"You don't?"

"Annja, I'm six hundred years old. Somehow that makes me a bit more than just another human, don't you think?"

"Well, you've certainly got the ego for it, I suppose."

Roux frowned. "The thanks I get for saving your life."

"Are we leaving?" Annja asked. The fire had started to die down and more rain was falling. Annja shivered and realized that she needed a hot shower and some serious sleep.

She glanced at Roux, who kicked sand onto the dying embers and then led her back down to the beach. In all probability, he wouldn't find anything at the dive site tonight. That meant Annja would have to try even harder tomorrow to come up with something.

But what?

She wasn't sure what she believed about the story of some lost civilization. Nor was Roux's tale that the pearl itself was twenty-five thousand years old particularly believable. How would people back then have made it? How could they have possibly created a round sphere like that?

The problem was, as much as Annja might not believe it, Roux did. Worse, if Spier got wind of that theory, it would drive him on like nothing else had before.

And Annja still didn't know what his motives were for possessing the pearl.

With Roux, that was fairly easy. Roux didn't want anyone to have anything remotely powerful. So he simply tried to grab everything he could.

But Spier...

"Let's get going. I want to dump you at the resort and then get back here before I lose the darkness."

"You might find more in the sunlight."

Roux shook his head. "As soon as the sun comes up, you and your merry band will be back out there. That's the last thing I need."

"Sorry to be a thorn in your side."

Roux eased the boat out into the waves and then hopped on board. Annja sat near the bow.

At once, the engine sputtered to life and Roux guided them away from the beach, pointing them out toward the bay. "Annja, you've been a thorn in my side before, but it hasn't stopped me from following my personal plans. And whether you agree or not, we are in this together."

"We are?"

Roux nodded. "You just don't see the situation for what it is. Yet."

"Yet?"

"But you will someday. I really do believe that."

"I guess I'll look forward to someday, then," Annja said. Because right then she didn't think she and Roux were on the same page at all.

14

Annja awoke the next morning to gentle breezes and brilliant sunshine spilling into her cabana. The storm clouds had vanished along with the choppy seas and driving rain.

Annja sat up and ran over the previous night's events in her mind. With Roux running around, she'd have to make sure that Spier didn't notice. The last thing she wanted was those two worlds colliding in a way that would force her to have to explain how she knew Roux.

She could always describe him as a work colleague or something, but there was no guarantee that Roux would go along with that. He'd delighted in thwarting her actions in the past. No telling what he'd want to do this time around.

After a quick breakfast of an egg-white omelet and oatmeal, Annja headed down to the dock, aware that it was getting late. As she approached the dock, she saw Hans and the rest of the men loading up the boat.

Hans didn't look up or smile in her direction.

"Good morning," she said brightly.

He glanced up at her. "I went by your place last night to say hello." He tossed a bag into the boat. "You weren't there."

Annja nodded. "I couldn't sleep. I went for a walk."

"Where?"

"All over."

Hans frowned. "I spent some time walking around, too. I thought that maybe you had gone for a walk so I looked around. I couldn't seem to locate you."

"We must have missed each other," Annja said.

Hans nodded. "I thought so, too. So I waited outside of your cabana until very late. Imagine my surprise when you came back with some old man, wrapped in a blanket and wearing nothing but your lingerie underneath."

Annja smiled. "Oh, Hans—"

He held up a hand. "Listen, Annja, I know we just met, so I'm not trying to be all possessive here. It's just that I thought you were different."

"Trust me, Hans. I'm as different as they come."

"Well, you can sleep with whomever you want, of course. I just wish you hadn't chosen to shack up with that guy. Honestly, he looked ancient."

If you only knew how old, Annja thought. "Hans, trust me, I didn't sleep with him."

"Annja, I'm a big boy. I can handle the truth. I know what I saw."

"You saw what you did, but not for the reasons you think."

Hans stopped loading the boat. "So, explain it to me, then."

Annja frowned. How exactly was she going to explain Roux, the dive master, the lack of oxygen, the pearl and all that stuff they were going to see when they returned to the reef? She couldn't.

"I don't know that I can," she said finally.

Hans sighed. "I thought so. Look, just be honest with me, Annja. If you want to fool around, then fine. I've done the wild stage of my life. I guess I was looking for a little something more…in-depth than just a good lay."

Annja smiled. "I didn't sleep with that guy, Hans. You've got to believe me. I can't tell you everything that's going on right now. Not because I don't trust you, but because it wouldn't make any sense to you. Just give me some time, okay? I promise it will all be clear in a day or two."

"Yeah, all right. Whatever." Hans went back to loading the boat. Annja stood there a moment longer.

"So, am I still welcome on the dive?"

"Why wouldn't you be?"

Annja turned and Spier stood there with a bright smile. He noticed the expression on Hans's face and sniffed. "Hans, stop acting like a little boy. The woman has a right to be with whomever she wishes. Don't pout."

Annja scowled. "You told everyone?"

Hans shrugged. "I was upset."

"Try devastated," Mueller said, walking over to grab the oxygen tanks. "Honestly, it got a little embarrassing."

Gottlieb chuckled. "I think, Annja Creed, that you may have broken our man Hans's heart with your cruel and calculating sexual escapades."

Spier leaned closer to Annja. "Hans said he was an old guy. If that's true, might I interest you in a little dalliance later?"

"Oh, for crying out loud." Annja stepped back. "I did not sleep with that man last night. Hans saw something he didn't understand. What looked like an obvious explanation is not what happened at all."

Spier and the rest of the team stopped. "So, what happened?"

Hans sighed. "She won't tell me."

"I can't," Annja said.

Heinkel snorted. "*Ja,* she slept with him."

Annja put her hands on her hips and glared. "I most certainly did not."

"She's telling the truth."

Annja groaned. She turned and saw Roux striding down the ramp toward the dock.

Spier and Hans stopped loading the boat. Spier said something in German to Hans, who only nodded.

Roux came up alongside Annja. "As delightful as a nocturnal interlude would have been—especially for Annja—we did not sleep together."

Annja rolled her eyes. "You're as bad as Garin sometimes," she said under her breath.

"Perish the thought," Roux said. To Spier he held out his hand. "I'm Roux. Very pleased to meet you."

"Joachim Spier. Very pleased to meet you. This is Hans, Gottlieb, Heinkel and Mueller."

Roux shook hands with all of them, but paused with Hans. "She's telling you the truth, my dear boy. We did not sleep together."

"Really?"

"Do I look as though I have the constitution to weather such an activity? Honestly, I'm far too old to indulge my libido these days. I live much more of a monklike existence."

Annja coughed, attempting to cover her uncontrollable laughter.

"And what is it you do?" Spier asked.

"Yes, Roux," Annja said. "What is it that you do?"

Roux winked at her and then smiled at Spier. "I'm interested in antiquities, of course. I gather you are interested in much the same thing."

"Do you now? And how would you know that about me?"

Roux smiled. "I make it my business to know about people. Usually long before I meet them."

Spier glanced at Annja but Roux held up his hand. "Annja

had nothing to do with this, I assure you. She and I are old friends. Nothing more."

"Since when do old friends parade around in their underwear?" Hans grumbled.

"Oh, yes, that," Roux said. "Well, Annja went for a walk last night and happened to take a rather nasty fall off the dock. She was soaked and I thought she might be swept out to sea."

"You saved her?" Spier asked.

"Indeed. We were at the far end of the island and I was forced to make a fire to warm her up. Imagine my surprise to find Annja here. We haven't seen each other in years, and of all the places to turn up, we find each other here."

"That's quite a coincidence," Spier said.

Annja grinned. "A lucky one for me apparently."

"You must remember to not be so careless," Spier said. "I hate to think what might have happened to you if your old friend was not nearby to save you."

"Me, too," Annja said. But Spier didn't look like he believed a word that Roux had told him. Despite that, he was warm and welcoming.

"Do you dive, Herr Roux?" he asked.

"I do indeed."

"Then you must join us on our excursion today."

Roux stepped forward excitedly. "Are you sure? I'd be honored, of course, but I don't want to intrude."

"Nonsense. We can always use another diver along with us. We are exploring a reef near here. It is uncharted and we hope to make some rudimentary surveys of the area to assist other recreational divers who might find it interesting."

Roux wiped his sunglasses on his T-shirt and smiled. "That's incredibly thoughtful of you."

"We do what we can," Spier said. "Now, you'll need diving gear, of course." He waved and Annja turned to see the dive master coming down the walkway. The dive master glanced hurriedly at Roux, who merely smiled at him.

"Yes, Herr Spier?"

Spier pointed at Roux. "Our new friend here requires gear for diving. Can you see to it that he's outfitted with the necessary equipment?"

"Of course."

"Excellent."

The dive master glanced at Roux. "This way, please."

Roux smiled at Spier and Annja. "I'll see you shortly."

Annja watched him turn and walk away. Spier watched, as well, and then regarded Annja. "I don't trust that man, Annja."

"That's probably wise."

He smiled. "Does he usually make a habit of lying to people he's only just met?"

"I think it depends on what he's up to."

Spier looked at her intently. "And you don't happen to know what he's up to, do you?"

"If I had to guess," Annja said. "I'd say he's probably after the same thing you are."

Spier nodded. "Thank you for being honest."

"I'm just along to see if this thing exists," Annja said. "I don't have any agenda for it if we find it."

Spier glanced up at the dive shack. "But something tells me that your friend Roux there does have an agenda. Is that so?"

"I've never known him not to have one," Annja said.

"Men like him are never without," Spier said. "I should know."

Hans glanced at Annja. "Was he lying about…that?"

"No," Annja said. "That was the truth."

Hans sighed. "I'm sorry."

"Forget it. I wasn't being up front with you because I

didn't know how to tell you what was going on without creating a lot of confusion."

"I understand."

Spier nodded at the boat. "Well, now that the two lovebirds are back together, I'm sure we can all agree to have a most productive outing? I'd like nothing more than to have a real reason to celebrate this evening over a hearty dinner."

Hans smiled. "That sounds good."

Roux came down the walkway already strapped into his oxygen tank and wearing a weight belt. "I'm all set."

Spier smirked. "Apparently."

Roux glanced down. "What—am I wearing it wrong?"

"Not at all. It's just that we don't usually gear up until we're at the dive site."

"Ah." Roux nodded. "Well, I like to get a head start. I'm simply brimming with excitement about this. And to think, I thought I'd be spending this day trying out windsurfing. This is much better."

Spier smiled. "I think it will be. Most definitely."

Annja hopped onto the boat and waited until Roux had settled himself nearby. While Spier and the others finished loading the gear, Annja elbowed Roux. "You know they don't believe you, right?"

"Of course."

Annja frowned. "Then why the pitiful charade?"

Roux sighed. "My dear girl, there are times when the appearance of a ruse is more powerful than the ruse itself. Spier will try doubly hard to locate the pearl. That means all I have to do is watch him instead of exerting myself on the hunt itself. It's much more convenient this way."

Annja shook her head. "I hope you know what you're doing. These guys won't mess about if they think you're trying to ruin their expedition."

"I don't doubt it," Roux said.

The boat wobbled as the rest of the team clambered

aboard. Spier settled himself by the rudder and smiled. "All set?"

Annja nodded.

Spier grinned. "Then let's be off."

15

The reef was fast becoming familiar territory for Annja. When Spier threw the anchor over the side of the boat, they quickly got ready and dropped into the much calmer seas. Annja was amazed at how much better she felt about diving in the daylight than she had the previous night. It had been virtually impossible to see anything without the arc lights that the dive master had set up for Roux.

Annja glanced down at the thought, but all traces of the lights had vanished. She frowned. Roux had probably removed them when he was finished diving last night.

She found it curious he was so eager to go along on this diving trip. That told her he hadn't found anything during his night dive. If he had, he'd be halfway home by now.

Hans glided near to Annja and winked at her as they descended. Again, life on the reef was abundant and incredibly active. Maybe the storm surges had churned up some extra food. The fish seemed to be out in force.

They drifted ever lower and Annja checked her gauges to make sure she was in good shape. Everything looked fine.

Spier and the team broke up as they had the previous day. Annja stayed with Hans and they started for the area where Hans had scraped some of the barnacles off the marble.

Annja was happy about that. She wanted to see if there was anything else there that warranted their attention.

They sank onto the reef and then made their way along it to the far end. Annja noted that Spier had brought along another clipboard and grease pencil for taking notes on the landscape. Also, Heinkel had brought along something that looked like a Shop-Vac. Annja wondered if they were intending to suck away part of the sand.

She and Hans made their way across to the outcropping they'd investigated yesterday. Hans found the location of his scraping and started again. Annja drifted nearby but soon found herself drawn to an opening that looked distinctly like an archway.

The interior was dark and she could see very little. It was large enough to permit entry if she squeezed through. But that would be foolish. The archway might be home to a moray eel or even a small shark. Sticking her head into the darkness would be inviting disaster.

Still, she wanted to see what was inside. All the more because she hadn't noticed the archway before. She ran her hands along the edge of the arch and found they'd been recently scraped clean.

Roux.

He must have discovered something last night but didn't have enough time to complete his work. That's why he wanted an excuse to come back here. She turned toward Hans, but he was engrossed in his work.

She felt a tap on her shoulder and turned to see Roux looking at her. He pointed at the archway and then produced a flashlight.

Annja shook her head. They couldn't go in there without

letting everyone else know. Roux nodded but Annja ignored him. She waved at Hans when he looked up.

Annja pointed at the archway and then at Roux and his flashlight. Comprehension dawned on Hans's face and he pointed at the area where Spier was exploring. He swam away to get them, leaving Annja with Roux.

Roux looked annoyed and shot Annja a look that said, This is a bad idea.

But Annja couldn't simply disappear on Hans and Spier. They'd done nothing to warrant treating them like that. They'd saved her life and they'd looked after her as friends.

Hans came swimming back, followed by the rest of the team. Spier's eyes widened when he saw the archway.

Roux switched the flashlight on, flooding the archway with light. It appeared to open up once one got past the entrance. Roux led the way inside.

Annja followed close behind and saw that they were in some sort of tunnel. The interior was filled with fish of all kinds. Annja froze when she saw a moray eel poke out of a nearby hole before retreating again.

Hans squeezed her ankle and she looked back with a grin. She was glad there were other people with her.

Roux led them farther into the tunnel, which now descended toward the seafloor. Or what would have been the seafloor if they had stayed out on the reef. But for some reason, this was something entirely different.

The tunnel widened and the water grew warmer. More fish shot past their face masks as Roux's flashlight illuminated the dark surrounding them.

This would be a horrible place to have to face a shark, Annja decided. With only a little room to maneuver, they'd be at an immediate disadvantage.

But they had yet to see anything more dangerous than the moray eel back at the opening. Maybe the sharks didn't like the tunnel any more than Annja did.

Their air bubbles drifted toward the top of the tunnel, and then back behind them. They were still descending, but at a gentler grade than at first.

How much farther did the tunnel go on? Annja wondered. And were they even still on the reef itself? Annja checked her oxygen gauge. If the tunnel kept going much farther, they'd have to turn back or else run out of air and die in this murky enclosure.

The path started to shift and ease them up at another angle. As they ascended, their air bubbles rushed ahead of them, seeking the top of wherever they might have been.

Fewer fish swam in this part of the tunnel and the water grew even warmer. Almost to the point of being uncomfortable.

Annja frowned. Strange that it should be so warm here, she thought. What could be causing the temperature to rise so much?

Roux's flashlight beam bounced off something light ahead. As they approached, Annja saw that it looked like smooth stone.

Roux ran his hand over it and glanced back at the team. As Annja grew near, she glided her hand along it and felt the smooth, cool surface like marble.

It was just like what Hans had unearthed outside on the reef. Were they in some type of ancient structure?

If they were, then there was definitely something to Spier's story about a lost civilization.

Roux kept leading them ahead.

Annja took another look at her oxygen gauge. They'd be approaching the point of no return soon.

She stopped and waited until Hans and Spier drew closer to her. Annja pointed at her gauge and they nodded. So, they knew. Annja held up her hands asking if they should go any farther or turn back.

She saw the answer in Spier's eyes. He wanted to go on.

Annja glanced at Hans and he, too, wanted to press on.

I hope you guys know what you're doing, Annja thought. She turned and kicked to catch up with Roux.

When she did, she tapped him on his ankle. He glanced back at her, perturbed with the interruption, but Annja gestured to his oxygen gauge and he checked it. His expression softened and then he nodded. They had time, he seemed to be saying. Let's move on.

He turned back and kicked his fins, putting a little distance between him and the rest of the team. Annja hurried to catch up.

And then she saw some measure of ambient light coming from somewhere up ahead. They were still a ways from the source, but Roux switched off his flashlight and stowed it on his gear belt.

They could see better the farther they progressed. Annja made out more of the marble stones that hadn't been covered by barnacles or algae. The angles were all extremely precise, as if someone had once used a laser to cut the blocks.

But that wasn't possible, was it?

Annja continued to swim. According to both Spier and Roux, there was a lost civilization at the heart of this mystery. A civilization that had somehow managed to create precision-cut marble blocks and the pearl itself.

Twenty-five thousand years ago.

And then something had happened to destroy that civilization. Annja was familiar enough with the various theories of prehistoric earth, especially where writers of fantastic fiction were concerned. Robert E. Howard's legendary Conan the Barbarian had lived during such an age. But not even Conan had had access to a laser. Then again, Annja had seen some fantastic things since she'd come into possession of the sword. Things she still struggled to believe, even though she'd seen them with her own eyes.

Roux led them along and the upward angle of the tunnel

seemed to be increasing. They swam higher. Annja checked her oxygen gauge again and saw they were reaching a critical point. They would need to turn back soon.

She looked back and saw the concern etched on Hans's face. Spier still looked excited about what was ahead of them.

Annja was, too, but she was also concerned they wouldn't make it back.

Where was Roux leading them?

Her legs started to ache from the swimming and even the warm water did little to ease her pain. She saw a few fish but nothing larger than her hand swam this far in the tunnel.

Annja wondered if she was actually starting to sweat underwater, or if that was even possible. The heat in the water seemed to sap her strength. She started to feel woozy.

She wanted Roux to stop. She wanted him to turn around and lead them back out. But he gave no indication that he would ever stop. At least, not until he reached the end of the tunnel.

She cursed him then. Why did he always have to be so driven? And why did she always end up in these situations? She'd come here to relax, not drown in some remote tunnel where no one would ever find her body.

Roux kept pressing forward. The ambient light grew stronger.

Annja saw more marble blocks now, each as precise as the others. They seemed to form giant steps that rose along the same angle of ascension as the tunnel.

Were they almost at the end?

They'd never have enough oxygen to reach it and make it back to the boat safely.

Annja tried to calm herself. Panicking would only use up her oxygen faster. And she couldn't have that.

Hans swam up next to her and looked concerned. His expression searched her as if asking if she were okay. She gave him a feeble thumbs-up and he nodded.

More light spilled into the tunnel now.

Roux stopped and hovered in the midst of the tunnel. He turned back and waved them all forward.

He pointed.

In the middle of the tunnel, they could see a round opening far above them where the light originated.

Their air bubbles raced toward the opening, and as they watched them ascend, the bubbles broke the surface.

Annja's heart raced. Finally!

They had to remember proper protocol, however, and despite the fact that they were nearly out of oxygen, they still had to time their ascents accordingly. After all, they had no real idea how deep they'd gone underwater or how much they might have ascended since going into the tunnel.

Roux led the way. Annja watched him journey up the slender tube and then saw Spier head up next. Annja waited until he had reached the top and clambered out of the tunnel before starting up herself.

She watched her bubbles rise.

She tasted stale air.

Again.

Next time, I'm bringing two tanks, she thought. Enough of this crap.

She kicked upward.

She felt her heart starting to race as her body experienced the lack of oxygen. Her lungs felt tight, constricted as they cried out for fresh air.

Annja felt the familiar feeling of blacking out, but clamped down on her mouthpiece and willed herself to keep going.

Stay awake!

Finally, she felt her head break through the surface of the water. She spit out her mouthpiece and sucked in fresh air, grateful—so grateful—to still be breathing.

When she finally climbed out of the tunnel and stood, she couldn't believe her eyes.

16

"What is this place?"

They were in a large, open circular room. Marble columns dominated the scene and huge blocks of the stone had been scattered about the room. It was as if they had walked into a temple after an earthquake.

Hans and the rest of the team climbed out of the tunnel and gasped at the sight. Spier and Roux, meanwhile, seemed to have found some common ground and were talking animatedly about the discovery.

Spier glanced over at Annja. "You still think the theory of a lost civilization is absurd?"

Annja shrugged. "I don't know what to think just yet. We haven't even explored the rest of this place."

Roux sniffed. "I told you she wouldn't be convinced. Annja's one of those types who often refuses to admit the truth even when it's staring her in the face."

"That's enough, Roux," Annja said. "Let's stow our gear and see what we can find."

They all took off their tanks and rigs. Annja pointed a

finger at Roux. "I hope you're planning on finding a way to refill our tanks. Otherwise, you'll need to figure out how you're going to get us all home again."

Roux waved his hand. "It won't be a problem."

"It won't be? How do you figure that?"

Roux was clearly more interested in exploring the ruins than thinking about getting them out safely. "Annja, if worse comes to worst, I'll simply swim back with all the tanks, use what air is left in them to breathe and then refill them once I get there. Then I'll come back down here and we all swim out again."

"You'll do that?"

"You don't trust me, Annja?"

She smiled. "Let's just say I might feel a bit better if someone else did it."

Roux nodded. "Fine, fine. Whatever. Now that that's settled, can we please get going? I'm dying to see what we've got here."

"As am I," Spier said. "I wish I'd thought to bring along a camera. But I didn't think we'd find something like this." He looked at Annja. "How did you ever spot it?"

"Oh," Annja said, casting a sideways glance at Roux. "I just happened upon it. It looked like someone else might have found the entrance to the tunnel, but for some reason stopped working on it."

Roux nodded. "Perhaps he got interrupted and was unable to finish."

"Perhaps."

"Well, no matter," Spier said. "We're here now and that's all that matters. The pearl must certainly be around somewhere."

Hans came up behind Annja. "You all right?"

She nodded. "Yeah. I'm anxious to see this place. I can't tell if we're still underwater or what."

"Does it make a difference?"

"Yes, actually. If we're only in a giant air pocket, then we'll need to be careful. Any sort of shift could bring the entire thing down on us. And we wouldn't have any of our gear with us to get out of here. That tunnel's too far to swim in one go. Even at top speed, you'd need at least ten minutes of air to reach the reef again and then up to the boat."

"We'll be okay," Hans said. "I promise you."

She looked at him. "Thanks."

Roux coughed. "Let's get going."

They followed Roux and Spier out of the room and up some intricately carved steps. Along the walls they spotted friezes showing people engaged in hunting and sports. They looked human enough, so Annja at least felt comfortable thinking they must have been related to modern people.

Roux ran his hands over the friezes. "Incredible workmanship. The level of detail here is astounding. Almost as if they had been etched with some type of computer-graphic tool."

"That would be impossible," Annja said.

Roux sighed. "You still cling to that assumption despite what you see before you? Really?"

"I haven't decided anything yet, but even if this is some sort of lost civilization, then I doubt very much they had computers."

Spier smiled. "You may be right, but you can't discount the level of craftsmanship."

"I don't," Annja said. "It's remarkable." She followed them up the steps and then into another antechamber. The interior walls were all an alabaster white. If you could have designed something to look like an ancient civilization, Annja thought, then this would certainly fit the bill.

A wide corridor stretched before them and Annja wondered what might lie down its length. She also couldn't figure out where the ambient light was coming from. As far as she could see, there were no windows.

"How is it that we have light here?" she asked. "Do you see any windows? Any source of light at all?"

Spier frowned. "An intriguing question."

Roux glanced about them. "Perhaps the stone itself radiates some sort of light?"

"The stone seems to be marble, though," Annja said. "I've never heard of marble giving off light."

"Nor I," Roux said. He pointed up near the cavernous ceiling. "Perhaps there's some sort of recessed lighting up where we can't see? It seems rather uniform throughout this entire structure."

Annja shrugged. "Something to keep in mind, I guess."

They moved on, entering the long tunnel, which wound its way along and descended something like a reclining snake. As they walked the corridor, their footfalls seemed to echo about them.

Spier and Roux stopped frequently, exchanging opinions about the nature of construction and the geologic qualities of the marble.

"Never seen anything like it," Roux said.

"A remarkable strain of stone," Spier concluded.

At the end of the tunnel, they stepped out into another chamber, this one complete with a marble altar of some sort situated above them, accessible by a circular set of steps.

"I wonder what the altar was for," Annja said. She'd seen a few altars in her time and most of them had meant some sort of sacrifices had taken place.

"Who knows what gods and goddesses these people may have worshipped," Spier said.

Hans and the rest of the divers had remained pretty quiet during the exploration. Annja caught up with him.

"You guys all right?"

He nodded. "Why?"

"You're not talking very much."

He grinned. "I think we're mostly just curious. We're waiting to see what the experts have to say about things before we contribute to the conversation."

"Is that it?"

He smiled. "Of course."

"Well, say something so I don't think I'm trapped with Spier and Roux over there, okay? That would not be a good thing."

"Herr Spier is a good man," Hans said. "A little crazy sometimes, but who isn't a little crazy by the time they reach eighty?"

"I don't know," Annja said. "I'm not there yet. But with a little luck I might make it someday."

Roux had already climbed the stairs and was examining the altar. Spier joined him and they ruminated over the carvings in the smooth surface. Annja went to investigate the carvings herself.

From what she could see, more people were depicted offering sacrifices to one god who appeared to have long flowing hair and horns. She frowned. It was an odd depiction of a god, unlike any she'd come across before, but then again, most of the races she'd researched in the past had their own strange ideas about what deities looked like.

"A sacrificial altar," Roux said. "Makes me wonder how many people may have lost their lives on this very slab." Annja continued to examine it and shook her head. "I don't think very many at all."

Spier looked up. "Why do you say that?"

Annja pointed. "There's no trough."

"Trough?" Hans asked.

"For the blood," Annja said. "Most altars have some sort of capacity for catching the blood that inevitably gets spilled and collecting it in some fashion. The blood is often more important than the act itself."

"Not all altars had such a device," Roux said.

Annja shrugged. "I don't see any stains, either."

"Bloodstains?" Spier asked.

"Exactly," Annja said. "Blood stains stone, after all. Shouldn't we see some sort of evidence of the sacrifices here?"

"Not necessarily," Roux said. "Maybe this race was meticulous in the cleanup after a sacrifice."

"Perhaps," Annja said. But she wasn't convinced. Something struck her as odd about the entire setup.

Roux and Spier didn't seem bothered by it, however. They ran all over the room comparing notes like a couple of schoolboys eager to discuss the latest action flick.

Annja wandered back down the altar steps and raced her way around the periphery of the room. The walls were all polished smooth. The stone felt cool to the touch. And again, there was enough ambient light to see extremely well.

But where did it come from?

She looked up at the conical ceiling above them. She could see it was equally light up there, but a lip of stone blocked her view so she couldn't tell if there might be recessed lighting, after all.

"I wish I could get up there," she said.

Hans glanced up. "A ladder would help, if we had one."

Annja nodded. "No matter. I'm sure we'll figure it out eventually." She looked around the room. Aside from the entrance, there seemed no other way out of the chamber.

That struck her as odd, too.

"Only one way in or out," she said to herself. "But why?"

"Maybe the people they brought here never came out alive afterward," Roux said. "Is it that important?"

"It could be," Annja said. She climbed the stairs that led to the altar again and examined the slab that would have supposedly seen victims lie on it. She ran her hands over it and, again, the stone felt totally smooth.

"No sign of a knife blade flecking bits of stone off this,"

she mused. She leaned against the slab and tried shoving it aside.

Hans saw what she was doing. "Annja?"

"Give me a hand with this, would you?"

He rushed up the steps and got behind the slab. "Do you think it will really move?"

"I don't know. But I feel like we're being fooled here."

Spier heard her. "Fooled? How so?"

Annja gestured around them. "This looks compelling. It feels compelling. But something doesn't add up. I don't know how to explain it. Maybe I can't. I just feel like we're missing something. And it could be important."

Roux sighed. "I think we're seeing what we need to see."

Annja glanced at Hans. "You ready?"

"Sure."

They put their strength into it and Annja grunted as they pushed.

The slab moved slightly.

"Ah!"

Annja looked at Hans. "We need more help here."

Hans called Mueller and Gottlieb over. The three men squatted and braced themselves as they shoved the top slab of the altar. There was a vague hissing sound and the slab slid away as if on a hinge.

"She was right," Spier said.

Roux frowned. "Lucky, more likely."

Annja peered into the opening. A set of stairs led down into a dark tunnel. She glanced up at Roux. "Still got your flashlight?"

He hefted it. "Right here."

"Then I think you should take the lead on this." Annja smiled. "It looks like we're going down again."

Roux climbed over the edge of the slab and dropped down

onto the stairs. Looking back up, he grinned at Annja. "You have to admit, this is incredibly fun stuff."

Annja nodded. "Just get going. I want to see where this leads."

17

The stairway corkscrewed down to another floor, depositing them all into a much smaller room. It was darker than where they'd come from and they were forced to rely on Roux's flashlight in order to see.

"There are sconces on the wall," Annja said. "But no torches anywhere."

"One floor has its own light source—as yet undetermined—and the next floor has to rely on torches?" Roux shook his head. "Mystifying."

"Not necessarily," Spier said. "What if the floor we just came from was more for the aristocracy and this one is for the servants? Perhaps they don't get the nice things that their bosses get."

"Or perhaps the upper floor is meant to be a sham," Annja said.

"Meaning what?" Hans asked. "This is not real?"

"Seems real enough," Mueller said.

"It's meant to look real," Annja said. "And probably display all sorts of power and wealth. But what if they received visitors on the upper floor, but in reality they lived down here? They concealed their weakness, in other words."

Roux shook his head. "I don't know. The more we explore, the less certain I am of anything."

He flashed his light on a round portal leading out of the room and they passed through it. Roux's light bounced along the smooth walls, still made of marble, and then gradually wound around to a blocked passage, completely caved in.

"More evidence of some sort of disaster," Spier said.

They progressed in single file, with Roux on point. Spier trailed him and then Annja, followed by Hans and the rest of the team.

Annja's mind raced. She couldn't imagine they were still within the confines of the coral reef. The structure they were in was far too large. What if the reef wasn't at the bottom of the seafloor, the way it appeared, but rather was the top of the structure they were in? That would account for the way they'd descended when they first entered the tunnel, only to have to then climb once they were inside the structure.

Was it possible, therefore, that this massive building had simply slipped into the sea? And over the years, the coral reef had simply enveloped the topmost portion?

If that was the case, that would mean they were buried beneath the sand of the seafloor at that moment.

But how was it that the corridors weren't flooded? What kept the ocean at bay and enabled them to breathe what tasted like fresh air?

"Look at this," Roux's light played over a massive painting of people charging into a terrifically violent battle scene. But they carried weapons that Annja had never seen before.

Spier peered closer at the painting. "It's incredible. They look Asian, but what are they wielding to fight with?"

"Like nothing I've ever seen before," Roux said.

Annja glanced at Hans and could see the mixture of curiosity and excitement on his face. But there was something else there, as well.

Fear.

"Are you okay?"

He looked around. "I may be overreacting, Annja. But I have the distinct impression that we are being watched."

"How long have you thought that?"

"Since we came up out of the tunnel."

Annja frowned. "That long?"

Hans nodded. "It has grown in intensity. Once you discovered the way down to this floor, it seemed to be more apparent."

Annja nodded. She suddenly felt uneasy. But was it legitimate? They were in the darkness and that could affect a person's sensitivity and paranoia level. Annja had been in many dark places before where she had felt like people were watching when they hadn't been.

"Let me know if you start to feel worse," she said quietly.

Annja moved back to the painting and studied it. There was an obvious leader riding in what looked to be a type of chariot. The wheels themselves looked as though they'd been hewn from the same marble that surrounded them now. Stone wheels? Not exactly the easiest or best source for transportation.

The leader of the warriors was a male with a youthful appearance. His long wavy dark hair stood out in stark contrast to his pale skin. In his hand he wielded a triple-barbed spear that looked more like it belonged to the god Neptune than a mere mortal. Swirling around him were his warriors, scores of men brandishing a host of strange-looking weapons.

Their foes across the expanse of the painting were darker-skinned Asians, wielding their own terrible weaponry. They were led by a woman with blond hair and Asian features.

In the middle of the painting, a horrific scene of carnage

unfolded as people were speared, mutilated and torn asunder in garishly recreated colors.

"It's excruciatingly violent," Annja said. "This battle scene, I mean."

Roux glanced at her. "You know how combat is, Annja. This is merely an authentic representation of it, it would appear."

Spier nodded grimly. "I can't decide what to make of the location they seem to be fighting in. Those trees don't look like any trees I know of."

Annja peered closer. Spier was right. The trees, such as they were, looked more like tall ferns without the benefit of any bark. Spindly tendrils that reminded Annja of sea grass were covered in blood and gore.

Roux chuckled. "Perhaps they were waging this war underwater."

"That would mean they would be able to breathe in the ocean," Spier said. "I don't see any gill slits on their necks."

Annja perked up. "Maybe they didn't need gills at all."

"How else would they be able to extract oxygen from the surrounding sea?" Spier asked.

"The U.S. government and a few others have conducted experiments on special-operations soldiers in the past decade or so where they have tested a means of enabling soldiers to breathe underwater. From what I've heard, it's a horrifyingly brutal process, but there have been some successes with it."

"Are you suggesting that perhaps this race, or races, even had that ability?" Roux asked.

Annja pointed at the painting. "If they're fighting in the ocean, then I'd have to imagine that would necessitate some type of breathing ability."

Spier nodded. "She's right."

Roux played the flashlight around and away from the painting. More sconces sat in the walls, but there were no torches in them. He glanced back at Annja. "Of course, if they were able to live underwater, then why would they need torches? Why would this place be in the open air like this?"

"I have no idea," Annja said. "I was merely offering up an opinion about the painting. Maybe we were looking at their ancestors? Maybe they made the move to dry land at some point in their history."

"Only to once again slip back into the sea when the cataclysm came," Spier said. "An interesting theory, Annja."

"I don't know if it's much of a theory," Annja said with a grin. "I'm trying to make sense of the situation just like you guys."

Roux's flashlight revealed another portal. This one wasn't as smooth as the others and showed that part of it had crumbled away. Roux ran his hand over the broken portion and shook his head. "It certainly appears to be stone," he said. "Marble, if I had to guess. It amazes me they were able to build such a place."

"It's no more incredible than what the early explorers must have imagined when they cast eyes upon the pyramids," Spier said. "It perhaps only seems wondrous because we have no reference point for any of this."

"Hopefully we'll get some answers soon," Roux said. "And I'd like to find the pearl, as well."

Hans nudged Annja. "Do you remember what I told you?"

Annja nodded. "Is it worse now?"

Hans nodded. "And there's something else."

"What?"

"Heinkel is gone."

Annja whirled around. "Roux, the light!"

"What?"

"Shine it back here, now!"

Roux did as she asked and Annja saw that it was true. Mueller, Gottlieb and Hans were with them, but Heinkel had vanished. "Where did he go?"

Hans shrugged. "We have no idea. We came down single

file, but when we stopped at the painting, I think we were all amazed by it and we lost track of Heinkel. He was last in line."

Spier called out to Heinkel but Annja put up a hand. "Stop shouting. It won't do any good."

"Why on earth not? One of my men is missing."

Annja looked at Hans. "Would he go back without us?"

"Where? Back to the tunnel?"

"Yes."

Hans frowned. "I doubt that. We have all been together for several years. Heinkel would not dare abandon his friends."

Roux scratched his chin. "Which leaves what possibility?"

"He was taken," Spier said quietly.

Annja nodded.

Hans eyed her thoughtfully. "You don't seem surprised?"

"I don't know what I am," Annja said. "When you told me you felt as though we were being watched, I had to agree with you. I've felt it, too."

Roux came closer. "Are you sure?"

"I'm not sure of anything, Roux. But I know when my instincts are telling me something. And they're telling me something now."

Roux gave her a searching look that seemed to ask if she could manifest the sword here. Annja shrugged. She didn't see why not, but until she actually did it, there'd be no way to know for certain.

Spier stepped forward. "We should double back and try to find him. He could be injured."

"He might be," Annja said, "but I don't think splitting our forces is a good idea."

"Why not?"

"Because if we are about to be attacked, it would be better to have as many of us here to fight them off, don't you think?"

Spier frowned. "I didn't think we'd be in any danger."

Hans reached down and unsheathed his diving knife. "We are armed at least."

"Those knives may not do much," Roux said. "Did you see what the weapons were in that painting?"

Hans shrugged. "Weapons don't make the fighter, spirit does. And if they have harmed my friend, then they will know the fear of facing me in combat."

Roux smiled. "All right, all right. I was just letting you know what you might be up against."

Hans turned and spoke quietly to Mueller and Gottlieb, organizing them accordingly.

Annja whirled at a sound coming from down the corridor. "Did you hear that noise?"

"What noise?" Hans asked.

Spier nodded. "I did. It sounded like something metallic."

Annja glanced at Hans. "If something strange happens in the next few minutes, I want you to promise that you won't be upset with me, okay?"

"Why would I be upset with you?"

"Just promise."

Hans looked puzzled. "All right, I promise."

Annja nodded. She closed her eyes and saw the sword hovering in the otherwhere. It was ready to be summoned if she needed it.

She opened her eyes and saw Roux looking at her with an inquisitive expression. She nodded at him.

She'd be ready.

"There it is again," Spier said.

Annja had heard it, as well.

"Definitely metallic."

"Circle up," Hans said quietly. The six of them formed a circle with their backs to one another so they could keep an eye on every approach. Annja wasn't ready to face whomever this was head-on. Especially if Heinkel had been taken from behind.

More sounds came at them from down the corridor.

But this time it wasn't metallic.

It was the sound of running feet.

18

Heinkel came running around the corner.

Fast.

Annja looked at him, saw the expression on his face and then glanced at Roux. The old man held up his hand. "Wait, Annja. Not yet."

Hans grabbed Heinkel. "What happened to you?"

Heinkel bent over double as if he'd been running a marathon. "They grabbed me from behind and there were too many of them to fight off."

"Who?" Annja asked.

Heinkel pointed. "Them."

Annja whirled. The corridor ahead of them was filled with angry-looking warriors similar to those depicted in the painting. There were at least a dozen of them, from what Annja could see. And each one of them carried a long triple-barbed spear. The weapons looked even more menacing than they had in the painting.

Hans stepped in front of Heinkel. "Who are you?" he demanded. "We mean you no harm."

"I don't think they will agree with that sentiment, Hans. And I am certain they mean us harm," Spier said quietly.

Hans gritted his teeth. "Then let them come."

Roux cleared his throat. "Hans, I don't mean to overstep my bounds here, but that knife is not going to do a thing to these chaps. You won't even get close to them before they have you on a spit like one of those delicious pigs they serve back at Club Noah."

Hans frowned. "You have a better idea?"

"Actually, yes." Roux smiled at Annja. "Now might be the time, my dear."

Hans looked at Annja. "What does he mean by that?"

Annja stepped in front of Hans. "I didn't want to have to do this, but it appears I have no choice. Not if we want to get out of here alive."

Hans stood there staring at her with a confused expression plastered on his face.

Annja saw the sword and then reached for it, felt her hands wrap around the hilt, felt the flow of power into her body as it suddenly appeared in her hands.

The sword gave off its own dull light, clearly showing Annja all the enemies she would face if this went to a full-scale battle.

Hans gasped as he looked at Annja. "How in the world did you do that?"

Annja smiled. "It's a long story."

Roux smiled. "All that matters is she knows how to use it well."

Annja stepped ahead of the rest of the team and held the sword high overhead, staring at the mass of warriors in front of her. They looked scared. They'd just seen the unthinkable occur in front of them. An unarmed woman had just conjured a sword out of thin air.

One of the warriors stepped forward and hurled his spear directly at Annja.

Hans shouted her name.

But Annja merely flicked the sword and cut the shaft of the spear in two. The pieces fell clattering to the floor.

Hans grabbed the end with the triple barbs on it and hefted it.

"It's got a good amount of weight to it."

Mueller grabbed the staff and twirled it in his hands. "Now we've got a bit more reach at least," he said.

Annja stood there as if defying the rest of the warriors to try something as useless as what had just been attempted. No one stepped forward. If anything, they seemed to be shrinking back from Annja.

She could hear mumbles from the crowd of warriors. It wasn't any language she recognized, and she found herself wondering if she had stepped back in time and this was really a long-lost civilization. If it was, the last thing she wanted to do was contribute to its extinction.

Unfortunately, if she had to kill some in order to get everyone out alive, then that's exactly what she would do.

"They seem a bit nervous around you, Annja. Perhaps you should press them a bit and see how they react," Roux said quietly.

"That could worsen the situation," she replied.

Roux shrugged. "I doubt it. If anything, it might show us exactly what they're planning to do with us."

"You mean if they wanted us dead, they would have already attacked?"

Roux nodded. "Seems to me they would certainly have killed Heinkel already if they'd wanted to kill us. Why simply grab him? Unless they're under orders to capture us and take us somewhere."

"Take us somewhere?" Spier asked. "You mean like in front of the people who rule this place?"

"It's possible," Roux said.

"So, what do you want me to do?" Annja asked. "Charge them?"

"No, but you might advance a few more steps and see what they do."

Annja took a swipe at the air in front of her with the sword and the result was immediate. The warriors retreated a few steps, pushing one another back.

Annja stepped closer to them, brandishing the sword in front of her and grimacing threateningly.

The warriors screamed.

Annja almost grinned. But then she imagined how she'd feel if she was in their place and had seen something so inexplicable happen right in front of her eyes.

Another warrior shoved his way through the crowd and twirled his spear menacingly.

Annja readied herself. There had to be one in every crowd.

The warrior in front of her stood only about five feet tall and his muscles extended along his limbs like thin ropes, stretched taut. A sheen of sweat covered him from head to toe, and he wore a simple loincloth around his waist.

He yelled at Annja, something guttural and not at all pleasant sounding.

"I don't think he likes you very much," Roux said.

"Apparently," Annja replied.

"Make an example of him and be done with it," Roux said.

Annja frowned. "I won't do that unless he leaves me no choice. We don't know who rules this place and the last thing I want to do is anger them by killing one of their own."

"She makes a good point," Spier said.

But in the end, it was the warrior who decided what would happen. He stepped forward and attempted to stab Annja with his spear. The triple barbs lunged forward, wicked looking at close range.

Annja jumped back and parried with her sword. The warrior had the advantage of distance, but he seemed ill prepared to utilize it in the close confines of the corridor. Annja had seen spear fighters in Japan who knew how to keep a sword-wielding opponent at the optimal length, never letting the sword cut the distance down to its effective range.

But this guy didn't seem to understand that. He cut back and forth, forever bringing himself closer and closer to Annja's blade.

Sweat broke out along her hairline as she fended off his attacks. There was strength behind them, and she realized that she would only be able to fend them off without harming him for only so long.

And then it happened.

The warrior stabbed in and attempted to leap around the point of Annja's sword to deliver another stab.

He miscalculated, however, and ended up running himself through.

A scream erupted from his lips and blood splattered the corridor as he sank free of the sword blade. His body was already lifeless by the time he hit the floor.

The warriors in front of Annja shrank away in terror.

Annja was angry. "That achieved nothing."

"Well, they're terrified," Roux said. "Should we press the advantage now?"

Annja hated to do it, but they had to get out of there. And slaying one of the warriors made her feel terrible, even if she hadn't intentionally killed him.

She stepped forward and the warriors shrank farther away from her. Several of the rearmost warriors turned and fled back down the corridor the way they'd come running.

"That was some magnificent fighting, Annja," Hans said as he came closer to where she stood.

Annja shook her head. "No. It wasn't. That was me trying to do the bare minimum necessary to get us out of this situation without having to resort to killing someone."

"It's unavoidable sometimes," Hans said. "As much as we might try to avoid it, sometimes there is no other way."

"Yeah, I guess," Annja said. But she felt awful. Killing someone who was intent on killing you was one thing if you knew who you were dealing with. But she had no idea about who these people were. They were probably just frightened at the thought of intruders and were doing their best to keep their home safe.

Roux came up alongside her. "Don't be so merciful that you expose yourself to attack, Annja. Some will look to exploit that weakness if you let them."

"Thanks for the advice."

"You're welcome."

Annja led them down the corridor. The warriors shrank back, several steps at a time. It was an odd dance of sorts with Annja advancing and the warriors shrinking backward.

But they progressed.

Gradually, the corridor turned and led them farther downward into a much larger room. It was still dark, but Annja's sword reflected some light. And it was enough to see for some distance.

"Now what?" Annja asked.

Roux sighed. "I don't know. I can see several doorways but I have no idea where they might lead."

"Great."

The warriors in front of her suddenly stopped backing up. And their faces no longer showed any fear.

"Roux," Annja said.

"Yes?"

"I don't think they're scared anymore."

"No?"

"Why wouldn't they be scared anymore?" she asked.

Hans was at Annja's elbow. "I see more of them."

"How many?"

"A lot," Hans said. "A whole lot."

The room blossomed into light at that moment and Annja could see it was filled with warriors, all of them brandishing the weapons they'd seen in the painting.

Roux whistled appreciatively. "Well, this is somewhat unexpected."

"Great plan, Roux," Annja said. "We walked right into their trap."

"I merely suggested one possible path we could take," Roux said. "You chose to follow my advice. I take no responsibility for that."

"Of course, you don't," Annja said. "Why would you?"

The circle of warriors surrounded them and pressed a little bit closer. The tips of their spears caught the light that spilled in from somewhere far overhead.

More of that seemingly sourceless light, Annja thought. I wonder what powers this place?

But she had more immediate concerns at the moment. Namely, the sheer number of armed warriors she faced.

"There are too many of them," she said quietly.

Hans nodded. "You can't be expected to fight them all."

Spier spoke quietly, as well. "I think it might be time for a strategic withdrawal."

"No good," Mueller said. "They've blocked us from behind, too."

Annja glanced quickly over her shoulder and saw he was right. The warriors had formed a complete circle around them. Every avenue of escape was closed. They were completely surrounded.

A sudden clap echoed across the chamber and instantly the circle of warriors backed away from Annja and the team.

"What was that?" Spier asked.

And then they heard a voice speak up from somewhere behind the mass of angry warriors.

"Why have you invaded our home?"

19

The group of warriors parted at that moment and Annja looked up at a throne sitting on a raised dais. A woman of indeterminate age sat on the throne. Her blond hair and Asian features reminded Annja of the woman she'd seen in the painting back in the hallway. Before Annja could say anything, Roux stepped forward. "We mean you no harm."

"You have trespassed in a place that does not belong to you. You have come into our home uninvited and, for that, you must be punished."

Roux stepped back. "We would prefer that you not punish us."

The woman ignored him and focused instead on Annja. "Come forward, sorceress. I will speak with you."

Annja approached the throne, keeping the sword in front of her. The rest of the team stayed close behind her.

The woman on the throne looked Annja over carefully, her eyes coming to rest upon the sword after a few moments. "What are you named?"

"Annja."

"I am Hsusia, ruler of this land." She pointed at the sword. "How is that you are able to conjure that weapon?"

"Don't say you don't know." Roux whispered to Annja.

Annja shrugged. "It is within my power to make the sword appear and disappear at will."

"And how came you by this skill?"

"I was chosen," Annja said. It isn't a lie, she thought. The sword did seem to choose me.

"Are you adept at its use?"

"I am."

Hsusia nodded. "Interesting. Female warriors are a rare breed in our kingdom. We let the men do the fighting, caring not if they are killed in battle."

"And yet you lead them," Annja said. "And judging by the painting in the hallway, you have led them into battle, as well."

"This is true," Hsusia said. "I am an old warrior, however. I spend my days now studying the ancient tomes and consulting with the oracle to divine how best to lead my people."

Annja looked around. "Are there more of you than this? I see only your warriors."

"There are," Hsusia said. "But our conditions here are troubling and we are forced to live as best we are able."

"How did you come to live in this world?" Annja asked.

"We have always been here. But long, long ago, a massive event shattered our world and caused us to slip into the sea along with several other nations of people. Resources became scarce and life was truly horrible. We were forced to battle and ended up killing the other races. We alone survive now in this place."

"You dwell beneath the ocean," Annja said. "How is this possible?"

"The oracle provides for us everything we need. Air, water, food, light. As long as the oracle is protected, we will never die out."

Annja frowned. "But don't you grow old and die?"

Hsusia shrugged. "Our lives are not measured by time."

"Do you have children here?"

"No."

Spier was fascinated. "How do you procreate?"

Hsusia fixed an icy stare on him. "Who are you to speak to me? I have no words with you. Only with the woman known as Annja."

Spier stepped back and mumbled something under his breath. Annja frowned. She could see that Hsusia would be tough to deal with. "We would very much like to leave your kingdom, Hsusia. We are sorry to have trespassed here."

Hsusia shook her head. "Things are not as easy as that. We have survived this long because our existence is a secret. If we were to let you go back to the surface world, we would be compromising our very existence."

"We would not tell anyone," Annja said.

Hsusia smiled. "Annja, I am not a fool. I know you might be able to promise that for yourself, but the men with you are likely to not honor that promise. What then? They would seek glory for themselves and lead others here to prove their outlandish claims. We would have to fight for our lives and at worst end up as a spectacle for those like you."

Annja glanced at Roux, but she knew Hsusia was right. There was no way she could keep control over any of the men with her. Roux especially would want to brag about what he'd found, if to no one else but Garin.

And then there was Spier. The spry eighty-year-old had already proclaimed a desire to leave a lasting legacy in his wake. What better accomplishment than being able to say he'd discovered a lost race of people?

Annja sighed. "You're right, of course. I cannot control what these men would do once we left. But neither can we stay here. We have lives of our own that we need to get back to."

Hsusia shook her head. "You will remain here. I will see

to it that you have comfortable lives out of respect for the power you command with that weapon."

"And if we refuse to stay here?" Annja asked.

"Then you will be put to death," Hsusia said. "It is the only way to safeguard our home."

"There must be another way," Annja said.

Hsusia's eyes flashed. "There is no other way! You will remain here as my guests."

"Prisoners, you mean," Annja said. "You would hold us against our will."

"I will do whatever is necessary to protect the sanctity of my kingdom. I am the chosen protector of this place. To let you go would be to deny my responsibility, my birthright and my very people."

Annja thought for a moment. "Perhaps you should consult the oracle and see what it has to say about this," she suggested, having no idea what the oracle could be.

Hsusia narrowed her eyes. "And what would you do if the oracle agrees with my decision?"

Annja shrugged. "We agree to abide by its decision."

Roux glared at Annja. "We will?"

"Shut up, Roux," Annja said. She addressed Hsusia again. "But if you are to consult the oracle, I must be present when you do so."

"You are not allowed to gaze upon it."

"Then how will I be able to trust you? I must be present when you consult with it."

"You think I would lie?"

Annja shook her head. "I don't know what I think. I only know what any rational person would demand if they were in my position."

Hsusia leaned back on her throne. "I suppose there is some merit to what you say."

Annja pointed at the rest of her team. "The men who are

with me will remain here with your warriors. Together, you and I will consult the oracle alone."

Hsusia smiled. "You would be alone with me with that weapon? How would I feel safe if that were so?"

"I will banish the sword," Annja said. When she allowed the sword to disappear to the otherwhere, she could see the surprise on Hsusia's face.

"Where did you put it?"

"It is back where it resides," Annja said. "But I can recall it instantly if I need it, or if I detect any betrayal on your part of our agreement."

Hsusia nodded. "I accept your proposition. Your men will remain here. I give you my word none shall be harmed provided they behave themselves."

"And they will," Annja said. She looked at the rest of her team. "Right, guys?"

They all nodded and Annja turned back to Hsusia. "We can proceed now?"

Hsusia rose from the throne and waved Annja forward. Annja approached and Hsusia came down to meet her. Up close, Hsusia was strikingly beautiful. Her eyes were a cool blue that seemed to be a direct contradiction to the obvious racial background she possessed.

Hsusia seemed to be appraising Annja's appearance, as well. "You're quite beautiful," she said after a moment.

Annja smiled. "I was thinking the same thing about you."

Hsusia seemed pleased with the comment and turned. "Come with me. We will walk together."

She led Annja toward the back of the room toward a portal. Two guards stood close by, but they snapped to attention as Hsusia passed through it. Annja thought they might tag along, but they stayed where they were.

She took one final look back at the throne room, at Hans and the rest of the team. I hope I see them again, she thought.

"Come, Annja," Hsusia said. "Your men will be fine. I gave you my word."

Annja hurried to catch up with Hsusia. "What is your kingdom called?"

"Why would you know this?"

"I'm curious," Annja said. "There are many among my people who think that there were many races of people who existed long before we came along. I have always wondered if they were right."

"What do those people call the lands that no longer exist?"

"Atlantis," Annja said. "Lemuria. Mu."

Hsusia nodded. "Intriguing names. I have never heard of them myself. But there might have been others long ago who knew of them. We were once known as the Jiao. Mighty warriors and brilliant scientists who straddled the realms of time and space. Our people built incredible structures all over this part of the world."

"What happened?"

"A terrible cataclysm shook our world to the very core. Everything we'd built, everything that we had developed, it all fell apart. Our kingdom slid into the sea. Over the eons, the ocean trapped us here, save for the one tunnel that leads to the upper world."

"Have you ever gone out there?"

Hsusia shook her head. "We would not survive out there."

"Why not?"

Hsusia sighed. "One of our kind once ventured into the upper world. He was never heard from again."

"So you simply believe he must have died?"

"He did die," Hsusia said. "Otherwise, he would have come back, such was his allegiance to us."

Annja said nothing for a while. "Have there been others who've trespassed upon your kingdom?"

"Many years ago," Hsusia said. "They seemed to find us

with startling regularity. We had little choice but to keep them here as slaves. Inevitably, they never survived for long."

"You killed them?"

Hsusia shook her head. "They all grew sick and perished."

"Why?"

"I do not know. Perhaps there is something about our environment that your kind cannot tolerate."

They emerged from the corridor and, at another portal ahead, Annja saw two more guards standing at attention.

Hsusia paused in front of the door. "There is something you should know."

"What?"

"You have demanded to see me consult the oracle. I will grant that request. But others of your kind who have seen the oracle have died as a result."

Annja paused. What would make the oracle so powerful that it could kill someone?

But she knew there was no other choice. "I'll take my chances, Hsusia."

"As you wish."

"But I thank you for the warning. I will relieve you of any responsibility should the same fate befall me."

Hsusia seemed satisfied with that. "Very well, then." She turned back and spoke to the guards. One of them moved aside and placed his hand on one section of the wall. Hsusia placed her hand on the opposite side of the wall.

Instantly, the portal slid open.

Hsusia turned to Annja. "Come with me."

They walked into the room and Annja saw the source of everything that the Jiao were.

The oracle sat inside the room on a pedestal surrounded by a basin of crystal-blue water. It was round. Black. Highly polished.

And Annja knew instantly she had found the Pearl of Palawan.

20

"Behold the oracle," Hsusia said reverently.

Annja looked closely at the pearl. It wasn't quite as big as she'd imagined—perhaps only about eight inches across. But its ebony appearance made her want to step back in awe of it.

It seemed to pulse in some way, as well. Annja watched as fresh water continuously bubbled around it. She could see that the mechanism brought fresh water in and transferred older water out, down the basin and into the floor. A constant stream of water surrounded it.

The light in the room was almost painfully bright, too. Annja had to squint or risk a horrible headache if she stayed much longer.

"It's incredible," she said.

Hsusia looked pleased. "It has been this way since our ancient elders molded this into what it is now."

"But it's not a pearl," Annja said.

Hsusia looked at her. "Of course not. What made you think that this was something so common?"

Annja smiled. "One of the legends I had heard before coming here was that there was a giant pearl hidden somewhere on the reef."

Hsusia sighed. "No doubt that legend was spread by one of the first people to ever intrude upon our kingdom. And the only person we ever granted freedom to. As you can see, it was a terrible mistake."

"Who was he?"

"A local diver," Hsusia said. "He found an opening in the reef and made his way here, somehow. He had the most amazing ability to hold his breath for what seemed hours. We were quite taken with him and showed him the breadth of our home. He took advantage of our kindness, tried to steal the oracle and then fled when he was unable to do so."

"He tried to steal it?"

Hsusia nodded. "He claimed he would make a gift out of it for some woman on the surface. What a fool."

"You stopped him from stealing the oracle?"

Hsusia shook her head. "No, we had no idea he would attempt such treachery. He came here during one of our rest periods and tried to pry the oracle out of its base. But while he may have had incredibly strong lungs, he lacked the physical strength necessary to carry the oracle. He was forced to abandon his attempt. And by that time, we knew what he was up to and chased him back the way he came in, through the cistern."

"I think that's how we entered, as well," Annja said.

"You swam through the waste water," Hsusia said with a grin. "But I wouldn't worry about it. I'm sure you'll be perfectly fine, provided you did not stay in it too long."

"What happens if we stay in the water too long?"

"Did you see any fish?" Hsusia asked.

"Not close to the entrance where the water was hot."

Hsusia nodded. "Exactly. The waste water kills everything

it touches. The fish know to stay away from that area. Once the waste water mixes with the sea, it becomes safe again."

Annja frowned. Something gnawed at her subconscious about the oracle. But she'd need to discuss it with Roux before she made any decisions.

The interior of the room felt warm. Annja put a hand to her head. "It is hot in here."

Hsusia nodded. "You've been exposed to the greatness of the oracle already. You should wait outside."

Annja shook her head. "No, I said we would consult it together. And I will stay until we do so."

"Very well." Hsusia knelt in front of the dais and bowed her head. From her pocket, she pulled out an assortment of long and short metallic objects. When she was finished with her prayer, she cast the metal objects on the floor in a way that reminded Annja of a shaman casting chicken bones and reading a fortune.

Hsusia looked at the metal objects and then back at Annja. "We have our answer."

"We do?"

Hsusia rose. "Come."

Annja followed her outside and back up the corridor to the throne room. "What did the oracle say? I didn't hear it speak."

"The oracle does not talk," Hsusia said. "It speaks in the way it manipulates the metal objects I cast at its base. The oracle uses its power to arrange them in such a way as to communicate a message."

"But I couldn't understand what it said," Annja said. "How do I know that you're telling the truth about what it might have said?"

Hsusia stopped in the hallway and looked at Annja. "Because none would ever lie about what the oracle says."

She strode on, forcing Annja to follow her. Annja felt grateful to be out of the room where the oracle resided. She'd felt feverish and clammy in the room and couldn't help thinking she was being exposed to something dangerous.

But how Hsusia was able to withstand the effects was a mystery. Perhaps, Annja mused, they had grown immune over time?

Back in the throne room, Annja saw Roux, Spier, Hans and the others standing in the circle still surrounded by Hsusia's warriors. They all looked bored. And even Hsusia's men looked tired.

But upon seeing their queen enter, they all snapped to immediate attention, their spears clanging as they brought them to bear on the intruding party.

Hsusia seated herself on the throne and gestured for Annja to stand beside her.

This is odd, Annja thought.

"Annja, you have asked that we consult the oracle and I have done so. Its words are profound and not even I expected the message that I received."

"What was the message?"

"As you know, my people have lived in secrecy for eons. We have only ever allowed one intruder to go free and that was a mistake that very nearly cost us our entire civilization."

Annja waited. Get on with it already, she wanted to say.

"The oracle, in its profound wisdom, has suggested that you and your friends might also be freed—"

"Thank you," Annja said. The room had erupted into startled murmurs and gasps.

Hsusia held up her hand. The throne room fell silent. "There are, however, conditions."

Annja frowned. She should have known better than to imagine she'd get out of here without some sort of penalty.

"What are the conditions?" she asked quietly.

"First, you, Annja, must battle my bravest warrior in a

contest to the death. If you prevail, then you will have to meet the other conditions set forth by the oracle."

"I have to fight someone?"

Hsusia nodded. "It will be a glorious bout and the honor of it will become legend."

"Who am I to fight?" Annja asked.

"There is but one warrior who would be able to stand before you," Hsusia said. "Only one who would wield enough power to match your skill."

Annja frowned. The last thing she wanted to do was fight. She wasn't feeling particularly well. "Who is that warrior?" she asked.

"Me," Hsusia said.

The room erupted as Hsusia's warriors cheered.

Annja stood there with her mouth hanging open.

"You?"

Hsusia looked at her. "Of course. Do not look as though you are surprised. I have led my people into battle many times before."

Annja nodded. "I know. And I saw on the painting in the hallway that you had. But I find it odd that the oracle would suggest we fight."

"You were expecting a male warrior?"

"Well, yeah."

Hsusia smiled. "In our society, female warriors are the best, Annja. We stand alone at the top. It is truly a great honor to be commanded by the oracle to meet in battle with a warrior such as yourself."

Annja took a deep breath. "Well, I guess I feel likewise. As surprised as I am, however."

"The oracle manifests its will in mysterious ways that defy comprehension sometimes," Hsusia said. "But obey it we must, for it is all-knowing and all-powerful. It provides us with everything we need to sustain ourselves."

Annja frowned. Fighting Hsusia wasn't exactly what she'd

had in mind. She'd only just met the woman, but somehow felt something of a kinship with her. And now they'd have to fight to the death.

"The contest shall occur in the time span of two turns," Hsusia said.

Annja frowned. "Does that mean we can rest before the battle?"

"Absolutely," Hsusia said. "You will need rest and nourishment from your journey to our home. To fight now would be to nullify the honor of a match fought on equal terms."

Annja nodded. Good, she could use some rest. And food didn't sound so bad, either.

Hsusia summoned three of her warriors. "These men will escort you to chambers where you may rest yourself for the coming battle. The other members of your party will also be placed there with you. Feel free to take advantage of our hospitality, Annja. This is a glorious opportunity for you."

"Not if I happen to lose," Annja said.

Hsusia laughed. "There is no such thing as losing when you are engaged in great battle. Honor is the only prize that exists. And we shall both have it regardless of who lives and who dies."

"If you say so," Annja said.

She stepped down off the dais and walked toward Hans and the rest of the team. He smiled as she approached.

"Glad you made it back in one piece."

"Me, too. Although I'm not so sure I'll stay in one piece when I have to fight her."

Roux grinned. "If it's any consolation, I'd put my money on you if I were a betting man."

"Gee, thanks."

Spier drew close. "Did you see the oracle, Annja?"

"I did."

"What was it like?"

Annja smiled. "The oracle is the pearl, Joachim. It's about

eight inches across, black, and immensely powerful for some reason that I can't quite figure out."

Spier gasped. "So, it does exist."

Annja nodded. "Oh, it exists all right. And it's far more potent than I think any of us ever imagined."

"Incredible," Spier said.

Roux looked fascinated, as well. Hans merely put his arm around Annja.

"Are you all right?"

Annja put a hand on her forehead. "I'm not feeling all that well, to be honest. It's a good thing I don't have to fight her right now. She'd win in a heartbeat."

"You need rest," Hans said. "And she mentioned food, as well, yes?"

"Yes."

He smiled. "Good. We'll get you fixed up and prepared for the match. I would battle for you if I was asked, but something tells me that she wants this to be between you two."

Annja nodded. "She does. Apparently female warriors are the top rung of the ladder here."

"Amazons," Roux said. "They're like the Amazon warrior princesses."

Annja shrugged. "I need to lie down."

Hsusia's men started to lead them out of the throne room. Hans helped Annja along, but at the portal to leave, Annja suddenly stopped him.

She turned back and called out to Hsusia. "You said there were other conditions to be met before we could go free."

"I did."

"What are they?"

Hsusia shook her head. "We will battle first."

Annja frowned. "And what happens when one of us dies? What then? Who will know what the oracle told you to do? We should know everything now."

Hsusia smiled. "Perhaps you are right. There is much wisdom in you, Annja. Much wisdom indeed."

"Thank you," Annja said. "Now, what are the conditions?"

"You must fight me."

"We already covered that."

Hsusia smiled. "And when the battle is over, all but one of you will be allowed to leave."

"All but one—"

Hsusia smiled even more broadly. "One of you must stay here forever."

21

Hsusia's warriors led them down another corridor to a comfortable room filled with cushions and a low table set with an incredible array of food and drink—none of which any of them recognized.

Annja lay down on the pillows and felt her forehead again. As far as she could tell, her temperature must have been running at least five degrees higher than normal.

Hans sat down next to her.

"Any better?"

"I feel like crap," Annja said.

Roux hovered nearby, munching on something that had been left out for them to eat. "No idea what this might be, but it's delicious." He glanced at Annja. "Would you like some?"

"I don't think that would be such a good idea," Annja said.

Roux frowned. "When did you start feeling sick?"

Annja sighed. "We were outside the oracle room and Hsusia mentioned that all of the surface dwellers who had ever viewed the oracle had become sick. I told her not to worry and we went inside."

"What happened then?"

"It was hot. I noticed that almost immediately. The pearl sits on a pedestal in this basin of water that is constantly renewed. Fresh water flows around it, and the old water, which is apparently very hot, flows down and into the cistern."

"There's a cistern?"

"We swam through it," Annja said. "When the water temperature was hot, that was waste water from what circulates around the pearl."

Roux rubbed his chin thoughtfully. "And this oracle—or the pearl, rather—it provides all the light and energy that they use here?"

"That's what Hsusia said."

Roux shook his head and spoke quietly. "It's not possible." He walked to the table and poured a glass of liquid before bringing it back to Annja. "You should drink this. Keep hydrated."

Annja accepted the glass and drank it, expecting it to be some strange beverage. It was cold water and she relished the feel of it on her throat. She downed the glass and asked for more.

Roux watched her intently and then sat down next to her on the cushions. "I think you might need to spend some time resting. Deeply, if you get my meaning."

She looked at him. "What do you mean by that?"

He smiled. "I know there's a lot we haven't discussed about the sword, Annja. I know there are things you can do with it besides just fight really well. The sword has other… properties. Doesn't it?"

Annja took another drink of water. "Like what, Roux?"

"Like it has the ability to heal you in some ways, correct? It's not merely an implement for killing."

"How would you know something like that?"

Roux smirked. "I've spent more lifetimes thinking about the sword than you can know, Annja. It's nothing to be so secretive about. But I'm right, aren't I?"

Annja thought back to the times when it had indeed seemed like the sword had healed her, or at least had accelerated the healing process of her own body. "I think so. Yes."

Roux nodded. "Then if what I think may have happened has indeed happened, you need to go to wherever it is you go in order to activate that healing. In fact, the longer you delay, the more you are in danger of losing your life."

Annja frowned. "Why is that?"

"Because you've been poisoned, Annja."

"Poisoned? She didn't touch me."

Roux shook his head. "Don't misunderstand me. Hsusia didn't do a thing to you. In fact, she warned you about it before it happened. But your exposure to the pearl has poisoned you just as it did those others. And the longer you linger here feeling sick, the more time the poison has to infect you."

Annja lay back. Roux's suggestion actually sounded appealing if only because she'd be able to sleep. "What sort of poison has infected me?"

Roux shook his head. "I'm not sure. I have a few theories on that, but I want to discuss them with Spier before I worry you too much. And we don't have a lot of time to spare. I think you need to do this right away in order to maximize your chances of survival."

"It's that bad?"

"It might be," Roux said.

"Okay." Annja closed her eyes and Roux moved away from the cushions. She could hear him urging everyone to remain quiet while she rested.

Annja had wanted to tell Hans not to worry, but even as she closed her eyes, she could feel her body sinking into the deep meditative reservoir of personal energy that seemed to be a part of being the owner of the sword.

Annja floated through a gray haze and saw the sword hanging in front of her, suspended, as always, by some unseen force. The blade glowed with its usual dull gray light.

She found herself drawn to the light and as she approached, the light intensity grew stronger. Annja tried to block it out, but the light glowed through every part of her body. She could feel its rays piercing her skin, down to the most minute cellular level.

She remembered reading about supposed healers who visualized white light pouring through their bodies, healing the sick and infected areas. Was there truth to that, after all? Or was this just a function of the sword's healing powers?

Annja didn't know. But she drifted through a between-world for what seemed like hours while the light from the sword continued to pierce her through and through. At times, she could feel the energy moving up and down through her body. In a way it almost felt like she was being cleansed from the inside out.

Bizarre, she found herself thinking. She didn't know exactly what was happening but she knew she should have faith in the power of the sword.

As the intensity increased, Annja felt her body temperature skyrocket. Sweat broke out all over her skin. She was drenched in it as more and more sweat spilled from her pores.

Her breathing came in hurried spurts. Her inhalations and exhalations fused together so there was no break in their timing.

And still the light from the sword grew even stronger. Annja felt as if she was being set on fire and in her mind's eye she saw an image of flames licking their way up her body.

Just like Joan of Arc.

But were these actual memories? Or was her body simply offering up a visual comparison of what it was experiencing at that moment?

The sword started to vibrate, giving off a constant humming sound like a tuning fork that had been struck and left to vibrate in the air. Annja felt the sound waves puncture her body and cause it to vibrate then, as well.

She shuddered and shook and continued to sweat. The humming continued. The light shone ever brighter.

And then everything went dark.

"I DON'T THINK I ever want to watch something like that again."

Annja's eye cracked open. Roux hovered over her, grimacing. "Seriously, that was not a pretty sight."

"This isn't exactly my Sleeping Beauty dream playing out here, either, Roux. What happened? Where's Hans?"

"He's in the corner having a heated conversation with Mueller, Heinkel and Gottlieb." Roux offered Annja some water. "How are you feeling?"

Annja sat up. She was tired, but she no longer felt sick. "Better, actually. Not one hundred percent, mind you, but a lot better than I was a few minutes ago."

"You mean two hours ago," Roux said.

Annja frowned. "What are you talking about?"

"You've been unconscious for two hours. It was all I could do to keep any of them from disturbing you."

Annja glanced around. Spier smiled at her and then went back to studying the construction of the room they were in.

Annja looked back at Roux. "Two hours? Really?"

"Yes." Roux mopped her forehead with a cool cloth. "I take it you achieved what I suggested?"

"I think so. It's not something I seem to be able to control. More a matter of presenting myself and the sword seems to sense what needs doing."

"Well, let's hope it worked."

"Let's hope." Annja took more water. "Have you given any more thought to what might have poisoned me?"

"I have. But I don't know if this is the time to discuss it or not."

"You said that before I went under."

"I haven't had much chance to talk it over with Spier. I've been tending to you. He's been absorbed in the construction of this place. He seems fascinated by it. I don't even think he wants the pearl any longer."

"Really?"

"He hasn't mentioned it. Much to the chagrin of Hans and the boys there. I think that's what they're discussing right now. They have been holding some sort of secret conversation since Spier started going on about how wonderful this place is. It's all a bit much, if you ask me. He's clearly lost his marbles."

Hans came over and smiled at Annja. "How are you feeling?"

"Much better."

Hans glared at Roux. "He would not let us help you when you appeared to be having a seizure."

Annja held up her hand. "It's okay, Hans. Roux knew what he was doing. You would have hurt me if you'd attempted anything while I was under."

"This thing," Hans said. "It happens a lot?"

"What—me being sick?"

"Yes."

Annja smiled. "Hardly ever actually. I get colds like anyone else, of course. But serious stuff like this? Never."

Hans nodded. "Good. That was not a pleasant sight to witness. I thought you might have been possessed by a demon."

"Not yet." Annja looked at Spier. "Is Joachim all right?"

Hans frowned. "He has become obsessed with this place. He no longer speaks of getting out of here. Nor of the pearl that we have traveled all the way around the world to find. I don't think he cares about it any longer."

"But you do," Annja said. "You and the rest of the guys."

Hans smiled. "We came here to find this pearl and we mean to do so. One way or another. To give up the quest now just because of the other things that have confronted us is not acceptable. We must have the pearl."

"What's so important about it?" Annja asked.

Hans leaned closer to her. "The pearl has the power to affect a great many people back in Germany. It has the power to right the wrongs of those who have forsaken their duty to the people."

Annja shook her head. "You're sounding a little bit like how I'd expect Roux to sound when he gets that maniacal look in his eyes."

Hans frowned. "Don't disregard what I say, Annja. You could help us obtain the pearl. You could be there when we use it."

"Use it?"

Roux held up a hand to silence them. "Did you hear something?"

Annja strained to listen and then she heard the approaching sound. "I think we're going to have some company any moment."

The portal to the room slid back and one of Hsusia's warriors strode into the chamber. "Annja, the queen would like me to inform you that the time of your battle has arrived. You are requested to follow me to the arena where you will fight. Your friends will also accompany us."

Annja stood and stretched her arms above her head. She glanced at Roux. "Thanks for suggesting that rest. I could use a few hours more of sleep, but beggars can't be choosers, I guess."

Roux smiled. "My pleasure. I wish there was more time for you to recover."

Annja walked to the front of the chamber and smiled at Hsusia's warrior. "I will follow you."

And together they walked out.

22

Hsusia's warriors led them down a long winding corridor that funneled them into a tight walkway. At the end, they emerged in a circular room almost a hundred feet across. Along the walls, rows of seats set above the field of battle waited. They were already almost completely filled. Annja saw the Jiao women for the first time. They looked almost exactly like Hsusia, their blond hair and blue eyes seemed so different from their male counterparts.

The lead warrior pointed to the center of the floor. "You will stay here and await the queen."

Annja nodded and waved to the rest of the team, who took seats in the row nearest to the action. They were perched about ten feet over the combat area.

Annja walked the length of the field, getting a feel for the arena. As far as she could tell, there was nothing to be suspicious of. The omnipresent light flooded out from the ceiling high above the field of combat. And like every other room in this place, the arena was constructed almost entirely of marble.

Annja shook her head. Who would ever have thought that she would end up in some underwater city, waiting for a fight to the death with a queen she didn't even consider an enemy?

It was too bizarre to believe. But then again, so were a lot of other aspects of her life, she decided.

The good news was she felt great. Her strength had returned. The fever was gone. Annja squatted a few times to test her legs and found them springy and responsive. She did a couple of arm circles to warm up those muscles and she felt great.

Ready.

She breathed deeply, oxygenating her blood and ensuring she didn't starve them unnecessarily.

The crowd watched her intently. This might be the first time they've ever seen anything like this, Annja realized. An outsider coming into their home to battle their queen.

She wondered if the Jiao were gamblers. Perhaps there were people in the stands eagerly taking bets on how long Annja would last against the might of Hsusia.

That was the problem, she knew. Trying to figure out how capable Hsusia was on the battlefield. If the painting in the hallway was to be believed, then she certainly knew how to fight.

But how did she fight?

If the circumstances were somewhat normal, Annja could have figured out if her opponent knew martial arts, was a brawler or just a gifted fighter. But down here? Who knew what they'd been exposed to or been forced to create out of the necessity for survival.

It presented a problem for her strategy.

As did the triple-barbed spear that she felt certain Hsusia would employ in her defense. Annja would have to figure out a way around that if she had any hope of surviving this fight.

The crowd suddenly fell silent.

Queen Hsusia entered at the other end of the arena. She was resplendent in bright green armor that seemed to cover her from head to foot. Annja frowned. She hadn't expected armor. Now she'd have to figure out how to penetrate it and see if it had any weak points. Most armor, as impenetrable as it seemed, had weaknesses. It just took a sharp mind to figure out how it was constructed. Oftentimes, the individual pieces would be joined to other pieces. The locations of those joinings were the best place to attack.

But Hsusia's armor looked as though it was one solid piece of a latexlike material.

Annja frowned. This would be tougher than she thought.

"Annja, we have been ordered to battle each other to the death by the glorious oracle that gives us life."

The crowd roared its approval and it sounded like a thunderstorm had taken root in the arena as Hsusia's people clapped and stomped their feet.

"There will be no quarter given."

"None shall be asked," Annja said. She figured she needed to at least be a part of the conversation. Maybe she could even win a few of the Jiao over to her side before this was over.

Maybe.

Hsusia looked immensely pleased. "It is my honor to fight you in this arena. I can see that you are a true warrior and you have my utmost respect."

Annja bowed. "As you have mine. I wish the oracle in its infinite wisdom had not seen fit to pit us against each other. I would have preferred to call you my ally rather than my enemy."

Again the crowd roared its approval. Clearly they liked what they heard from Annja. Well, that was one thing at least, she figured.

Hsusia held her hand up for quiet and the arena instantly

fell silent. "When the signal is given, we will come out and not stop until one of us is dead."

Annja nodded. "I understand. Are there any rules?"

"There are none."

"So be it," Annja said. "I have prepared myself."

"As have I," Hsusia replied. "Have you any final words before we begin?"

"I would ask one thing," Annja said. "That you let my friends go regardless of the outcome of this battle. We have abided by your laws and the wishes of your oracle, but my friends do not deserve to be imprisoned here any longer than is necessary for us to battle."

Hsusia considered this. "There is the final condition that must be met. One of your people must remain here. The others will be free to go, no matter the outcome. You have my word as ruler of the Jiao."

"And if you are defeated in battle? Will your successor honor your wishes?"

Hsusia looked amused. "In the unlikely event that happens, my successor will indeed honor my final edict."

Annja nodded. "Then the time for talking is finished."

"It is indeed. Good luck to you, Annja." Hsusia turned around and ordered the portals to be closed.

Behind Annja, the opening to the arena slid shut.

Annja took a few deep breaths and summoned the sword. An immediate gasp arose from the crowd. Annja had to smile. So they didn't know that she'd come in here armed.

Well, that was one point in her favor at least.

Hsusia brought out a larger and longer version of the triple-barbed spear that Annja had seen in the painting.

Annja frowned. Apparently the artist got the dimensions a little incorrect, she thought. Oh, well.

Hsusia spun the spear as she stalked across the floor toward Annja. Annja kept the sword up in front of her. The goal was to close the distance quickly, get inside where the sword would be most effective and cut her down without giving Hsusia time or space to impale Annja.

Easier said than done, she decided.

Hsusia leaped into the air, twirling the spear as she did so. Annja saw her cut down the distance so fast that she barely had time to react. Hsusia seemed to be moving faster than anyone Annja had ever fought before.

That was confirmed less than a second later when the butt of the spear slammed into Annja's ankle, sweeping the leg and knocking Annja flat on her back.

Wind rushed out of her lungs and Hsusia spun the spear, stabbing straight down with the tip.

Annja rolled backward over her right shoulder, came up and sliced at the head of the spear. Her blade connected, but rather than cut it in two, the spear shaft clanged and held.

Annja redoubled her attack, charging to keep the distance tighter. But Hsusia flipped the spear up and brought the butt down on the back of Annja's head.

Annja saw stars and heard the roar of the crowd. They must have sensed that Hsusia could end this quickly.

Annja fought off the encroaching loss of consciousness and flicked her blade up and under Hsusia's arms. She felt the blade connect, and despite the armor, Annja's blade cut Hsusia's left arm above the wrist.

Blood spilled on the alabaster-white surface of the arena.

A gasp erupted from the crowd.

This must be a first, Annja thought.

But Hsusia only smiled and nodded at the wound. Annja looked and saw the armor instantly seal itself up again. If there was an injury there, the armor would keep her from bleeding out.

How the hell did she do that?

Hsusia leaped away and immediately flipped the spear over so its point faced Annja. Then she charged and jabbed at Annja again and again.

Annja backpedaled away, using the blade of the sword to deflect. But the barbed heads were a double threat. Annja was able to deflect them but she also had to make sure the spearhead didn't catch her blade on the pullback. Otherwise, Hsusia could easily and quickly disarm Annja.

Not that Annja would be unarmed for long. She could instantly regain the sword, but Hsusia was so fast that any moment unarmed would be a bad time.

Annja brought the sword up and feigned a downward cut. Hsusia stepped to the side and made ready to bring the butt of the spear down on the back of Annja's hands. If the strike connected, it would crush the bones on the backs of Annja's hands.

But Annja pivoted and dropped to one knee, slicing in a wide horizontal arc at Hsusia.

The move caught the queen by surprise. The edge of Annja's blade cut into the armor again and she saw more blood flow.

But just as quickly, the armor resealed itself and any blood vanished from sight.

I wish I had a suit of armor like that, she thought.

"The oracle gives us many things," Hsusia said. "Including this incredible suit of armor that has been handed down for many, many years."

"Nice of you to offer me one of those," Annja said.

But Hsusia merely smiled. "I think your time is almost at an end, Annja. It has been my honor to battle you."

And then she spun and drove the spear in deep. Annja gasped, having missed the move entirely. She felt the metallic head of the spear pierce her side, turn and then rip outward.

Annja sank to one knee, clutching her side. That hurt like hell, she thought. Sweat ran down her face.

The roar of the crowd thundered in the arena and made Annja's head swim. She was losing a lot of blood. It ran all over her hands, pooling around her feet. The sword dropped to her side.

Hsusia spun away and stood watching Annja for a moment.

Annja's breath came in spurts. She tried to flush her system with oxygen, tried to energize herself, but she felt weak.

Hsusia sensed an opening and came running right at her, the spear point poised to pierce Annja through her heart.

Annja looked up and saw Hsusia rushing her full on.

At the last minute, Annja rolled and brought the sword up from the ground.

Hsusia ran right onto the blade.

There was the briefest resistance from the armor, but then it yielded to the sword and Hsusia slid down until her face was mere inches from Annja's. The sword punched through her back, having pierced her heart.

Hsusia's breath froze. Her eyes went completely black.

But a smile played across her face. Annja rolled her off and got to her feet, wobbled and then collapsed next to the prone form of Hsusia.

It was over.

The arena went deathly silent.

And then a roar went up from the crowd. The thunder grew in intensity until Annja thought the roof might cave in completely.

Hans rushed out of the stands and came to Annja's aid. "Are you all right?"

Annja shook her head. "I'm losing a lot of blood. I need to get bandaged up or I'm going to die, I think."

Hans clamped a hand over the wound and waved the rest of the team down from the stands. Annja heard him giving orders, but her world was drifting away.

Hsusia lay on the ground, an ever-widening pool of blood spilled out of her armor. Annja frowned. It was a shame that it had to end this way, she thought. Hsusia was a good woman.

And I've just killed her.

The blackness came again for Annja.

And she succumbed.

"Wake up, Annja."

Annja groaned. "This is getting old, coming to like this." She sat up and winced as pain lanced through her side. She looked down and saw the wad of bandages wrapped around her waist.

"Did it stop bleeding?"

Hans nodded. "We stemmed the flow and stitched you up. Not sure how long it's going to hurt, though. Could be a while."

Roux stood nearby. "You gave us all quite a scare, Annja. We thought you were dead."

"Felt like it," Annja said. She looked around, but the body of Hsusia had been taken away. The arena itself was empty. Apparently none of Hsusia's people had stayed after the battle was over. "Where is everyone?"

"Holding a funeral for Hsusia," Spier said. "There is a time of mourning for the Jiao now. I have no idea how long it will last, but we've pretty much been left alone because of it."

Annja shook her head. "I wish this had gone down some other way. Killing Hsusia wasn't necessary."

"Apparently the oracle thought so," Roux said. "And they do seem to do whatever it tells them."

Annja frowned. "I'd like to know exactly what that oracle is. And how it's able to exert so much influence here."

Roux nodded. "Well, I may have the answer to that question. I've been thinking about it ever since you told me you were feeling sick."

"And what did you come up with?"

"I believe that it is some type of radioactive device."

"How is that even possible?"

Roux held up his hand. "Hear me out. The oracle supplies a constant stream of power to the Jiao. It powers everything here—the lights, the plumbing, everything. You reported that it needs a constant source of water around it. Water flows in cold and leaves hot. Much the same way the water is superheated in nuclear reactors, right?"

"I guess."

"And then there's the fact that Hsusia said that every surface person who comes in contact with the oracle gets sick and dies. You got sick, as well, and nearly died if not for the fact that you had some extra help in the matter."

"But how would they have ever gotten their hands on radioactive material?" Annja asked. "It's not the sort of thing you just find lying around on the street somewhere."

"True," Roux said. "But some things do occur naturally. It would obviously be a very rare occurrence, of course, but suppose they did find it and were able to refine it in such a way that it became an object of fascination first and then, over time, an object of worship."

"It makes sense," Spier said. "Especially since the cataclysm might well have destroyed the official records that were kept pertaining to the object. Without the background, the Jiao would have concocted some other story that would fit with the nature of it. Thus, it became deified as a matter of course."

Roux nodded. "It's an evolution of a fascinating, naturally occurring object that then gets transformed into something godlike."

"So, why don't the Jiao get sick from it?" Annja asked.

"Who knows? Gradual exposure over the millennia? Perhaps they have evolved to be able to withstand the level of radioactivity without succumbing to it. Of course, whenever someone from the surface comes here, they obviously lack that immunity. So they get sick and die," Roux said.

"You really think it's radioactive?"

Roux nodded. "I'm convinced of it."

"Well, that certainly explains a lot."

Hans helped Annja to her feet. "You still need to rest, Annja."

"What I'd like," Annja said, "is to get the hell out of here. See the sun again, not some nuclear-powered light."

"That's a good idea," Roux said. "What are the odds that the Jiao will keep their word and let us go?"

Spier shrugged. "I don't think it will be a problem, provided one of us stays behind like they said."

Annja shook her head. "No way. We all get out of here together or we all fight our way out."

Spier frowned. "You're in no shape to fight these warriors. They'd overwhelm us with sheer numbers and then what good would that do? Senseless violence is a silly thing. And our deaths would be for nothing."

"So, what, you're saying that we should leave someone behind?"

Spier shrugged. "We could draw straws or something."

"Annja is excused from the draw," Hans said. "She already put her life on the line for all of us. Several times over, if I recall properly."

Annja shook her head. "Nice of you to say so, but I'm in this with you guys. I'll take my chances like anyone else."

Roux glanced around. "We seem to be a bit short on straws, however. Anyone have any ideas on how we'll figure this out?"

"No clue," Annja said. She looked at Hans. "Got anything you can use?"

"No."

Annja looked at Mueller and Gottlieb but neither of them

had anything, either. She looked back at Hans. "Hey, where did Heinkel go?"

Hans looked at her. "What?" He glanced around and then saw that Heinkel was missing. "I have no idea."

Roux frowned. "I'm afraid we were all a little concerned about the state of your health, Annja. Heinkel might have slipped out during the confusion."

"Why?" Annja asked. "Where would he go?"

Hans glanced at Spier. "Do you think?"

Spier shrugged. "It's possible. But how would he know how to get there?"

"He's a smart man," Hans said. "He could figure it out easily enough."

"What are you two talking about?"

Hans looked into her eyes. "He may have gone for the pearl."

"What? No," Annja said. "And, of course, he has no idea that it's radioactive. What's he going to do, bring it back here and get us all sick?"

"We'll find him," Hans said. He nodded at Gottlieb and Mueller. They all left the room together.

Annja looked at Roux. "How would he transport the pearl if he finds it?"

"The only safe way," Roux said, "is with a lead-shielded bag or something similar. But he doesn't have anything like that."

Spier shook his head. "He has no idea it's radioactive, anyway. He'd have no reason to think he has to be careful with it."

"This is not good," Annja said. She turned and winced as more pain lanced through her side. "If the Jiao find out one of us is trying to rob them of their precious oracle, I think we can kiss our chances of escape goodbye. They'll kill us all, for crying out loud."

"This is my fault," Spier said. "If I hadn't been so obsessed with finding the pearl, Heinkel would never have taken it upon himself to go after it."

"Heinkel bears responsibility for this," Annja said. "After all, you didn't tell him to go get it, did you?"

"Of course not."

"Okay. Let's just hope that Hans and the others can find him before he gets us all killed."

Roux sighed. "We might be too late for that." He nodded toward the entrance to the arena area and Annja followed his gaze. A dozen of Hsusia's warriors stood with Heinkel in their custody.

The lead warrior came over to Annja. "We caught this man in the oracle room."

Annja looked at Heinkel. "What were you doing?"

He frowned. "I was doing what we came here to do."

Annja looked back at the warrior. "He acted alone. He was under no order to disturb your oracle. Any damage he caused was due to his actions alone."

The warrior considered this and then frowned. "The rule of law is that anyone attempting to take the oracle will be put to death."

Annja shook her head. "Whose rule of law was that?"

"The queen's."

"The queen is dead," Annja said. "So, too, must her laws be struck down."

The warrior shook his head. "We have yet to elect a new ruler. Until such time as we do, the old laws remain in effect. Your man here must be executed for his crime."

"I cannot allow that," Annja said.

"Yours is not to say," the warrior replied. "If you attempt to stop us, you will also be killed."

Annja shook her head. "Did you see me battle your queen?"

"Of course."

"And I bested her in armed combat, correct?"

The warrior nodded. "You defeated her according to the rules of the bout. Yes."

"So you're well aware of what I am capable of as a warrior, like yourself. You know that I will not simply let you kill one of my men."

The warrior considered this for a moment. "I would not be in a hurry to fight against you, if that is what you mean."

"It is."

"What do you propose, then?"

But the answer came to Annja in startling detail. As she looked at Heinkel, he seemed to pale, and then he slumped over, vomiting.

Annja waited until he was finished. "Did you touch it?"

Heinkel took a breath and then nodded. "I removed it from the basin. When they came into the room, I accidentally dropped it."

"You dropped it?"

"Yes."

"You've got radiation poison, Heinkel. The oracle is some sort of naturally occurring radioactive substance."

"Is that why you got sick earlier?"

"Yes."

Heinkel looked at her. "But you got better."

"I got better because of the sword," Annja said. "I don't know how to help you battle the sickness that is ravaging your body right now."

The warrior frowned. "It would appear that the oracle is dispensing its own justice here."

Annja nodded. "It seems that way."

The warrior seemed satisfied. He turned to his men. "We will return to the oracle room and make sure that the oracle is once again properly positioned."

But as they turned to leave, a thunderous sound echoed across the chamber. The lights flickered and went out briefly before coming back on.

The floor shuddered.

Roux frowned. "Annja?"

Annja looked at Heinkel. "What the hell did you do?"

He shook his head. "I put it back after I dropped it. I'm telling you the truth. Honestly."

Annja shook her head while Heinkel slumped to his side moaning in pain. She glanced at Spier. "You'd better hope your guys get back here soon. Something tells me this place isn't going to be very hospitable once they figure out what happened."

Hsusia's warriors ran out of the room. Annja looked at Roux. "What are the odds we can find our way back to the cistern?"

"I don't know, what are you thinking?"

"That we need to leave. Our time seems to be almost up."

Roux frowned. "We don't have enough air in our tanks to make the journey back."

"Then we'll have to share as we swim."

"What about that hot water? It's bound to be radioactive."

Annja shrugged. "I'm open to suggestions, Roux. I think we can stand the exposure provided we get through the tunnel as fast as possible. If we stay in the hot water, we'll be cooked. But once we get free, we should be all right."

"In that case, we'd better get going."

The floor beneath them rumbled and shook. Annja fell and hit her side, crying out as she did so. The pain was incredible, but she closed her eyes and took a deep breath, willing the agony to subside.

Spier knelt over Heinkel, but then shook his head and stood. "He's gone."

A giant crack appeared in one of the walls of the arena, running from the ceiling to the floor. Again, the lights flickered.

"We need to leave," Annja said. "Now!"

Hans, Mueller and Gottlieb came running back into the

room. They took one look at Heinkel and then kept moving. Hans rushed to Annja. "The entire place is falling apart. We have to try to get away!"

Annja leaned on him. "Lead on, Hans. We're right behind you."

23

The corridors of the underground kingdom were filled with the Jiao people, screaming and huddled in corners away from the falling debris. Chunks of marble tumbled to the ground as the very foundations themselves seemed to be rocked to their core.

"What the hell did Heinkel do?" Annja shouted.

"He may have upset the very thing that has kept this place in a state of suspended safety for all these years," Roux said as he dodged a chunk of marble. "By dropping the oracle, he may have severed the sense of balance and containment this place has."

"Great." Annja clutched her side, which ached terribly, as they threaded their way through the corridors.

Hans seemed to have an innate sense of direction and led them back toward the corridor where they'd first seen the painting. As they passed it, Annja looked upon the face of Hsusia and frowned. I wish there'd been another way, she thought. Then she ran on amid the showering stones.

The Jiao themselves seemed woefully unprepared for their

destruction. None of the mighty warriors seemed to have the first inclination on how to lead their people to safety. But even if they had, where would they have gone? How would they have escaped? Annja wasn't sure they would survive on the surface world. Just as she knew that none of them would have ever been able to survive trapped down here.

They reached the corkscrew staircase and dashed up it. At the top, the altar slab had to be pushed aside from inside the stairs. Hans and Gottlieb were able to shove it out of the way, finally, and then they spilled out.

Things on this floor weren't much better. Giant cracks split the walls, running ragged down toward the floor. Worse, Annja tasted salt in the air. "The ocean is breaking in," she said. "We've got to hurry!"

They made it back to the cistern and saw that the floor was already a few inches under water. They grabbed their gear and slid into it.

"How are we going to do this?" Roux asked.

"We share the air we have left," Annja said. "It's the only way we'll make it back alive."

She grabbed Heinkel's tank. "We've got one extra. We ought to have enough to get free of the tunnel."

The water rose to their knees and Annja felt its warmth, although the heat seemed to be dissipating. "I wish they'd get the oracle back into position. It might stop this destruction."

Spier appeared before Annja with his oxygen tank in hand. "Take this."

Annja looked at him. "What are you doing?"

"I'm staying."

Annja shook her head. "Don't be a fool. This place is coming down around us. If you stay, you'll die."

Spier smiled. "I'm eighty years old, Annja. I don't have much time left, anyway. I might look healthy, but I've been living a lie. You asked about my diet and how I could eat like that? It's because I've got terminal cancer. Doctors gave me a few months to live and I came here." He shrugged. "And now I know how I want to go out. By giving you all a better chance to live."

Hans appeared next to Spier. "This wasn't part of the plan."

"I changed the plan. Take the tank and go." Spier smiled. "Besides, according to the oracle, one of us was supposed to stay, anyway. I'm fulfilling that request."

"The oracle wasn't a prophecy," Annja said. "It was only Hsusia casting the bones."

"Doesn't matter," Spier said. "You don't have much time. Now go!" He turned and pushed his way through the waist-deep water, up the stairs and out of the room.

Gottlieb went to follow him, but Hans merely shook his head. And in the next instant, a giant chunk of ceiling came down, blocking the exit from the cistern.

Their mind was made up for them.

"We go now," Roux said. "Or we all die here."

Annja nodded and they descended into the tunnel. Annja could taste the stale air in her lungs, but they'd have to make do. The water grew hot again, but they sank quickly with their weight belts.

As they descended, more rocks and marble came crashing down through the water. Annja risked a glance up and saw that the top of the tunnel was now blocked.

Even if Spier wanted to get out, it was too late. The finality of it weighed heavy on Annja's mind as they continued to sink.

Spier and Heinkel were gone forever.

They dropped closer to the bottom of the tunnel and then turned. The temperature of the water increased as they did so, but then started to cool off. Annja saw her first fish. But even still, the walls around them continued to shudder and shake, and Annja felt that at any moment they might be crushed by the falling debris.

As they ascended through the tunnel, they saw more fish, but the walls still shook violently. Annja had been in an earthquake or two in her lifetime, but being in one under-water was a new experience entirely.

And it wasn't one she wanted to repeat any time soon.

Annja took a breath and nothing came out. Her tank was totally empty. She ripped the mouthpiece out and dropped the tank. It was useless now.

Hans shoved his into her mouth and she sucked deep, tast-ing the same stale oxygen. But it was air and her lungs took it greedily.

Behind her, Gottlieb and Mueller were already sharing Heinkel's tank. Out of all of them Roux seemed the only one who wasn't having a hard time breathing.

Annja frowned. He's probably half fish, anyway, she thought. After all, when you've been around for six hun-dred years, you've got time to evolve some gills.

Hans pointed suddenly and Annja saw it. The opening archway where they'd first come into the tunnel.

They pushed for it and then Hans went through first, helped Annja through and then Roux, Gottlieb and Mueller followed. They headed immediately for the surface.

As they ascended, Annja looked down at the reef but the shaking had apparently stopped. She saw no signs that there was any type of earthquake at all.

That's strange, she thought.

But she didn't have time to dwell on it. Her air bubbles stopped coming and she realized she'd just taken her final breath on that oxygen tank, as well.

Hans was already holding his breath and rising toward the surface. Annja had to do the same.

She ditched the tank and watched it fall toward the ocean

floor. Unburdened by her gear, she rose quickly and then broke the surface.

The sun was setting and the choppy waves showed signs that a storm was on its way.

Hans gasped in the surf next to her. "You all right?"

Annja brought her hand away from her wound. Only a small trace of blood showed. "I think so. The seawater seems to have helped stop the bleeding."

"Either that or the radiation," Roux said, having suddenly surfaced next to her. "But that's a good thing. I don't think any of us are eager for a confrontation with a shark right now."

"I'm certainly not," Annja said. "I want to sleep for about a thousand days."

Gottlieb surfaced next and then a minute later Mueller bobbed up alongside of them. Annja frowned. "What took you guys so long?"

Mueller smiled. "I was appreciating the view on the way out. I'm happy never to have to go back to that place."

"Dinner's on me tonight," Annja said. "We just have to get home now."

"Where the hell is the boat?" Hans asked.

They bobbed in the swells and Annja turned around trying to see their sloop. But Hans was right. The boat was gone.

Roux frowned. "That damned dive master probably came out and towed it back into shore. We've been gone far too long, after all."

"Yeah, but if they thought we were dead, wouldn't they have a recovery team out here looking for our bodies?" Annja asked.

Roux sniffed. "I think you might be giving him too much credit. Odds are he was more concerned about his boat and gear than he was us."

"But the other people of the resort would want to know,"

Annja said. "Dr. Tiko would make him launch some sort of rescue."

"Perhaps," Hans said, "they simply don't know yet."

Mueller frowned. "Regardless, we are without a boat. And we are perhaps a mile away from shore. Anyone up for a swim."

"Not a mile-long swim," Roux said miserably. "My old bones won't take it."

Annja clutched her side, but the pain was quickly dissipating. "Well, in that case, you can always stay here and act as bait for any sharks we happen to attract."

Roux shook his head. "You're just trying to rattle my nerves, Annja Creed. I'll have you know that I once battled a shark myself. In the waters of the Mediterranean, on a dare no less."

"Awesome," Annja said, already starting to do a breast stroke toward the shore far in the distance. "You can tell the tiger sharks all about that. Me? I'm going to get a good meal and a stiff drink."

Hans swam next to her. "You don't think he'll stay, do you?"

"Not a chance. Roux hates sharks. Despite what he says. It's false bravado."

Sure enough, Roux started swimming toward them, pleading for them to slow down so he could catch up. Mueller stopped and treaded water until Roux was safely in the midst of them. Then they all started swimming together toward the shore.

Annja heard the boat motor long before she could see it over the cresting waves that swirled around her. "Someone's coming!"

Hans bobbed up and then waved his hand high in the air. "It's one of the resort sloops."

They stopped and treaded water while Hans flagged the boat. It drew alongside them and the smiling face of the dive master appeared above them. "I thought I'd better come back and find my gear. Those tanks are expensive, you know!"

"Great, he wasn't concerned about saving us," Annja said. "He just wanted to protect his investment. What a humanitarian."

The dive master helped them on board, one by one. When they were seated, he looked at them. "Okay, where's all my stuff."

"Down on the reef," Annja said. "If you like, you can go back and get it. We'll wait here."

The dive master looked at the darkening sky. "It'll keep until tomorrow, I think. Besides, the night is coming and that's when the sharks come out to feed. It would be better for all of us if I got you back to Club Noah."

"You sure?" Annja asked. "I can see how much it would hurt you to lose a buck."

The dive master shook his head. "I will get it tomorrow." He turned back to the rudder but then stopped. "Where are the other two?"

Hans shook his head. "They didn't make it."

"What?"

"They're dead. Now get this boat going. We need to see the doctor and then we need to get food."

"Dead?" The dive master shook his head and gunned the engine. "This is what happens when you foreigners don't listen to me."

They cut through the waves toward the shore. As the boat skipped over the water, Annja finally caught sight of Club Noah in the distance. I never thought I'd be so happy to see that place again, she thought.

The dive master brought them into the dock and then they tied off. Hans helped Annja off the boat. "You'd better see the doctor—get your wound looked at. Make sure it hasn't gotten infected."

Annja felt the puncture and then shook her head. "I actually think I'm all right for the moment. Something tells me that the water down there maybe have helped kill off any infection. I'll go see the doctor after we get something to eat."

"You're sure?"

"Yeah."

Roux stepped onto the dock next to Annja. "Well, that was a little more adventure than I was actually intending to have."

"There's an understatement," Annja said.

"Shame about Heinkel and Spier," Roux said. "But I guess there's no accounting for what some people will do."

"Spier gave his life for us," Annja said. "He should be honored for his sacrifice."

"He lied to us, as well," Roux said. "Had we known about the cancer, would you have gone diving with him?"

"Sure, why not?"

Roux just shook his head and walked away. Annja looked after him and sighed. As if Roux had never told a lie in his life.

Hans came over to her. "We're going to get cleaned up and then have dinner. Will you dine with us?"

Annja nodded. "Absolutely."

Together, they walked off toward their cabanas.

24

By the time Annja emerged from the hot shower in her cabana, she felt almost human again. As far as she could tell, her wound from Hsusia was already almost fully healed. That was odd. Annja had been injured many times in the past, and while her recuperation time might have been less than normal, it was still necessary. Yet here she'd almost been run through with a spear and she seemed to be healing at an extraordinary rate.

No need for Dr. Tiko, she decided after checking herself in the mirror. She redressed the wound with a fresh bandage and then got ready for dinner.

To say she didn't have any regrets about the Jiao and her experiences there would have been wrong. Annja was keenly aware that Hsusia had died for no good reason. If the oracle or the pearl or whatever it was hadn't led them to believe it was some sort of all-powerful object, then Hsusia and her people might still be alive right now.

But the act of Heinkel when he dropped the pearl from its basin had clearly caused massive destruction in the underwater city. And Annja didn't think there'd be any chance of coming back from that.

She thought about how Spier had volunteered to stay behind. It was admirable, she supposed. But it didn't completely make sense. Annja had known plenty of cancer patients before and none of them exhibited the level of vitality that Spier had. Was it possible that he was really that close to death? Or had he simply said that to get Annja to leave him behind?

With a few blush strokes and some eyeliner, she felt ready for a much-needed meal. Outside, the weather seemed to be getting angry. More dark storm clouds roiled in the distance and the seas echoed their counterpart by churning to and fro. Annja could see the resort's boats jostling over by the dock.

But there seemed to be a few missing.

Putting it out of her mind, she considered grabbing an umbrella from her cabana for the walk to the main pavilion. But she decided against it. It wasn't raining just yet.

The walkway felt firm under her feet, unlike the ground in the underwater city. She shivered. How would she even go about telling anyone about their adventure there? Who would ever believe her?

She could lead an expedition to excavate the reef, of course, but what was the point. As Annja had seen many times, some of the secrets in the world were better left as secrets.

Besides, she liked the idea of knowing that the Jiao would remain protected in their final resting place. She had no doubt that the earthquakes would have reduced the city to rubble and allowed the ocean to flood it.

She shuddered at the thought. Nothing could be worse than being trapped without any way to escape.

As she approached the dining pavilion, she spotted Roux sitting alone at a table. He glanced up as she approached.

"You're looking quite fetching this evening," he said with a smile.

"Such an antiquated term," Annja said. "But a nice one, nonetheless. Thank you, Roux."

"You're welcome."

Annja sat across from him and ordered a glass of wine when the bartender swung by. She looked at Roux and smiled. "Still thinking about where we were a few hours ago?"

He shrugged and helped himself to a sip of his whiskey. "I don't know. I've been around many, many years and have seen quite a bit in that time. That was something else, however. I'm glad you were there with me."

"Likewise," Annja said. "It always amazes me how a little danger can turn enemies into allies and vice versa. You never know who you'll have to trust with your survival, right?"

"Well said. Hans certainly seems to have taken a liking to you," Roux said.

Annja smiled. "Has he now?"

"Of course, I'm not telling you anything you don't already know. I can see it in the way you look at each other. Dare I suggest that wedding bells might toll in your future?"

Annja waved him off. "Stop it, Roux. You're being silly. Hans is a nice diversion right now. I'm not much for serious relationships. How could I be, what with the sword and all?"

Roux shrugged. "I don't know. But the responsibility of carrying that blade shouldn't mean you have to sacrifice your happiness."

"That's kind of you to say, but I don't know if it works that way."

"No?"

Annja sighed. "I wonder what I would do if I were ever free of it. If I could ever go back to being normal. And what would happen the first time I got into trouble and went looking to pull the sword out, only to have nothing in my hands when I expected it to be there."

"You're presuming that you'd get into trouble again," Roux said. "Maybe that's being a bit harsh on yourself."

"Hardly," Annja said. "I know myself, if no one else. I know where my life has taken me to this point and I know what I'm liable to be involved with in the future."

"Do you?"

"Sure. Chaos."

Roux smirked and looked up. "Here comes your wine."

Annja accepted the glass and raised it to Roux. "Well, here's to us being a couple of survivors."

"And unlikely allies sometimes," Roux said.

"And that," Annja said. She took a sip of her wine and sighed as she set the glass down on the table.

Roux glanced at his watch. "I do wish the boys would hurry up and get here. I'm afraid I'm absolutely starving and that buffet looks utterly astounding."

Annja glanced at the walkway but saw no signs of Hans or anyone else. She frowned. They'd agreed to meet for dinner. So where were they?

"Let's wait five more minutes, and if they don't show up, I'm getting some food. I'm famished," she said.

"Deal," Roux said. He leaned back in his chair. "So, what will you do with Hans? Kiss him goodbye when this is all over? How do you see it playing out? I'm curious."

"You're nosy," Annja said. "And to be honest, I haven't really given it a lot of thought. We've got a few days left here and I intend to use that time to do what I came here to do initially—relax."

Roux smiled. "Nothing wrong with that. I myself will be leaving tomorrow morning, I expect."

"Really? So soon?"

He shrugged. "Well, there's really not much left for me here now, is there? The pearl is still buried underwater and I don't think there's much chance of getting it out now with all that coral lying atop it."

"Plus, there's the whole radiation thing."

"Indeed," Roux said. "How fascinating, though. What are the chances of something like that occurring naturally?"

"I have no idea," Annja said.

"Nor do I," Roux said. "But I intend to find out. It's a shame there wasn't some way to test it and find out exactly how old it is. I imagine that would tell us an awful lot about life on prehistoric earth."

"So you believe that there were other races before us?"

Roux nodded. "Most definitely. And I'd be willing to bet that they were rather advanced in several areas of mathematics and science. Perhaps not as advanced as we are today, but a good deal more advanced than just sitting about in caves somewhere in France."

Annja leaned back. "I've never given it much thought, to be honest. I mean, I've been fascinated by ancient peoples for so long. But I've always looked at them as having a finite length of time to peer back into. The thought that there was a whole other history to earth prior to some sort of apocalypse and that we know nothing about it is incredible to me."

"And yet, you've been exposed to the proof of its existence." Roux finished his whiskey. "That ought to be rattling a few of your preconceived notions about, eh?"

Annja shrugged. "The sword already took care of a lot of that."

Roux laughed. "I'll bet."

"I'll have to give it a lot of thought. And I wonder why we haven't found more evidence of this prehistory before now?"

"Perhaps the apocalypse that we speak of was so total that it simply erased the evidence. Turned the earth into a blank canvas, so to speak."

Annja nodded. "It must have. But what could have caused such a level of destruction?"

Roux fiddled with his empty glass. "I don't know. Perhaps some sort of nuclear Armageddon? I mean, we've just seen evidence that it occurred naturally in some form. Perhaps the people who populated the earth before us had learned to harness it?"

"Weaponize it, too?"

"It's possible."

"And that might mean they somehow lost control of it at some point. And it unleashed hell."

Roux sighed. "Ah, but for the curiosity of man, the universe might be a safe and peaceful place."

"And boring," Annja said. She looked at her watch. "That's five minutes gone now. I'm hungry."

Roux frowned. "And I'm curious." He stood and smiled at Annja. "I'll be back shortly."

Annja wandered over to the buffet. She grabbed a plate and started piling the food on. Tonight, they had several varieties of fresh fish, sushi, Filipino noodle dishes, more flank steak and a fresh *lechón*.

Annja grabbed a little bit of everything. She smiled to herself. Got to keep my strength up, don't I?

She saw Roux having a rather animated conversation with the desk clerk. What's he doing now?

Finally, she saw his shoulder droop in acceptance and he nodded several times before thanking the man. Looking rather dejected, he came walking back across the food pavilion.

"You all right?"

Roux pointed at their table. "Finish getting your food and then come sit with me, all right?"

"Sure."

She watched Roux walk away and then turned back to finish filling up her plate. She felt like she could single-handedly polish off everything they had available.

A flash of lightning followed by a crack of thunder split the sky overhead and then buckets of rain started pouring down.

I guess I should have brought that umbrella, she thought with a grin. Oh, well, maybe Hans will let me take refuge in his cabana later. The thought of it made her happy.

Annja walked back to the table she shared with Roux. He laughed at the amount of food on the plate.

"You eating for two already?"

"Oh, hush," she said as she sat down. "What's with you, anyway? I saw you speaking with the desk clerk. You don't look too happy."

Roux had a fresh whiskey and sat there nursing it. "Well, there's nothing that can be done about it now, anyway. The weather has certainly seen to that. This storm's going to be with us for some time apparently."

"What are you talking about?"

"I made some inquiries at the main desk."

"About what?"

"About leaving, of course."

Annja bit into her steak and shrugged. "I thought you said you were leaving tomorrow?"

"I was," Roux said. "But I asked if there was any way possible that I might be able to leave tonight."

"Why would you want to do a thing like that? It's pouring rain out and you'll be traveling in terrible weather."

"I'd want to leave," Roux said, "for the same reason you'll want to leave."

"Who said I wanted to leave?"

Roux smiled. "I'm sorry to have to be the one to tell you this, Annja."

Annja stopped eating. "Dammit, Roux, if you've got something to say, just spit it out, would you?"

"All right," Roux said. "Hans is gone. Along with Gottlieb and Mueller."

"What do you mean they're gone? They're meeting us for dinner any moment now."

Roux shook his head. "No. They're not. It seems our German friends checked out immediately after we got back. And as far as anyone seems to know, they're already heading back to wherever they came from."

25

The last thing Annja wanted to do was make this particular phone call. The problem was, she had nowhere else to turn. Hans and his team had vanished and Annja had no clue where they might have disappeared to. Germany was a reasonable assumption, but Annja needed to be sure.

Roux stood nearby. "We don't even know what they're up to."

"But they're up to something," Annja said. She'd managed to quell most of the rage she felt at Hans for deceiving her. But she was still angry. And annoyed enough to want to figure out exactly what the hell was going on.

"This guy can do it?" Roux asked.

"If he can't, no one can," Annja said. "The problem is, he's got a big crush on me. It gets a little awkward sometimes."

"Awkward? How? Do I need to excuse myself if you two are going to engage in a little telecommunications dalliance?"

"Don't be gross," Annja said. She made the call and waited for the phone on the other end to ring. It took several tries before he finally picked up.

"Hi, Annja."

She sighed. "How did you know it was me?"

"I hacked your email the other day. Saw you were going over to the Philippines. Besides, I don't get many international calls unless it's you."

"You hacked my email?"

"I'm kidding. Seriously. I wouldn't invade your privacy like that. At least, not unless I had access to some mini-high-def cameras that I could implant in your shower."

"You're making me regret calling," Annja said. "Seriously. Tone down the creepiness, okay?"

"What can I do you for?"

Annja sighed. George was one of the most talented hackers she knew. He'd gotten his start busting into places like NORAD and the Pentagon. When the government found out what he could do, they decided it would be better to pay to have him on their side than against them wreaking havoc.

"I need to know where a few friends of mine went. They've disappeared."

"Maybe you were rude to them."

"That's not it, George. They were here in the Philippines and now they've taken off for someplace else. Presumably home to Germany, but I can't be sure."

"Were they German?"

"Yes."

"Okay, feed me their names and I'll see what I can do."

Annja paused. "That might be a problem."

"How so?"

Annja ran a hand over her forehead. "I don't have their last names."

"Any of them?" George paused. "I can only work miracles in so many ways, Annja. I need at least some basic information if I'm going to turn dead ends into fruitful leads."

"Almost poetic," Annja said. "I don't have any of the names of the guys who are traveling right now. But I do have one last name of a man they came in with. Could that help?"

"I don't know. I might be able to trace the arrival data and then work from there. What's the name?"

"Spier. First name Joachim." She spelled it out for him.

She heard the clacking of keys and George started to hum bad show tunes as he usually did when he worked. After a few seconds he started whistling, which Annja knew meant that he might have something.

"Okay, hang on…"

Annja held the phone. Next to her Roux rubbed his chin thoughtfully. He'd managed to polish off several glasses of whiskey and Annja wondered if he might be drunk. She shook her head. Only my life, she thought. A drunk six-hundred-year-old man on one side and a perpetually horny geek hacker on the other. No wonder she'd been so attracted to Hans. He was the most normal man she'd come across lately.

At least until he deserted her.

"What have you got, George?"

"Joachim Spier. Flew from Frankfurt to Delhi and then on to Manila. Traveled with four men: Heinkel Guttiger, Gottlieb Schwarzwalder, Hans Schmidt, and Karl Mueller. Those names sound right?"

"Yes, they do. Can you work back and see any departing information on where Hans, Gottlieb and Mueller went?"

"I'm assuming they booked round trip tickets…hang on."

Annja heard more keys clacking as George worked his magic. "Well, that's interesting."

"What is?"

"Seems your boys didn't head back to Germany, after all."

"Where did they go?"

"Hang on, it's coming up. Lessee…Manila to Osaka, then on to Minneapolis. From there, they are booked to fly into Logan International Airport in Boston."

"Boston? Why would they be going there?"

"Search me, babe. I can't divine that kind of information. But I can tell you that they are currently on a layover in Osaka. You want me to have security pull them and hold them in custody for you?"

Annja frowned. "You can do that?"

"Technically? Yep. But it's usually done at the behest of my esteemed employers, not on an individual basis. You'd owe me really big if I did that."

Annja shuddered. "I don't want that kind of debt on my shoulders, George."

"Gee, make it sound less pleasant, why don't you."

Annja sighed. "George, don't be like that. But seriously, I don't need them pulled off the plane. Not yet, anyway."

"Who are these guys?"

"I don't really know," Annja said. "I got mixed up with them over here and we went diving a few times. One of them is supposedly ex-German special operations."

"Really?" George sounded interested even more now. "Tell me more."

"He saw action in Afghanistan. I did some Google searches but couldn't find out anything."

She heard George snort. "Google. Please. You civilians think it's the be-all-end-all of searching. That's like comparing a tricycle with a Ferrari. It's almost damned near insulting."

"We don't all have access to the same stuff you do, George. Us civilians have to make do with what we can get our hands on."

"Oh, I know. Trust me. I was out there before. I know what it's like. But it sure is a lot nicer being here where the real information is."

Annja took a breath. "So, prove it."

"Prove what?"

"Prove how nice it is. Dig me up something on Hans and tell me why he's in such a hurry to get to Boston."

George paused on the phone. "Why would I do a thing like that?"

"Because you happen to be completely and totally crazy for me."

Roux stifled a laugh and Annja had to shoo him away. On the other end of the line, George didn't say anything for a moment.

"You still there?"

George cleared his throat. "If I do this for you, I'm going to expect something in return."

"Don't be crass, George. It's not charming."

"I'm not being crass. I just want a little compensation."

Annja sighed. "Fine, how much?"

"You insult me," George said. "I've got more money than I know what to do with right now. I don't do this for the money."

"All right—what, then?" But she had an idea of what was coming.

"Dinner. Just you and me. For real this time. No more standing me up like the last time."

"George, there really was an emergency. I wasn't lying."

"I don't want to get back into that whole mess. Just promise me that we'll go out for a nice dinner. Anywhere you want."

"In Washington?"

George sighed. "No, *anywhere* you want. Anywhere. Any city, any country. I don't care. It's on me. I've got all this cash in the bank and no one to spend it on. I eat microwavable meals while I work. It'd be good for me to get out and enjoy a real meal for a change. And the fact that you're so incredibly beautiful wouldn't hurt, either."

"Well, thank you."

"I mean it," George said. "I'll be happy to dig up every little juicy tidbit on this guy and, in exchange, you agree to let me take you out for a fabulous meal." He paused. "Look,

Annja, I'm not under any illusions here. I know I'm not your type of guy. I don't expect you to fall madly in love with me. But I would like the honor of taking you out for a proper meal."

Annja smiled in spite of herself. "You know what, George? I think you may have just convinced me to give you a shot."

"Yeah?"

"Yeah."

"Sweet. I'll call you back as soon as I have something."

"Thanks." Annja hung up the phone and looked up at Roux. "He'll get to work digging up stuff."

"And you're going to voluntarily carbonate his hormones. How utterly altruistic of you."

Annja sighed. "He's not that bad."

"I'll bet you a thousand dollars he lives in his mother's basement," Roux said. "And eats cheese puffs for breakfast."

Annja smirked. "You owe me a grand. He's got a high-rise condo on the Potomac."

"Really?"

Annja shrugged. "We'll call it even at five hundred. I think he does eat cheese puffs for breakfast."

Roux nodded. "Fair enough. How'd you find this guy?"

"He found me while I was working a story on black helicopters and conspiracy theories about Area 51."

"Not exactly your usual fare for that television show of yours."

Annja nodded. "I know. The producers wanted a show to coincide with the fiftieth anniversary of the supposed Roswell Incident. I started poking around and George found me after I sent a few emails to some supposed authorities on the matter."

"And the course of true love has run smooth ever since." Roux licked his lips. "How touching."

"Oh, be quiet already. George is a valuable contact. God

knows why Hans and the rest of them took off like that. I don't suppose you have anything to add to the conversation?"

Roux shrugged. "I don't know, to be honest. I'm standing here thinking to myself what would make them leave without saying goodbye? What would make them simply drop everything and basically run away? I mean, Hans seemed genuinely smitten by you. Unless it was all an act."

Annja frowned. "I've considered that, as well."

"I realize it's not a nice thing to have to consider, but given the reality we currently face…"

Annja nodded. "Yeah, he may have been playing me. I know. But to what end? Why?"

"Perhaps we have to go back and reexamine why they were here in the first place."

"You mean the pearl?"

Roux nodded. "They traveled here to obtain it, didn't they? So did they know more about it than we did? Was there more to their quest than they led us to believe?"

"Anything's possible," Annja said. "I just wish I knew what was improbable so I could eliminate the chaff and figure this out."

"I think we'll find out before too long," Roux said.

"You do?"

He smiled. "Oh, yes, I'm an eternal optimist. Didn't I ever tell you that?"

"Uh, no."

He nodded and looked into his empty whiskey glass. "Oh, yes, I find it's much more compelling to be an optimist, especially when you've been dealt a particularly bad hand of cards."

"If you say so," Annja said.

The phone rang and she picked it up. "Hello?"

"Annja?"

"Yeah, George, what's up?"

"Annja, where the hell did you find these guys?"

"What's that supposed to mean?"

George sighed. "It means get ready for me to lay some really heavy shit on you."

26

"Tell me," said Annja. "And don't hold anything back."

George's voice came over the phone line and delivered the news. "These guys are all ex-KSK. Do you know what that is?"

"I know KSK stands for *Kommando Spezialkräfte.* So they're special ops. Tough guys."

"The toughest," George said. "KSK is what became of the West German GSG-9 unit after the fall of Communism, except that KSK is more badass. These guys are the Kraut equivalent of our Delta Force and then some. They've been on secret missions all over the world, even if the German government doesn't admit it. They've been in every major conflict and a lot more of the lower-intensity ones, as well. Rumor is there have even been a few that the Germans started deliberately just to get their guys some practical real-world experience."

"So, what Hans told me about Afghanistan was legitimate?"

"Oh, he was there all right," George said. "And he was the

only member of his team to come back from a mission. But it isn't a very nice story. There was suspicion that he killed the other members of his team himself."

Annja felt her stomach drop. "Why would he do a thing like that?"

"Well, here's where it gets a little wonky. Seems like there was a rabidly nationalistic splinter group within KSK. These guys were so far right wing they made Hitler look like he spent his summers working for Greenpeace. They wanted the expulsion of all foreigners from German soil. Seriously antiimmigration. They wanted to dismantle the Turkish neighborhoods in German cities and send them all packing. Crazy stuff."

"Maybe not as crazy as it used to be," Annja said. "That kind of stuff is happening everywhere, even in the U.S."

"Good point. Anyway, the group was exposed and those who had pledged loyalty to it were booted out of the KSK with orders that if they ever spoke about their time inside the unit, they'd be arrested for treason."

"That didn't seem to stop Hans from fabricating a story for me the other night."

"Was he trying to get in your pants?"

Annja sighed. "When you put it in such crude terms like that, George, it's really unpleasant."

"Sorry."

"Never mind. Just keep going."

"Well, your boy Hans kicked around in a couple of grunt jobs for a few months after Berlin heaved him. But just as his savings accounts started to run out, he got a payday in the form of about fifty thousand dollars."

"Sign-on bonus?"

"That's what I thought, too. You know a lot of these former special-ops guys go into security work. Close protection stuff that takes them abroad. Either that or mercenary work. The jobs pay well, so the influx of funds didn't set off any alarms in Berlin. It probably should have."

"So how do you know about it, then?"

"I can't actually tell you, because it's classified. Let's just say that our government likes to keep tabs on the most highly specialized units all over the world. If you're in one of those units or one of those teams, chances are pretty good we have a file on you."

"Why would you care about who is in special operations?"

George sighed. "You have any idea what these guys are capable of, Annja? With their skills and know-how, they could literally bring down governments in weeks if not days. It's not just the fact that they know how to use explosives, it's that they understand the fragility of government bureaucracies. How they work, what it takes to bribe the right people and how best to cripple them. These guys get sent abroad to be fifth columns within the shadows of certain nations. At any time, they can pull the trigger and collapse whomever they want. They're not just dangerous in conventional terms— they're dangerous in unseen intangible terms, as well."

"Never thought of it like that," Annja said.

"Well, trust me, we have." George sighed. "So, where was I?"

"About fifty thousand dollars into the story."

"Right, so anyway, your boy Hans comes into that money and then the next day disappears. We lost him."

"You lost him?"

"Surveillance in the program isn't like a stakeout. We don't have people sitting on these targets. We keep tabs on the stuff we can monitor with a few keystrokes and a software package. So if someone decides to drop out of circulation, we don't usually sound alarm bells nor do we know about it until something sparks our interest."

"Like, say, a long-lost friend calling you up from the Philippines and asking about one of your targets."

George chuckled. "Now you're getting the hang of things."

"And I'm thrilled," Annja said. "Where did he go? Do you have any idea?"

"Austria. A small town there named Kitselplatz. Try to find that on your precious Google and it won't even show up. That's how tiny and insignificant it is. At least to them."

"But you know about it."

"Yeah. Hans traveled there to meet with his friends."

Annja sighed. "Let me guess—Heinkel, Gottlieb and Mueller."

"Bingo. Win a prize. They stayed in a small bed-and-breakfast and had long walks in the woods, longer dinners and lots and lots of beer."

"So, what's the deal on Heinkel, Mueller and Gottlieb? Were they in the KSK, as well?"

"Yep. And they were also part of the same fringe group. So when Hans got the boot, so did they. Needless to say, the rage they must have felt at being kicked out of the unit they so obviously loved must have been intense."

"What happened at that meeting?"

"We're not sure," George said. "We know that they stayed in Kitselplatz for about three days. Then they drove in a single car back into Germany and all the way to Munich without stopping."

"Without stopping?"

"Well, except for gas and stuff."

Annja nodded. "Who did they meet with in Munich?"

"Joachim Spier."

Annja's frown deepened. Roux, who had gone to fetch himself another whiskey, came back, saw Annja's face and promptly downed his drink in one go.

"And what's Spier's role in all of this? The most I could find was that he was a former German paratrooper who made his money after he got out of his service by investing."

"That's all true. Spier was an investment genius. They

said he picked stocks the way some guys know how to pick horses at the track. But Spier didn't need someone paying off a jockey to pick his winners. The guy had a feel for the markets. Knew just where to stick all his cash. He made a fortune and then doubled, tripled and quadrupled it in just a matter of a few years."

"I'm surprised there isn't more information about him on the web. I couldn't find all that much."

"Spier's notorious for avoiding the limelight. Wants nothing to do with the high-society scene, movie premieres, any of that junk. Spier's main goal in life is to not be seen at all. If no one knew who he was, he'd be a million times happier."

"He seems to have succeeded admirably in that goal," Annja said. "When was he diagnosed with his cancer?"

There was a pause on the phone. George said, "Huh?"

"Cancer. He said he had cancer. He told me to my face that his doctors had given him months to live."

"Annja, Joachim Spier is in perfect health. I have his latest physical records here—ran them through the translation software—and there's not one mention of cancer. The guy's the poster child of longevity. As far as anyone is concerned, Spier ought to live into his hundreds, for crying out loud."

"Why would he tell me that?"

"I don't know. Maybe he had an alternate agenda? Something that necessitated him lying to you about it?"

Annja put her head in her hands. This was all coming undone far too quickly. Had the vacation really dulled her senses to the point she'd let these guys pull a fast one on her? Or was she just getting tired of the game?

"Can you do me a favor?"

"Sure."

"See if there's any indication that the area I'm in experienced any type of earthquake earlier today."

"Hang on a second." Annja heard him typing on several keys and then punch one final key. "Palawan, Philippines…

nope. Nothing registered on any of the Geological Service monitors. If you felt something, it must have been highly localized."

"How could that be?" Annja asked. "It felt like a massive earthquake underwater. Things were shaking. Ceiling collapsing. Walls splitting. How could that have been fabricated?"

"Explosives," George said.

"Really?"

"You'd need an expert in demolitions to pull it off, but if they knew what they were doing, sure."

"And a former KSK operator?"

"Yeah, he'd have all the know-how to do something like that."

Annja shook her head. "We really got played here."

"So, getting back to Spier for a moment?"

"Yes?"

"Turns out he's something of an ultranationalist himself. Really appreciated the fascist point of view. Began espousing it to several people close to him. But they just branded him a lunatic. So he started frequenting the hangouts of special-ops guys."

"So it appears he found himself an audience, huh?"

"Yep. Hans and the others became Spier supporters. But Spier didn't publish papers or do anything to call attention to himself. That would have gone against the desire for no publicity. Instead, they started meeting in secret, planning God knows what."

"We don't know what they were up to?"

"No."

"Damn," Annja said. She rubbed her temples and tried to imagine what could have been going on here these past few days.

"Was Spier into archaeology?"

"Almost as much as you, it would seem," George said. "He

amassed quite a collection of relics that were all supposed to have mystical powers or something attached to them."

"Really?"

"Yeah. Maybe he's as zealous an occultist as Hitler was. I don't know. But he seemed to have this strange belief that these relics had powers he could tap into."

"And what would he do with that power if he could tap into it?"

"Good question," George said.

Annja looked up at Roux, who had a puzzled look on his face. She knew he'd been able to piece some of the conversation together, but key parts were missing and he was anxious to hear what George was telling her.

Tough, she thought, you'll have to wait.

"Are they still in Osaka?"

"For another three hours," George said. "Then they fly into the U.S."

Annja nodded. "I need to get back to the U.S., too, apparently."

She heard George take a sharp breath. "You're not going after them, are you?"

"Yes. I am."

"You'll need tickets."

"I'll need a lot more than that. It's raining here to beat the band. They say they can't get us out for a day at least. By then this could all be over."

"Let me see what I can do about that," George said. "And by the way, you can't go after these guys by yourself."

Annja looked at Roux. "I have a friend with me. I think he will be willing to help."

"Yeah, is he any good?"

"He's kind of old," Annja said. "But I think he's still got some fight in him."

"Well, you're going to need it. Trying to take down five guys isn't something you do without a lot of support."

Annja frowned. "What did you just say?"

"Support. You'll need support."

"No, before that. You said *five* guys?"

"That's right. Hans, Mueller and Gottlieb. They're waiting with Heinkel and Spier for the flight to the U.S."

27

"I must say I'm quite impressed with the capabilities of your would-be suitor, Annja."

They zoomed through the air, cruising at thirty-eight thousand feet in the Gulfstream G650, close to the speed of sound. The interior cabin boasted luxurious leather trim, a stateroom and even a pair of beds in the aft of the cabin for sleeping on long flights.

"I mean," Roux continued, "it is a sixty-million-dollar plane, after all. The boy obviously has style."

"What he's got is connections," Annja said. When she'd told George that they needed a way out of the Philippines, he hadn't wasted any time. Using his government credentials, he'd managed to have a military helicopter fly out in the midst of the storm, no less, to pick up Annja and Roux and take them back to Manila where the Gulfstream was idling on the runway, courtesy of the United States government. Annja had looked at the tail numbers and wondered if they even corresponded to a legitimate entity back in the States. Probably a CIA front company, she decided.

No matter, George had been good to his word and got them out of the Philippines within three hours of Annja's phone call. The Gulfstream could cruise at speeds in excess of what the commercial airlines flew. That would give them a chance to catch up with Hans and his team, although Annja still had no idea what they might be up to.

Roux sat next to her, swiveling in his chair and enjoying the view out of the twenty-eight-inch windows that ran down the sides of the fuselage. "Marvelous plane. Marvelous. I hope you treat this kid well, Annja."

"You want to date him?"

Roux grinned. "After all of this, I just might." He took a sip from the bottle of water he'd received from the flight attendant. "Now, let's try to figure out exactly what we've stumbled on to here, shall we?"

Annja frowned. "I have to admit, I'm a bit curious as to why you're still along on this ride. Doesn't this violate your usually sacred rule of letting the rest of us get on with destroying ourselves? I thought you'd prefer to stay in your ivory tower and come down when we're done making a mess of the planet."

Roux shrugged. "Hey, I wanted the pearl for myself, if you recall."

"I do. But you never told me why."

Roux sighed. "It was my belief that the pearl might enable the wielder to possess some type of power. Personal power. I thought it might be a means of bridging our world and the next. Of elongating life."

"Elongating life? Roux, you're almost six hundred years old. How much longer do you want to live?"

Roux's eyes sparkled. "Who knows. Why not forever?"

Annja shook her head. "You'd really be happy living forever?"

"I don't know, but it might be nice to have the option."

"What about the people you grow to love? What happens when they die and move on to whatever comes next?"

Roux nodded. "The first time it happened was the hardest. But, over time, you somehow get used to it. You ask why I'm usually so reluctant to get involved with others? That's why."

"Yet you still want to prolong your life? I don't get it."

"Well, you haven't yet lived beyond your own lifetime. There's a certain novelty to being a witness to history."

"Yeah, but that history is still only the blink of an eye. Six hundred years as compared with the eons that the planet has been around…it's almost nothing. Look at the discovery we just made of the Jiao. They survived until we came blundering into their lives."

"I have been thinking about that," Roux said. "And in some ways, you might be right about a life being but a breath. But I do so enjoy seeing what the next generation will do on this precious chunk of rock that hurtles through the universe."

Annja sighed. "Sometimes I think death can't come soon enough for some people."

"Including yourself?"

"I'm not suicidal," Annja said.

"The dive master back in Palawan would probably disagree with you on that."

Annja ignored that statement. "But there have been times when I wondered whether it would be better just to lose my life and move on. Especially when I find myself questioning exactly what my purpose is here with the sword at this point in our history. Why now? Why me?"

"So you'd hope to find the answers once you arrived at the pearly gates, is that it?"

"It would be nice."

"I think you'd be in for a disappointment," Roux said bitterly.

"God doesn't give out answers to our deepest questions."

"How would you know? You're not dead."

Roux frowned. "I may as well have died fifty times by now. I've gone through so much soul searching and pleading for answers from above that it no longer concerns me in the slightest."

"You've got a faith problem," Annja said. "Don't project that on to others. It's not fair."

"Nothing's fair," Roux snapped. "Don't be a child, for God's sake. This idea that you'll find your answers when you die—it's silly. And it's naive to think that death presents some great opportunity. What if we're only destined to break down and become fertilizer for those who come after us?"

Annja smirked. "You don't believe that nonsense. You know there's something more to all of this than just one time around."

"Do I?"

Annja nodded. "Your own life has been stretched—not due to something amazing you did—but because of the will of God. In much the same way I now have the burden of this sword. It's all part of a bigger plan."

"So we don't get a choice?"

"We get to choose," Annja said. "But I think the choices are predetermined. The outcome is uncertain, but the paths are already laid out."

"How does that even make sense?" Roux said.

Annja leaned back. "You're just upset you didn't get the sword. You'll get over it someday."

Roux shook his head. "I hate it when you get insufferable like this."

"So, let's take our minds off this discussion and try to figure out what Hans and the boys are up to."

"Spier must be heading it up. No offense to your afternoon delight, but I don't think he's got the brains to spear-head something like this."

"I agree," Annja said. "His talents were obviously designed for more primal activities."

"Oh, please, that's the last thing I need to hear about now." Roux sighed. "Honestly."

Annja laughed.

Roux rolled his eyes. "You're starting to sound like that beast Garin. How that boy ever apprenticed under me is beyond me. You would have thought a libido like that would be sent from the devil himself."

Annja changed the topic. "So if Spier is behind all of this, what's the point?"

"I think we've got to accept the fact that they knew a lot more about things than they let on. They may have even let us believe that we were doing the work for them. That way, we'd make the wrong assumptions."

"So, let's go back to the pearl. What do we know about it?"

"It's radioactive," Roux said. "So obviously it's a potent thing to have."

"Is it possible Spier knew about it being radioactive? I don't recall him saying anything specifically about that, but it did seem that anyone who came into contact with it in the legend he told me about suffered from misfortune."

Roux nodded. "So, again, he's leading us in what we might come up with relating to the pearl. He told you that story and put the suggestion in your mind that something bad would happen. And then when Hsusia told you as much, it simply strengthened the suggestion. Almost like hypnosis."

"But the danger was real," Annja said. "I did get sick."

Roux nodded. "And we thought Heinkel did, too."

"He must have faked it," Annja said. "And when he went missing those two times, was it to plant explosives? To simulate the earthquake?"

"So they could grab the pearl," Roux said. "That's really what they wanted all along. Spier does his heroic role that we both fell for. Here we were thinking he'd sacrificed himself for the team, but in reality, he and Heinkel secured the pearl and got it ready for transport."

"But how could they transport it? It's radioactive."

"We don't know the nature of the radiation coming off it," Roux said. "But they could have simply brought along a storage container that we didn't even see."

Annja shook her head. "How would they have carried that? We were with them the whole time."

Roux smiled. "Do you remember seeing magicians perform? All those wonderful tricks they like to do?"

"Sure."

"They rely on misdirection. Watch this hand while the other is doing all the work. Spier took the lead right after me going into the tunnel, right?"

"Yes."

"So we tended to be focused on him while Heinkel, Gottlieb and Mueller were relegated to the background. You focused on Hans and I focused on Spier. The real threat was always out of our awareness."

Annja shook her head. "So Heinkel and the others could have brought everything they needed with them."

"Sure. And when Heinkel disappeared the first time, he could have gone back into the tunnel, for example, and brought up both the explosives and the protective container and we wouldn't have been any wiser. It appeared that he'd been grabbed. But he hadn't. He'd simply gone back, grabbed the gear and come back along a different route."

"Spier would have had to guess that the pearl was radioactive in some way."

Roux shrugged. "Maybe he did. Maybe he simply thought it would be some sort of energy device. And being intelligent—because he certainly is—he simply took steps to cover any contingency. The radiation may have been as much a surprise to him as any of us. But he would have planned ahead for that possibility."

"We're playing a bad game of catch-up here," Annja said. "And I don't much care for it."

"The real question now," Roux said, "is what do they hope to achieve in America? And Massachusetts, no less."

"George said he'd try to work on that and have something for us by the time we land in Boston."

"Let's hope he doesn't take too long," Roux said. "Time doesn't seem to be a luxury we have a great deal of at the moment."

"I know he'll work his ass off," Annja said. "Especially if he happens to think that dinner is riding on it."

"Stop using sex as a weapon, Annja."

Annja looked at him and broke out into a grin. "What did you say?"

Roux waved his hand in the air. "Oh, nothing. I heard a song the other day and I've been dying to say it ever since."

"Well, glad I could oblige."

The flight attendant stopped by to ask if there was anything they needed. Roux asked for a glass of whiskey. Annja asked for a pillow. When the attendant left, Annja looked at Roux and frowned.

"You've been drinking a lot lately. You okay?"

He frowned. "Why? Do you want to be my sponsor?"

"Do I need to be?"

"I enjoy my drinks, Annja," Roux said. "Leave me to them, if you please."

"Fair enough." Annja looked out of the window and watched the clouds pass by for a few moments.

The attendant returned with Roux's whiskey. He took a sniff and nodded as if he approved. Then, just before he took a sip, he made a very subtle gesture. Annja caught the movement.

"What was that?" she asked.

"What was what?"

"That movement you made, like you were toasting someone."

Roux frowned. "You've just spent the past several days being completely unaware and now, what—you're making up for lost time?"

"You were as unaware as I was. Now spill it."

The attendant brought Annja her pillow.

Roux nodded at it. "Today happens to be an anniversary of sorts. For a special someone I lost a long time ago. Now put your head on that pillow and go to sleep. Allow me to enjoy some memories in peace."

28

Annja slept through the refueling in Honolulu and only woke when Roux tapped her on the arm. She was alert immediately. "Where are we?"

"Boston, according to the pilot. We're starting our preliminary approach. But we're not landing at Logan."

"Why not?"

"Apparently this plane is more welcome at military fields. So we're landing in Bedford, Massachusetts, at Hanscom Field. Part of an Air Force base but it also handles civilian planes like this one."

"Civilian. Right." Annja stretched. "I've been out for a while, I guess?"

"Hours and hours," Roux said. "It was pleasant being alone with my thoughts. Did you get some good sleep?"

"Actually, yes. I feel like I slept better on this plane than I have in months."

Roux nodded. "Strange how that happens sometimes."

Before Annja could respond, the flight attendant came

toward her with a phone. "Excuse me, Miss Creed? I've got a phone call for you."

Annja took the phone. "Hello?"

"How's the flight?"

Annja smiled. "It's amazing, George. I can't thank you enough."

"Oh, sure you can," George said. "But we'll talk about that later. For right now, we've got other things to discuss."

"Did you find a connection?"

"And how. Turns out the German chancellor is vacationing in Massachusetts. On Martha's Vineyard. The president is supposed to join her in a few days."

"Well, that's good news, right? I mean, if the chancellor is there now and our president is coming in soon, then that means the Secret Service will have that place buttoned up so much a mouse couldn't sneak through."

"Presumably," George said. "But it depends on what your team of lunatics might be trying to do. If they're going for a kidnap, then, yeah, it's probably almost certainly not going to work. But if they're looking to blow them all to hell, for instance, then depending on the explosive, they wouldn't need to breach the perimeters that the Secret Service will have set up."

"That would mean a lot of explosives, wouldn't it?" Annja asked.

"Usually. Unless they had access to, say, something nuclear. Then they could be back on Cape Cod and set the thing off and it would vaporize everything within twenty miles, depending on the yield."

Annja's stomach sank. That had to be it. A nuclear explosion.

But George interrupted her thoughts again. "Or they could use a dirty bomb. Set it off and make everyone ill with radiation sickness. That's pretty nasty stuff, too." He paused. "So, what do you think they're up to?"

"I don't know," Annja said. "There's a chance they might have access to nuclear material, though."

George paused. "Are you serious?"

"I think so."

"Annja, I'm going to have to escalate this accordingly. You know that, right?"

"Yes," Annja said. "But the thing is, we need to get these guys now. If they get wind that we know about it, then they'll go to ground and we'll never find out where that nuke is."

"Are you sure they've got a nuke?"

Annja paused. "I don't know."

George sounded impatient. "Well, what the hell does that mean?"

"It means I don't know, George. I wish I did. We were in the Philippines to find some long-lost giant pearl, but it turns out that it wasn't a pearl, after all. It was some sort of naturally radioactive object that could power lights, supply oxygen and all that stuff."

"Are you messing with me, Annja?"

"Definitely not."

George groaned. "I don't know how I'm going to take this to my bosses. What am I supposed to say, that I think there might be a band of crazy ex-special-ops guys looking to take out the German chancellor using some sort of naturally radioactive globe of something?"

"I know it's not the best scenario."

"It's not even close."

"So what do we do?"

"Fortunately for you, you happen to be friends with a pretty incredible guy. Leave it to me and I'll get something cooking on this. You guys are slated to land at Hanscom. Stay there until I contact you."

"You sure?"

"Yeah, gotta run."

The phone disconnected and Annja slumped back in her

seat. She looked at Roux. "This whole thing sounds ridiculous."

"Not necessarily," Roux said. "There are such things as naturally occurring radioactive materials—they're called NORMs—and they're a by-product of the oil and gas industry. You don't normally find them in such a form as the pearl, but the concept at least is not unbelievable."

"What a relief."

"Even more," Roux said, "the U.S. government doesn't actively regulate NORMs at all. Someone with enough creativity and ingenuity could theoretically put enough together to at least create some type of dirty bomb. It's not as though this whole thing is completely crazy. There are precedents for it."

"Really? Another band of ex-KSK commandos got their hands on a radioactive relic and planned to kill someone with it? When did that happen?"

Roux sighed. "You should really restrain that sarcasm of yours, Annja. It does get tedious after a while."

"I'll keep that in mind. In the meantime, George wants us to stay put once we land at Hanscom."

"Why?"

"He's putting something together."

Roux yawned. "Wonderful. No doubt it will be a platoon of government bureaucrats all jockeying to further their own careers while a potential disaster looms. I've always found it so fascinating that these people are supposed to be keeping others safe and yet, at the end of the day, they're exactly like the very people they claim to keep us safe from. Everyone's out for their own good. That bottom line is all-powerful."

"Well, I don't hear you coming up with any excellent plans of your own. I'm all ears if you've got one formulating."

"What's the target?"

"As far as George can tell, it's on Martha's Vineyard."

Roux smiled. "Really? How nice. Charming little island.

I used to visit it frequently back in the 1980s. I had quite a nice sail in Nantucket Sound with a very prestigious television news anchor who used to summer there. Oh, the stories he would tell me over a few bottles of wine. Fascinating stuff. Truly."

"Roux!"

"Oh, all right. Let me think about it. We should be on the ground fairly soon, right?"

The plane banked at that moment and started to descend at a steep angle. The flight attendant came around. "Seat belts, please. We've been directed to come in fast."

"Why fast? What's wrong with slow?" Annja asked.

But the attendant had already walked past her so she could strap herself in. Annja heard the flaps come down and then the landing gear descended from the bottom of the aircraft.

Outside her window, trees and buildings and highways and cars came into view all at once. She saw other planes nearby, including several fighter jets. They must use those to scramble in case of a terrorist incident on board a civilian plane.

And then the plane was coming in and Annja felt the first touchdown as the wheels made contact with the tarmac. The nose of the plane came down and they were back on the ground after nearly twelve hours in the air.

Roux breathed a sigh of relief. "I happen to hate airplane landings. Truly awful things."

"I didn't think you were afraid of flying," Annja said.

"You would be, too, if you were around during the initial days when no one knew what the hell they were doing."

Annja smiled. "Good point."

Roux stood and stretched as much as he could. "Let's get out of here. I need to feel solid earth under my feet again."

They thanked the pilot and crew and stepped off the plane.

Hanscom Field had been converted to a mostly civilian airfield, although it was adjacent to the part used by the U.S.

Air Force. Annja looked at the line of corporate jets parked near hangars. She thought she spotted a movie star walking toward one of them.

"It's a lot less busy here than at a regular airport," she said to herself.

From the nearby terminal building, a young man ran up to the aircraft. "Welcome to Hanscom, Annja."

She couldn't believe it. "George?"

He grinned. "Figured it would be better if we did it this way."

"How'd you get here so fast?"

"It's a skip from Washington. A little less time than coming across the Pacific Ocean."

"I guess." She looked him over. George had trimmed down and cleaned himself up considerably since the last time she'd seen him. He still had thick glasses perched atop his nose, but she could see evidence of an exercise routine. And his clothes looked clean and fit him properly.

"You've been made over, huh?"

He smiled. "You like? Pretty different from the last time you saw me."

"Definitely," Annja said.

"If we could skip the fashion pleasantries," Roux said. "I think we have more pressing matters to discuss."

George held out his hand. "You must be Roux."

"I am."

"Nice to meet you," George said. "Why don't you guys come into the building. I've commandeered a corner office so we can talk this out. We've only got a little time before this turns into a three-ring circus so I want to be sure I have all the facts straight before the clowns get here and ruin everything."

"Sounds good," Annja said. They walked into the main building, but aside from a lone state trooper, Annja saw little in the way of security.

George led them up to the second floor and into an office that he promptly locked behind them. On the table was a state-of-the-art computer. George sat down behind it and typed in his password.

"All right, so let's go over this again."

Annja took him through everything that had happened over the past several days. Roux interrupted at key points, including taking five minutes to describe how Annja had apparently single-handedly killed a massive tiger shark intent on devouring her.

"A tiger shark?"

Annja sighed. "Roux, you're not helping matters."

When they were finally finished, George leaned back and put his hands behind his head. "That's pretty crazy shit."

"I know," Annja said. "But it's the truth."

"Oh, I know it's true. I mean, we've got the trail to prove these guys aren't good eggs. But the facts surrounding the situation are just bizarre. I mean, how the hell would they transport something radioactive on a civilian bird? They'd set off all sorts of alarms. I don't know if it could even be done."

"Unless they had someone helping them on the inside," Roux said. "For a team of experienced operators like these guys, that wouldn't be too difficult to obtain."

George nodded. "Good point." He checked his watch. "Their plane ought to be landing in the next thirty minutes. That means we've got a small window to plan our strategy. Any flaws with the plan will mean we'll potentially be turning a picturesque seaside tourist attraction into a glow-in-the-dark hunk of barren rock."

"Not if we have anything to do with it," Annja said.

George looked at his watch again. "In about five minutes, this place is going to be overrun with suits looking to get their next promotion based on how well this operation unfolds."

"Wonderful," Roux said.

George smiled at him. "Welcome to my world. For the most part, I love what I do. But having to deal with these idiots is the low point of any day for me."

"Why is that?"

"They don't trust the opinion of a tech guy like me." George smiled. "Which is why we need someone whose opinion they will respect." He stood and walked to the door.

"You have someone in mind?" Annja asked.

"An old friend of yours, Annja," George said. He opened the door and Annja saw a face she hadn't seen since the jungles of the Philippines a long time ago.

"Vic?"

The Marine sniper walked in with a big wide grin on his face. "Hi, Annja, long time, no see...."

29

Annja looked at George. "This is your doing?"

George grinned. "Think of it as me stacking the deck in my favor, that's all. These suits need someone whose opinion they respect. I'm just giving that to them. When Vic tells them the facts surrounding this situation, they'll listen. If I tell them, they'll ignore it."

Annja nodded at Roux. "This is Roux. Roux, this is Vic Gutierrez, gunnery sergeant with the Marine Corps."

"Ex-Marine, actually," Vic said, shaking Roux's hand. "I'm with another agency at this time."

"Which agency?" Roux asked with a thin smile playing out across his face. "Or can't you say."

"Exactly," Vic said. "And besides, it's not important. When George called me and told me what was up, I got here as soon as I could." He smiled at Annja. "You're looking good. Still getting into all sorts of trouble, I see."

Annja nodded. "I was on vacation, I swear it."

"Weren't you on vacation the last time you were over there? Right before the Abu Sayyaf grabbed you?"

"That poor country has a bad reputation with me," Annja said. She looked at George again. "How did you know about Vic?"

George shrugged. "I told you that I've followed some of your adventures with great enthusiasm. You know how some people search Google to find references to themselves? I did that only on my computers. I wanted to see if you'd had any dealings with the government. Imagine my surprise when Vic's name came up."

"I've had plenty of dealings with spies and soldiers," Annja said. "Sometimes they don't end all that well."

"Sometimes they do," Vic said. He smiled and turned to George. "So, bring me up to speed here. I'm hearing chatter that there's a phalanx of bureaucrats on their way here to ruin any hope of resolving this thing intelligently."

George led Vic over to his computer and Annja watched as the former hacker briefed the former Marine sniper. Vic looked different in his suit, but Annja could tell the heart of a warrior still beat proudly in his chest. He listened intently as George briefed him, waited until he was done and then asked several pointed questions that George answered as best he could.

When they were finished, Vic looked at Annja and Roux. "Well, this is something to tell the grandkids, huh?"

"Something like that," Annja said. "Will it be a problem?"

Vic shrugged. "Depends on who walks through that door. We could get lucky and score someone with half a brain they don't mind using. Chances are, however, that we'll get a boatload of idiots looking to rubber stamp their own careers even at the cost of thousands of lives."

"That's not exactly doing a lot for my morale," Annja said.

Vic smiled. "Which is exactly why you and your buddy Roux are leaving. Immediately."

"What are you talking about? We brought this to you." Annja frowned. "I want in on anything that happens."

Vic held up his hand. "Relax, Annja. I'm not cutting you out completely. I just don't want you guys around when the bullshit brigade arrives. The less they know of the situation, the better off we'll be."

"That doesn't even sound like it's supposed to make sense," Roux said.

"Smart man," Vic said. "It's not. I'll give them the barest amount of intel on this so they can see how bad it is. Once they realize that, they'll want to stay far away from it, which means they'll turn over command to me."

"You've got that kind of sway?" Annja asked.

Vic grinned. "Been a few years since the jungle, Annja. You wouldn't believe what kind of pull I can get if I ask real nice."

"Okay."

Vic continued. "The problem with these idiots is that if they see you guys here—civilians, in other words—they'll go nuts and start parading around trying to impress one another and you, not to mention they'll start poking into the story details. And once they learn this came from you, they'll start overstepping their bounds, dismissing facts and pretty much doing everything in their power to give this guy Spier exactly what he wants—a genuine clusterfuck."

"So where are we going, then?"

"Martha's Vineyard," Vic said. "I want eyes on the ground there. George and I will join you, along with a select team of operators, once I get this mess cleared up."

Roux glanced out of the window. "Speaking of which, I think your brigade just arrived."

Annja looked out and saw a fleet of black SUVs had rolled into the parking lot. From within, dozens of suits with phones stuck to their ears spilled out and stalked toward the terminal building.

Vic frowned. "Shit, that was fast." He looked back at Roux and Annja. "All right, you two, get the hell out of here.

You're just two people catching a flight to somewhere. Take the back stairway down and find hangar five. There's a chopper there already spinning its rotors."

"That'll take us to Martha's Vineyard?"

Vic pushed them toward the door. "Yep. Now go!"

Annja and Roux stepped outside and the door locked behind them. From down below they could hear the commotion. Roux glanced at Annja. "I guess we should get lost."

They hurried down the back stairway, as Vic had told them. Outside on the tarmac, a stiff breeze blew in from the west. As they wandered the flight line, Roux pointed at a hangar on their left. "There it is."

Just outside the hangar, a Bell Helicopter painted blue with yellow trim sat spinning up its rotors. The pilot waved them aboard.

Annja climbed in and slid over so Roux could sit next to her. The pilot motioned for them to put on headsets.

When they had, he spoke. "Welcome aboard."

"Thanks," Annja said. "You know where we're going?"

The pilot nodded. "Sure do. Sit back and enjoy the ride. We'll be there before you know it."

Annja heard the air-traffic controller come on the headset, directing the pilot that he was cleared for takeoff. The pilot responded, and then instead of racing down the tarmac toward liftoff, he simply pulled back and the helicopter lifted off the ground. Annja looked out the window and saw the ground falling away fast.

They skimmed at treetop level until the pilot adjusted his heading and increased their altitude. Then they were off on a straight course bound for Martha's Vineyard.

Annja had been to Massachusetts a few times, but she couldn't recognize any landmarks as they flew farther southeast. She watched the cities and towns fall away beneath her.

Roux, for his part, looked annoyed at having to be in the air again so soon after the ride across the Pacific.

"You okay?" she asked.

He nodded. "Tired of flying. If God had meant us to do this, he would have given us wings."

"But the view is incredible," Annja said. "You've got to admit that."

"My eyes are closed," Roux said. "Wake me up when we get there."

Annja leaned back and looked out toward the horizon. She could already see the Atlantic Ocean far off to the south. The pilot pointed ahead of them.

"That's where we're going. Beautiful day for flying!"

Annja agreed. She hoped Vic was right about the bureaucrats. They couldn't afford to screw this up; everything had to work out perfectly or else Spier and his gang of ex-special-ops commandos could succeed in killing the German chancellor, and possibly the American president, as well.

Anger bubbled to the surface as she thought about Hans. He played me, she thought. And I fell for it. I made it so easy.

But could she blame herself? All she'd been looking for was some companionship. And a vacation is the perfect place to have a little uncommitted involvement, right?

Imagine if they hadn't been around after the shark attack, she thought. She owed him that at least. He had saved her life.

Unless he caused the shark attack in the first place, she thought. She frowned. How could he have done that? They would have had to chum the waters. And she'd seen no evidence of that.

Besides, deliberately setting up a shark attack would also have meant they had to be certain Annja could kill the shark. And how would they have been able to predict that?

None of them knew who she was, after all. And they certainly hadn't known about the sword.

At least, she hoped they hadn't.

The thought that they might have researched her before

they traveled to the Philippines was disconcerting, but at the same time, she disregarded the fear as completely unsound. There were too many factors at play for anyone to control completely.

The shark-attack save had to have been legitimate, she figured. Probably it was the only thing that was in this whole vacation.

Beneath the helicopter, the landscape changed from taller trees to shrub pine and sand.

And then they were out over Nantucket Sound, flying into Martha's Vineyard. Annja could see the boats in the water, the sandy beaches and the darker blue of the Atlantic Ocean far below. It was so different from the Pacific Ocean and the Philippines, she thought.

But just as beautiful.

"We should be down in five minutes," the pilot said. "Stand by, okay?"

Annja responded and then nudged Roux awake. "Almost there," she said. "I thought you'd want to see us land."

"Ugh, no," Roux said. "Why do you torment me so, Annja Creed?"

"Because I love it."

"Apparently."

The helicopter flew over a small airfield and then slowed, started to rotate, and the ground came up at them with a suddenness that made Annja's stomach drop slightly.

The skids of the chopper touched down. The pilot switched the rotors off and they waited until they'd stopped turning.

Annja removed her headset and stepped out of the chopper. The pilot smiled. "Thanks for flying with us."

"Thanks for the lift."

Roux stepped out behind her. "Thank God that's over."

"I wonder where we go from here," Annja said. "You think Vic's got something set up already?"

"That would require quite a bit of planning on his part,"

Roux said. "And considering George only just filled him in on things, I'd say it's doubtful we have a solid plan in place."

"I guess we should do as he says and just look to get some eyes on the target. See if Spier and the gang show up."

Roux checked his watch. "They'd need to either drive or fly down here. If they drove, they'd have to catch a ferry. If their plane landed on time and if they flew, then they could already be here."

"I think they'll probably drive down and take the ferry. Blend in more that way," Annja said. She pointed near the terminal. "See the people here hoping to catch a glimpse of a celebrity flying in on a private bird? Spier won't want that kind of attention."

Roux nodded. "Good point."

"We need to get into town and find out where the chancellor is staying on the island. Once we get that information, we can plan accordingly."

Roux frowned. "You know any sort of action we take is going to immediately put us on the radar of the chancellor's security people and possibly also the Secret Service, right?"

"What about it?"

Roux put a hand on his chest. "I'm as attention averse as Spier. The last thing I want is people looking into my background and figuring out that I should have died about five hundred and twenty years ago."

Annja smiled. "You really think that they'd be able to find that kind of information?"

"It wouldn't be the first time someone tried," Roux said. "And you don't need anyone looking beyond your lightweight celebrity, either. Now come on, let's find a shuttle so we can get this game afoot, shall we?"

30

Annja and Roux caught an airport shuttle into Edgartown, but even as they drove closer to the outskirts of the town, they could see the increased security was going to be immense. The local police had been supplemented by a serious state police presence as well as federal agents with the Secret Service, State Department and a few other organizations.

Annja shook her head as they approached the crowded sidewalks of Edgartown. "I can't even imagine why they'd try anything here. They'll never get anywhere close to where the chancellor is staying."

Roux shrugged. "Maybe they don't need to. If they've figured out how to weaponize that pearl, then all they'd need to do is detonate it from somewhere they can be certain will take out their target."

Tourists clogged the streets, mostly couples with children, and Annja frowned. A nuclear device of any type would result in an untold number of casualties. Among them, innocent children. It was unacceptable. And it was unthinkable that someone like Hans would find it so easy to forsake his military background and kill civilians who had nothing to do with his past. If he has a beef with the German government, then he should have simply waited until he could get to the chancellor without needing to threaten the lives of so many kids.

Her anger grew until Roux put a hand on her arm. "I can feel the rage boiling off you. I know what you're thinking. Just try to control yourself. Otherwise, we'll end up drawing too much attention to ourselves. We've got a job to do."

"*I've* got a job to do," Annja said. "I'm the one with the sword, remember?"

Roux nodded. "That doesn't mean you can't have a friend along to help, as well." He grinned. "Or a few, for that matter, since George and Vic will be along, too."

Annja took a calming breath. "Sorry. I just can't fathom how they could rationalize hurting so many innocent people. This island is filled with kids!"

"I know," Roux said. "But don't drive yourself crazy trying to figure it out. The minds of those who are committed to death and mayhem can't be swayed by rational discourse."

Annja nodded. "In that case, I'll have the sword do my arguing for me."

ANNJA'S CELL PHONE purred a few moments later as they got off the shuttle in front of a souvenir shop.

"Annja? It's George. You guys get there okay?"

"Yes, we caught a shuttle at the airport. We're in Edgartown right now."

"Good. We're coming to you. Don't move, okay?"

Annja started to say, "You're here?" but then she saw the black SUV across the street and George waving them over. She nudged Roux. "There they are. Let's go."

They climbed into the backseat. George was driving. Vic was dressed in black assault gear, load-bearing equipment and had enough ammunition on him to outfit a small revolution. But he smiled when they climbed in.

"Welcome to Martha's Vineyard."

Annja shook her head. "How did you guys get here so fast?"

Vic shrugged. "F15. It's a little faster than a helicopter."

"I thought an F15 could only seat two people."

George groaned. "I had to sit on Vic's lap. Don't ask. It's not an experience I ever want to repeat."

"All in the name of national security," Vic said. "But anyway, we flew into Otis on the cape and then choppered over. I briefed the Secret Service and grabbed one of their war wagons."

"How did it go with the suits back at Hanscom?"

"They moved the incident command center into Boston, so they could have easier access to good places to drink and massages at their hotels," Vic said. "But otherwise, I managed to convince them that this would be better handled by a small unit who could close on the assassins and deal with them without the need for any artillery strikes."

George grinned. "What he means is he got them to sit the hell down and shut the hell up while we went to work."

Annja looked at George. "Are you trained for this?"

"Technically? Nope. But Vic says on-the-job training is the best kind there is, so here I am."

Annja looked at Vic. "You're not serious."

Vic shrugged. "My man wanted to come along. Says he's qualified on firearms, so who am I to deny him some fun."

"This isn't fun, Vic," Annja said. "These guys are professional operators. I know they have your respect."

"They do. I've heard of the KSK guys before. I know we're not dealing with any slouches here."

"In that case," Annja said, "why are you bringing along an amateur—no offense, George."

George frowned. "Annja, you're not exactly commando grade, either. So how is it that you get to be here and I don't?"

"There are some things you don't exactly know about me, George," Annja said. "Things that will actually make me an asset to the team."

"That's harsh," George said. "If it wasn't for me, you guys wouldn't even know where to begin. You'd be home wondering where they were when this thing goes boom. You owe me and you know it. And I'm here and ready to go."

Vic looked at Annja and shrugged. "He says he wants in. I'm fine with it." He looked back out of the windshield. "Besides, I've got a few more friends scattered about the island. And a few others making their way here right now."

"Operators?"

Vic nodded. "Surgeons, as it were."

Annja noticed the rifle in between Vic's legs and wondered if he had brought additional snipers in to help. If they could engage the targets from a distance, that would be all the better. Plus, it would mean that George wouldn't have to be exposed to fire up close.

George steered them through traffic, occasionally flashing the red-and-blue lights on the war wagon. People got out of his way and they left the town behind and got on the road heading out toward the residential areas.

"The German chancellor is staying in Gayhead," Vic said. "It's the same home that the president stayed in when he was here last summer. It's got a commanding view of the Atlantic and it's fairly well isolated. Not as much as we'd like obviously, given the nature of the island, but enough for us to put some hides in and make sure we don't let those guys get close."

"How did the Secret Service take to your briefing?" Roux asked. "I imagine they wanted to spearhead the operation."

Vic shrugged. "I had to juggle the State Department with them, but fortunately, I'm with an agency that overrules those guys on a routine basis. They'll cooperate as long as things don't get too hairy for their taste. If they think their principals are in danger, they'll evacuate immediately. The Secret Service has moved a chopper onto the property and the pilot's on a five-minute standby at all times."

"Fun for him," Annja said. "Has the chancellor been briefed?"

"I don't know if State passed along the intel," Vic said. "I imagine they will, because if anything does happen, the Germans will want to know why they weren't told their leader was in grave danger. State will go to all lengths to avoid that kind of diplomatic faux pas."

"I don't blame them," Annja said. "The last thing we'd want is the same situation to unfold on foreign soil around our president."

Vic nodded. "Exactly." He pointed ahead to where they were approaching a vehicle checkpoint. "You guys stay cool back there and let me do the talking as we get through this. Once we're on the grounds, we'll have a bit more freedom to do our thing."

George slowed the car and slid the window down as two agents stepped forward with guns ready to bear on the SUV. One of the agents leaned forward but kept his distance. "Identification?"

Vic leaned over George and showed a laminated ID card. "Day word is Cherokee."

The agent looked at the card and then nodded. "Have a good day."

Two more agents by the roadblock raised the barrier and let them pass through. Annja looked back as they drove past. "Is that normal security for something like this?"

Vic shrugged. "It's a little tighter. I had to compromise somewhat with the Service. But it's not overboard as yet. If our hit team does surveillance, it shouldn't alert them that we're on to them. Remember, we want them thinking that they've left you far behind in the Philippines and no one knows they're coming. The last thing we want is for them to get spooked and vanish with that nuclear whatever-it-is."

Annja watched as the main compound came into view. The Secret Service and State Department had obviously tried their best to blend in, but concealing two dozen agents, plus the German chancellor's own security detail, was a little difficult in the bucolic estate setting. Annja could see the war wagons—SUVs packed with all sorts of high-powered weaponry for repelling an assault—and the escape cars, as well.

Across a field sat a gray shingled weathered barn that had probably stood for a hundred years. And yet now, she could clearly see the rotor blades of a helicopter sticking out of it. All it would take was two men to shove it clear of the roof and they could be airborne within five minutes.

She knew there'd be other precautions, too. Looking out at the sea, she spotted a few boats. One was a Coast Guard cutter, and the others were apparently civilian sailboats and yachts. Annja didn't believe they were all civilian, however.

Vic confirmed it. "Some of my people will be offshore. They'll have eyes on the grounds here all the time. Staggered shifts, that sort of thing."

Annja was impressed. "So where do we fit into all of this? I mean, it looks like you've got this entire place sealed up tight as a drum."

Vic nodded. "We do. But there's always the chance that they'll get through. We have no way of knowing what type of assault this will be. Frontal? Suicidal? There are too many variables at this point. So we try to cover as many possibilities as we can. But we can't outthink these guys because they're the only ones who know what they'll do."

"So we're here to help you think of any possibilities that you haven't covered, is that it?" Annja asked.

"Yep."

Annja nodded. "Well, I'm glad you could make all of this happen so quickly, Vic. And you, too, George. I hope you weren't too offended by what I said back in Edgartown."

"I was," George said. "But I understand why you said it." The small grin that played across his face told Annja that he was only fooling around, but she decided not to pursue it any further.

Vic pointed over near the barn. "Put it there, George, and then we'll get you all suited up."

George wheeled the war wagon in close to the barn and Vic led them around to the trunk. He smiled as they approached. "Ever seen what the Service carries in these things when they're trailing the president around?"

Annja shook her head. "Nope."

Vic opened the tailgate and threw back the tarp. "Behold."

A dizzying arsenal greeted their eyes. Annja saw several LAWS rocket launchers, two M60 machine guns, two SAW machine guns, three sniper rifles and an assortment of close-quarters submachine guns like the MP5 and the LRWC PSD. A dozen pistols and ammunition of varying kinds rounded out that part of the truck. Vic showed them where the body armor was stored and the medical trauma packs.

When he was finished giving them the guided tour, he stepped back. "Pretty incredible stuff, huh?"

Roux looked like a child at Christmas. "So many fun toys to play with in here."

George grinned. "That's a helluva lot of firepower."

"They take their job seriously," Vic said. "They protect the most powerful man on the planet and have to be able to repel an invasion force, if necessary. They've got my respect, that's for sure."

He reached back in and came out with several duffel bags. "Gear for you guys to change into. We're a little short on accommodations around here, so duck into the barn and get into the coveralls. Meet me back here and we'll arm up."

The three of them walked into the barn past the chopper and dropped their bags. Annja frowned. "George, would you mind turning around?"

The disappointment on his face was clear. Roux chuckled to himself, but then Annja looked at him. "You're turning around, too. I don't want to be responsible for resurrecting your libido."

31

"We've got agents everywhere all over the island. Plus a whole ton of them back on the mainland. If they take a ferry over here, we'll know it." Vic shrugged. "At least, that's the plan."

"The odds of you catching them are pretty slim," Annja said. "These guys aren't amateurs."

Vic nodded. "I know. But I have to set it up so that everyone back in D.C. is happy. And who knows? We might get lucky."

Roux frowned. "You would have to be extraordinarily lucky. Something tells me that Spier has somehow thought this entire matter through."

Vic eyed Roux. "Who exactly are you again? I mean, I realize Annja vouched for you and everything, but I don't know you from Adam. How do you know Annja?"

Roux crossed his arms and simply stared at Vic. "If not for me, Annja would be less of a woman than she is today."

"What the hell does that mean? You were her first lover or something?" Vic shook his head. "Seriously, what the hell?"

Annja held up her hand. "It's okay, Roux. He knows about the sword. We go back a ways."

Roux shrugged. "Fine."

Annja looked at Vic. "Roux was with me when the sword chose to become a part of me."

George stood nearby with a look of confusion crisscrossing his face. "Sword? Excuse me?"

Annja sighed and looked around. Seeing no one nearby, she quickly manifested the sword in front of George. His eyes went wide and Annja quickly made it vanish.

George looked like he'd seen a ghost.

"How the heck did you do that?"

Vic chuckled. "That never gets old."

Annja looked at George. "I don't know how to explain it, so please don't bother asking me all these detailed questions. It's part of me—I can draw it out and use it to defend myself. But other than that, I'm still figuring things out, okay?"

George nodded his head quickly. "That is the coolest thing I've ever seen."

Annja rolled her eyes. As if George had needed another reason to pine over her, she'd just given him one.

Vic nodded at Roux. "So he was with you when that whole thing went down?"

"You might say," Roux said, "that if it wasn't for me, Annja would never have had the sword become part of her."

"Not like I was asking for it," Annja said. "It just seemed to happen. Rather unexpectedly, I might add."

Vic took out a stick of gum and bit into it. "All right. Fair enough. You've got history, I can dig that. And I'm assuming you were involved with this Spier guy, too?"

Roux nodded. "I accompanied them on the dives, yes."

Vic chewed thoughtfully. "All right, then. So you think this guy is too smart for us?"

"He's very smart," Roux said, "but he's not infallible. You may indeed get lucky, as you say. But I wouldn't bank on it. What bothers me is that Spier seems to have known a lot more about the pearl—that is to say, the nuclear device—than any of us knew about. Strange, too, considering I make a hobby out of studying such things."

Annja smirked. "Admitting he pulled one over on you, Roux? That's got to be a first for you."

"I can admit when I've been bettered," Roux said. "The job now is to make sure it doesn't happen again."

IN THE HIGH GRASS overlooking the bluff that the main estate house sat on, Annja lay next to Vic. Vic scanned the area of the beach with his binoculars. On the horizon, the sun had started to set, staining the sky with a crimson hue that bled into the sea.

"Anything?"

Vic set the binoculars down. "Not a damned thing." He glanced at Annja. "You're sure about this target, right? I'd hate to think we were sitting on the wrong target here, you know?"

Annja nodded. "George assured me this was the only one that makes sense. There's no other reason for them to be in Massachusetts."

"I'm still foggy on motive," Vic said. "So, what—they get revenge for a KSK mission gone awry or something?"

"Either that or because they all got the boot from the KSK for harboring radical beliefs."

Vic snorted. "That's not exactly a rare occurrence. I know plenty of special-ops guys who have some serious political leanings. For the most part, they can separate their personal beliefs from the jobs they're tasked to do, but every once in a while one of those guys will go bat-shit crazy. Not a good scene to be a part of."

Annja sighed. "George said that Spier espouses a far right-wing political ideology. Maybe they're after the chancellor because she's too liberal? I'm not up on my German politics, so I can't say for certain."

Vic shook his head. "So, get rid of the current chancellor and then what—establish yourself as the new leader of Germany? These guys are already off the deep end, huh?"

"They certainly seem to be, although at the time, they struck me as being perfectly normal."

"Yeah, that's the problem with psychotics. They look normal at first. And then once you get to know them…look out."

"Where'd you position George and Roux?"

Vic nodded toward the house. "Closer to the rest of the protection detail. I hope you don't mind but I wanted George a little bit closer to the professionals."

"I thought you said—"

Vic nodded. "Yeah, I know what I said. But I wasn't going to tear the guy down in front of you. I mean, it's obvious he's crazy about you. Wouldn't do his ego any good if he knew I thought he was a detriment to the operation."

"You old softie."

Vic eyed her. "Hey, don't let that get out, okay? I might not be in the Marines anymore, but I've still got a rep."

"Your secret's safe with me," Annja said. She scanned the beach, but it was becoming too dark to see much of anything.

"Here," Vic said. "Use these."

He handed Annja a pair of night-vision binoculars and she turned them on. There was a brief burst of a high-pitched whine and then it settled into nothingness. Annja brought them up to her eyes and the beach stood out in brilliant lime-green luminescence. She scanned up and down the beach, but didn't see anything but crashing waves as the tide rolled in.

She sniffed the air. "Nothing out there, Vic."

He nodded. "That's what's got me worried. I can't sense anything. They could be anywhere. But we wouldn't know it until it's too late. And no offense or anything, but I don't feel like dying on Martha's Vineyard. Kinda not the cool death I'd always envisioned for myself."

Annja grinned. "I take it back, you're still the same old Vic."

He smiled. "Thanks."

Annja shook her head. "No, thank you for coming up here like this. I'm happy to see you again."

The waves continued to crash on the shore. Annja and Vic continued to lie amid the high grass, watching the surrounding area.

And night fell.

VIC'S PHONE PURRED an hour later. He opened it up and spoke for a few seconds to someone on the other end. When he snapped it shut, he seemed annoyed.

"What is it?" Annja asked.

"Field report from the agents looking for these guys. Seems they had one guy matching a description who took an earlier ferry. Gottlieb. But then he disappeared."

"What about the others?"

Vic shook his head. "That's just it. No one seems to know where they might have vanished to."

"Well, that's not good."

"No," Vic said. "It's not."

"If Gottlieb came over to the island, then he must still be here somewhere."

"Unless he's meant to be bait to see if we know they're coming," Vic said. "Send him in advance, test the waters, so to speak, and if we snatch him they know we're on to their plan."

"And then they can regroup and plan another attack."

"Right, and we get nothing."

Annja took another look through the night-vision binoculars, scanned up and down the beach and then back toward the main house. "I wish I knew how many ways there were to get to this island."

Vic sighed. "Probably more than we could count. I mean, you can take the ferry, the plane, a chopper—"

Annja shook her head. "No, I mean how many other ways could you get here if you really wanted to."

"I'm not following."

"Boats, Vic. What's to stop Spier and his team from traveling down the southern coast of anywhere in New England, renting a boat—hell, they could buy one if they wanted—and simply sailing over here? It's not like we're out in the middle of the ocean. It's a pretty accessible place if you've got the equipment to get here."

Vic frowned. "That's true. But we've got boats out monitoring the maritime traffic."

"Yeah, but how many boats can they check out? There will always be some that slip through."

Vic took the binoculars from Annja. "So, you think we might be staging this wrong? That they'll come in by boat?"

"It's a possibility, right?"

"Anything is at this point. We're flying blind."

"The only thing we have working for us is that they don't know we're on to them."

Vic shrugged. "Yeah, but any team worth its salt will always assume that the opposition knows about them. Otherwise, you get sloppy. Take things for granted. And that's when things go to hell."

"I wish we knew," Annja said. "I wish we knew for absolute certain where they were."

Vic's phone buzzed again. He took it out and listened for a moment. "Okay, thanks."

"What?"

Vic stood and brushed the dirt off his coveralls. "We just picked up Gottlieb in a bar downtown."

Annja frowned. "Bait?"

Vic nodded. "Almost certainly. But I've got to take a crack at him. We don't have anything else to go on."

Annja stood. "Let me go with you."

"You sure?"

Annja nodded. "He knows me. I might get him to reveal something that he wouldn't say otherwise."

"He might not."

Annja grinned. "Like you said—what choice do we have?"

32

Vic drove the SUV like a madman over the quiet roads of Martha's Vineyard, skirting disaster at every moment. Annja fought to hold on while he navigated the winding roads. "Where'd they grab him?"

"Having a drink in a bar." Vic shrugged. "What do you make of that?"

Annja frowned. "I don't know. Strikes me as a little odd. Was it a rendezvous or something?"

Vic shook his head. "Don't think so. My guys sat on him for a while. If he was there to meet someone, they stood him up."

"Or you were right and they set him up as bait."

"If that's true, our boy might just be willing to talk to us about Spier and his plans."

Annja watched Vic round another curve and narrowly miss hitting a mailbox. "Or Spier has sent him here to throw us off the trail."

"Well, I guess we'll just have to be smarter than him." Vic steered them into Vineyard Haven and parked close to the bar in question. When they got out, Vic nodded at Annja. "We've got him set up next door at the hotel. I'll go in first. You wait outside until I bring you in. Since he doesn't know me, it might give me some leverage—he might say something that you know isn't true that we can then use against him."

Annja nodded. "Okay. I'll hang outside until you come for me."

She watched Vic disappear inside the hotel and eased herself back into the alley running next to the hotel. The night might have fallen but Vineyard Haven, like Edgartown, still bustled with tourists and residents eager for a late-evening dinner. She could see across the street to the little harbor. Small sailboats jockeyed for position next to expensive sleek yachts sailing in from Newport and farther away in the Hamptons. Celebrities and the megarich partied together while the regular folks gawked from afar.

Annja considered that. She'd never understood the lure of celebrity, but she'd gotten a small taste of it by hosting a television show. Spier recognizing her in the Philippines was just one example of how it could work against her. She'd been asked for autographs in plenty of surprising places.

Annja shook her head. She couldn't imagine a real celebrity having to deal with the camera hounds and people prying into her life at any opportunity. Still, she wondered if that was the trade-off. If you wanted celebrity, you had to be willing to embrace the negative aspects, as well.

A couple walked past her arm in arm and Annja smiled. They'd obviously enjoyed a good bottle of wine somewhere nearby. She could smell the aroma around them. But at least they weren't driving.

She glanced up at the hotel. Yellow light bled out of one of the windows facing the street. She wondered if Vic was inside that one with Gottlieb. Gottlieb wouldn't tell him a thing, of course.

But maybe Vic had a few more skills than Annja knew about. Maybe he knew how to drag information out of an uncooperative captive.

She leaned against the building and watched the boats in the harbor. What if Spier was out there somewhere? What if he was waiting to blow up the chancellor?

She frowned. Somehow they had to get to Gottlieb.

"Miss Creed?"

She turned and saw a young man dressed in a blazer and khaki pants. Definitely a fed. She smiled. "Yes?"

"Mr. Gutierrez would like you to come inside now."

Annja followed the man inside the hotel. She'd noticed that Vic hadn't been referred to as "special agent." She wondered exactly which agency he was working for.

They walked upstairs to the second floor and the young agent paused, looked at Annja and winked once. Then he knocked on the door and waited until he heard Vic call out, "Come."

He opened the door and Annja walked inside. She saw that Gottlieb was seated with his hands cuffed behind his back positioned in front of the window looking out over the harbor. He couldn't see Annja.

Vic stood in front of Gottlieb and nodded for Annja to stand behind the prisoner. Annja did as he suggested and waited.

"So, Gottlieb, we know you're up to something here on the island. What we can't seem to figure out is why you're doing it here. Is it about the chancellor? You want to take her out?"

Gottlieb said nothing.

Vic continued. "We know about the pearl, Gottlieb."

That got a reaction. Gottlieb's head snapped up and then he quickly regained control of himself. His mind must be racing, Annja thought. He'd want to know how Vic knew about it.

Vic kept up the pressure. "We know it's radioactive. So what did you and the KSK boys do? Did you figure out how to weaponize it? Turn it into a dirty bomb, maybe?"

Gottlieb shook his head. "You won't get anything from me. You should know that right now."

Vic shrugged. "Well, see, here's the thing. I don't really need you. I've got a pretty reliable source of information already."

"You're lying."

Vic smiled. "Am I? Then how did I know about the pearl? How did I know it's radioactive? How would I know all that unless someone inside your merry little band of terrorists was actually a double agent? Ready to betray their friends. Huh? Ask yourself that."

Gottlieb stayed silent for a moment. Then he looked directly at Vic. "None of us would betray the cause."

"And what cause is that? Spier's fruitcake right-wing ideology? What—you guys want to pick up where Hitler left off? Resurrect the Aryan nation?"

Gottlieb shook his head. "You would never understand."

"Why? Because I'm Latino? You think my blood doesn't bleed the same as a white man? You people make me sick with your bullshit." He slapped Gottlieb across the mouth and the sound of the flesh on flesh shocked Annja.

But Gottlieb just laughed. "Your attempts to get me to talk are pathetic. You know I'm former KSK. You know I've been trained to endure torture."

"Endure it, yeah. But the thing about torture is everyone has their breaking point. It's just a matter of finding out what makes you tick. I'll find it," Vic said. He grinned. "I'll find it for sure."

Gottlieb shrugged. "You're wasting your time."

Vic stepped back and looked at Annja. "You know what? Maybe you're right. Maybe I am wasting my time here. You won't talk. You won't tell us anything. Or so you think…"

"What do you mean?"

Vic shrugged. "Maybe it doesn't matter that you haven't told us anything. Maybe if I let you loose and tell everyone that you talked, it'll be just as good."

"I'm *not* talking," Gottlieb said.

Vic shrugged. "Yeah, but they won't know that, will they? Not when we start releasing juicy details of your little plan, your ideology, where you were before this trip to Martha's Vineyard, that sort of thing."

Gottlieb laughed. "You don't have that kind of information."

Vic leaned back in. "That's where you're wrong, pal." And then he spun Gottlieb's chair around so he faced Annja.

The expression on Gottlieb's face was one for the ages. "You!"

Annja smiled. "Hi, Gottlieb."

Vic turned him around again. "So, you see, I don't really need you to talk. Annja here has plenty of information to share all about you guys. And it's the kind of stuff that someone on the inside would know all about. So when we feed that to the media, they'll be all over it. And then what do you suppose Spier will think when it gets back to him and you're all of sudden walking free? Why, he's going to think that you turned on them and gave us everything we wanted."

Vic leaned back against the window frame and popped a piece of gum into his mouth. "I sure as hell wouldn't want to be in your shoes when that happens. I don't imagine your leader is going to be a compassionate soul when he gets his hands on you."

Gottlieb laughed. "He will never believe it. He knows me."

"Aw, Gottlieb, you know that's bullshit. Y'see, I know a little about paranoia. I was a sniper. It was my job to instill paranoia into the enemy I hunted. Make them think that anywhere they poked their head out there was going to be one of my Lapua rounds just waiting to take their head clean off their spinal column. I saw what my presence could do to even the most grounded enemy. They start wondering. They start asking themselves questions. You get that shit in your head? Forget it. And even the most trusted associate starts looking like a Benedict Arnold when grade-A intel starts flowing into the papers. You think I'm lying?"

Gottlieb stayed quiet for a few moments and the only sound was Vic chewing his gum. Occasionally, he would snap it loudly, breaking the silence in the room.

Gottlieb stayed very still.

Vic checked his watch. "So, here's how this is going to go down, Gottlieb. Me and Annja are going to go have a late dinner at a cute little Italian joint around the corner. Over some meatballs and linguine and a nice bottle of merlot, we're going to talk about what you guys did in the Philippines on your hunt for the pearl and how you saved her from sharks and all that good shit. And then I'm going to hold a press conference and announce we've dismantled a terrorist cell operating with the purpose of assassinating the German chancellor. I imagine they'll gobble that right up." He smiled at Gottlieb. "And I'll make a point of telling them that all of our golden information came from one of the terrorists who is now cooperating with us."

"You lie!" Gottlieb said.

Vic stood unfazed by the outburst. "And then, say about twelve hours from now, I'm going to spring you loose. I'm going to take the cuffs off, give you a friendly pat on the back outside the hotel where all these awesome tourists can snap their pictures and videos, and then you and I are going to walk away from each other. Me? I'm going back to the mainland to hop a plane back to Washington. And you? Well, that's where this picture gets kind of interesting. Because I don't know how long it'll take Spier to find you. But I feel pretty strongly that he'll want to have a few words with you. Y'know, reconnect, as it were. He'll want to find out all the cool stuff that went on while you were in federal custody. And you'll tell him you told us nothing, that it was Annja here who spilled the beans. But you know what? It won't matter. Because even if Spier believes you, there's going to be a part of him that isn't entirely sure. It'll be a small part of his brain at first. Just that niggling little voice that whispers, 'What if?' every so often.

"But then you know what will end up happening? That little part is going to grow into a bigger part. And that little voice is going to get louder. Spier's going to start connecting all sorts of shit that a normal person wouldn't equate with betrayal. But Spier will because of that little 'what if?' And sooner than later, he's going to start looking at you like a traitor. And then he's going to put two bullets into that thick skull of yours."

Vic blew a bubble and let it pop for effect. "And that, my friend, will be that."

"It will never happen that way."

Vic shrugged. "I'm glad you're an optimist. Really. Almost restores my faith in humanity. But I'm a realist. And I know what happens when that shit starts rattling around in your head. Gets you all jacked up, worrying all the time. And Spier will want to get rid of that worry. That's you, pal. Better safe than sorry."

Vic stood and nodded at Annja. "So, let's you and I go have a nice dinner and have that talk. I've got a hankering for some good merlot. Been a long day."

Annja nodded. "Okay. See you, Gottlieb."

Gottlieb spun his chair around. "You can't leave me here like this."

Vic looked at him. "Of course I can. I can do anything to you, Gottlieb. That's the thing you haven't grasped yet. If I wanted to, I could make your ass disappear into some hellhole third-world country that no one even knows about. You'd eat maggots and be grateful about it for the rest of your life."

Vic smirked. "But I like my idea better. There's some kind of universal justice to it. You getting topped by your own team works for me. Nice and neat. And when they do you, we're going to be right there to kill the rest of them."

"You wish," Gottlieb said. "Spier is smarter than any of you. This is all false bravado."

Vic shook his head. "A loyal guy, I like that. Keep dreaming, Gottlieb—"

But in that instant, the door to the room blew off its hinges and Annja saw something small and black float into the air.

Unable to take her eyes off it, she watched it burst into the brightness of a thousand suns while her ears felt the thundering concussion of sound.

And then everything exploded.

33

Annja's head was a swirl of confusion. She heard voices speaking in gruff German and English. Fragmented speech. Urgency. But she heard it all like it was being said underwater. And there was a constant ringing in her ears.

She still couldn't see clearly. She made out forms rushing into the room. Scattered bursts of what sounded like gunfire.

Someone ran over her, their boots knocking her down and then stomping on her back.

She tried to fend them off but could only move slowly and without any sense of coordination.

A hand slapped hers away. Someone was speaking to her close by.

"Her, too."

Strong hands lifted her off the floor, where she thought maybe she'd curled up into the fetal position. They dragged her toward the door. She saw it was off its hinges.

Annja risked a glance back, and saw several bodies sprawled on the floor. The stench of cordite, burned wood and spent shells hung in the air.

And something pooled on the floor.

Blood.

Her last thought was of Vic and what might have happened to him. But then she was being dragged, force-marched down the stairs.

People were screaming.

Smoke hung in the air.

And then they were outside. Annja was still being pushed and prodded but her legs seemed to have turned to jelly.

She smelled the salt air, knew they were down by the harbor close to the sea. And then someone tossed her through the air. She landed, rolled onto her left shoulder and gasped at the pain that shot through her body.

An engine sounded somewhere near her head and she had the most indescribable sensation of being on something moving.

A boat, she decided.

A hood was forced over her head. Slowly, she heard more sounds.

"What do we do with her?" a voice said.

And then someone knocked her on the back of the head.

ANNJA CAME TO, sputtering and alert again. Finally. They'd dragged her down into the galley and threw water on her face to wake her up.

Spier's face hovered in front of hers. "Welcome back to the land of the living, Annja."

She spat in his face.

Spier smiled. "Is that any way to address your elders?" He backhanded her across the face, snapping Annja's head back. Again, Spier's strength surprised her.

"Wow, that cancer really took a lot out of you, didn't it?" Annja spat some more water out of her mouth. "I hate liars."

Spier shrugged. "The lie was necessary to get you out so Heinkel and I could finish our work."

"Robbing the Jiao of their power supply. Very nice of you to leave them in the literal darkness like that."

Spier shrugged. "They had no idea of what its true power could be. But we will show them, I assure you."

Hans came belowdecks and glanced at Annja. "I thought you would have been back in the Philippines."

"I don't like being stood up," Annja said. "It's rude and boorish behavior."

Hans feigned offense.

He frowned and said something to Spier that Annja couldn't hear. Spier nodded and then looked back at Annja. "It would probably be smart not to upset him too greatly. He's already highly annoyed that Gottlieb was picked up by those government agents."

"He should be. Gottlieb sang like a canary to them."

Spier smiled. "Funny, Gottlieb said that you would probably say exactly that very thing."

"Of course he did," Annja said. "He's trying to cover his own tracks. When the lead agent brought me in, Gottlieb was standing over a map pointing out how you guys came to the island and where you're planning on setting off the pearl."

"And that's why when we stormed the hotel, he was sitting in the chair handcuffed? Nice try, Annja. I know you're resourceful and I respect that, but try to remember you're not dealing with an idiot here."

Annja shook her head. "Gottlieb was recuffed just prior to the lead agent moving him to a safe house. He figured it would keep up appearances if you happened to be doing surveillance on the place."

"We were," Spier said. "From out in the harbor. Gottlieb was supposed to go ashore and meet a contact of ours, but instead, your government decided to ruin the party."

"So you took Gottlieb back," Annja said. "But now you've got a traitor in your midst."

Spier shook his head. "I don't think we do. What we do

have is a very determined woman who should have stayed behind and finished her vacation, rather than put her mind to causing trouble where none is warranted."

"You're planning on setting off a nuke in my country. I sorta think that means I ought to get involved."

Spier frowned. "You have no idea what we are attempting to do. You have no clue as to how we have suffered under this administration or what we hope to achieve by liberating our countrymen of it. You only know what you think and that is not the reality of the situation at all."

Annja sighed. "I get so tired of megalomaniacs who drone on and on about their plans to rule the world."

"Would you prefer I simply tossed you overboard, then?"

"Depends on what's for dinner later."

Spier smiled. "Indeed." He climbed back on to the deck and left Annja in the galley with her hands tied behind her back. But at least the hood was off.

She tried to make sense of the situation.

Clearly, they had stormed the hotel after seeing Gottlieb being taken there for questioning. The disorientation and confusion Annja had experienced was due to the flash-bang grenade they had thrown upon breaching the room. The magnesium flare effect would have blinded her and the concussion blast would have deafened her. It would also have made her uncoordinated and easy to maneuver.

She remembered seeing bodies and frowned. They had probably killed Vic and the young fed who had been assisting him. Annja felt a heat rise within her as her rage bubbled to the surface.

Gottlieb ducked belowdecks looking none the worse for wear. He grinned at her. "Still peddling that story, huh? I told that guy it would never work. And they don't believe it, either. So give it up already, Annja."

Annja smiled at him. "You're a traitor, Gottlieb, and

sooner or later they're going to find out. And when they do, they'll kill you for betraying them."

Gottlieb smacked her on the chin and Annja tasted blood. She spat a puddle of it onto the galley floor. "You hit like a suburban housewife."

Gottlieb laughed. "We'll see who enjoys this day, Annja. And I happen to think it will be me."

Gottlieb vanished up onto the deck and Annja looked around. She needed to cut her hands free. She'd done it once before, manifesting the sword and cutting her ropes, but was there enough room in the boat itself to do so?

She didn't know.

She'd also have to time it just right or else she'd be discovered. And she didn't think that they'd take any chances with her. They all knew about the sword. They'd simply kill her and be done with it.

The boat engine drew to a stop and the boat seemed to bob in the swells slightly. Outside, the dawn sky brightened, but Annja couldn't see nearly enough yet to make out where they were. She couldn't even see the coastline from where she was being held.

If she could, perhaps she could throw herself overboard and swim for shore? Annja frowned. That would be tough under the best conditions. The water in Nantucket Sound was much colder than in the Philippines. And she'd have to take care of her hands first. Plus, the currents here were terribly strong.

She sighed. Doing this was going to take a lot of work and she'd have to make sure she had half a chance before she attempted anything.

Mueller ducked below and walked past Annja on his way to the bow of the boat. When he came back out, Annja saw that he had diving gear on. Along with that, he carried out oxygen tanks one by one.

They were going diving?

She frowned. Then it all made perfect sense. They'd plant the device and then swim away. Meanwhile, all the units on the ground on Martha's Vineyard would be expecting some type of obvious assault.

But there wouldn't be one.

And when the countdown expired, the device would blow and vaporize the intended target.

I've got to get out of here, she thought.

Hans and Gottlieb returned several times for more oxygen tanks. By the looks of it, they were planning on an extended stay underwater. Annja counted ten tanks in total, which would mean two each. That would give them plenty of time to plant the device, swim back and then hop on the boat and vanish.

She wondered if the Coast Guard cutter she'd seen patrolling yesterday was still in the area. Chances were it was, but unless they saw something suspicious, would they even challenge a vessel like this? Probably not, especially if the boat made no obvious approach to the coastline near the target's residence.

With those tanks they can swim miles and back and no one would know they were planting the explosive.

Would a nuclear device cause much destruction if it detonated underwater? She had no idea. She did know that water acted like a tamping agent to explosives, forcing their blast into a certain direction, but what about a nuclear device? Would it be enough to cause the death and destruction they sought? Or would it simply be like setting off a dirty bomb?

Annja strained against her ropes but they were tied by someone who knew what they were doing.

Mueller came by and noticed her struggle. "I wouldn't bother. I studied rope restraints with a Peruvian Indian who knew so many ways to tie up a person that you'll never figure it out, Annja." And then he walked back onto the deck, laughing.

Annja frowned. I've still got a few ways to get free, she thought.

Spier came down into the galley. "So, you've no doubt noticed that we took great pains to make sure you couldn't use that wonderful sword of yours to get free and cut us all to ribbons."

"Mueller's handiwork," Annja said. "Whatever."

"In any event," Spier said. "It won't matter much in a few minutes. We'll be gone and then, tragically, so will you."

"You're not taking me with you?"

"I think you'd rather spoil all the fun," Spier said. "No, no, you'll be staying here, my dear."

"Shame," Annja said. "I was looking forward to seeing you guys fail utterly and completely."

"In which case you'd be severely disappointed," Spier said. "We won't fail."

Hans ducked his head down and spoke to Spier. "All is ready."

Spier nodded. "Very well." He turned to Annja. "I'm afraid it's time to say farewell. At least this time we got to say a proper goodbye, hmm?" He grinned. "We won't be seeing each other again, Annja, so I hope you've made peace with your life."

"Not until I kill you," Annja said.

Spier laughed. "Indeed. Maybe in the next life."

He turned and walked back onto the main deck. Seconds later, Annja heard a series of splashes.

They were gone.

And she was alone on the boat.

As the boat bobbed, silence settled over it. Annja took several deep breaths.

And then heard something out of ordinary.

Beeping.

Steady and measured.

From somewhere far below her.

Her heart rate quickened as the realization set in. The boat was rigged to blow up.

34

Annja tested the ropes but they held fast. She struggled to get to her feet and nearly lost her footing as a wave rolled under the boat and it dipped to the left.

She twisted and tried to get a look at the knots, but she wasn't nearly flexible enough to do that. Looking around the galley, she searched for anything sharp but saw nothing immediately available.

Without knowing how long she had before the bomb went off, Annja knew she had to get out of there in a hurry.

She concentrated and tried to manifest the sword in her hands. Nothing happened.

Suddenly she realized why. Her hands had been tied back to back so the palms didn't face each other. She couldn't grasp the sword between them.

She wondered if she could control the sword single-handed. Annja closed her eyes and concentrated on seeing the sword. Then she tried to feel the hilt only in her right hand. She felt her hand close around the hilt and then opened her eyes again.

She felt the sword's weight in her hand and then allowed it to fall to the floor, embedding itself into the wood of the galley floor.

Annja leaned down carefully and felt the honed blade bite into the ropes. It slid through them like they weren't even there. The ropes fell away and Annja massaged her wrists gratefully.

She pulled the sword out of the galley floor and ran for the upper deck, unsure what she would find there. The boat was indeed abandoned. As she looked around she spotted a pair of oxygen tanks, a regulator, a mask and fins discarded on the deck. I guess I know where I'm going now, she thought with a grin. She returned the sword to the otherwhere.

Now the question was how much time had Spier left on the bomb? Was it even worth looking for it and trying to disarm it?

The answer came to her quickly when she heard the beeping sound suddenly increase in tempo.

She grabbed the diving gear and ran hard for the stern, driving with her legs, churning and breathing hard, and then she launched herself into the air, gaining height and passing the apex of her dive as the boat behind her blew apart.

Annja hit the water as the debris from the explosion showered the sea around her. Shards of wood and metal speared through the water.

Annja swam deeper, trying to stay clear of the lethal fragmentation. Her lungs screamed for air and she was forced to ascend faster than she wanted to. There was no time to use the oxygen tanks. She could barely hold on to the gear and swim.

She broke the surface about a hundred feet away from the smoldering wreck. Flames danced over what remained of the boat, smoke billowing in the air. Around the boat, a pool of oil coated the surface of the water, already alight.

Bobbing in the surf, Annja strapped herself in the gear and

looked at the coastline in front of her. It was tough picking out topographical features from the ocean, but she figured they must have been about five miles south of the German chancellor's residence.

That meant Spier and his team were swimming north underwater.

She frowned. It made sense. They'd never be able to be detected underwater unless Vic had deployed a defensive string of divers in the area.

And that was highly unlikely.

Annja figured she could have waited for the Coast Guard to show up on scene of the flaming wreck, but what good would that do? Her heart ached as she thought about it, but in all likelihood, Vic was dead.

That meant someone else was now in charge. And the chances of that person taking any sort of advice from Annja were slim.

She'd have to do this on her own.

Annja thought briefly about Roux and George and how nice it would be to have some company along on this part of the trip. But she couldn't contact them. She'd have to do what she could—alone.

Unaware of the depths she'd be diving at, Annja decided to swim farther out and try to cut her travel distance down to straight line shots up the coast.

It occurred to her that she was swimming in waters known for abundant numbers of great white sharks. And they were potentially far more dangerous than tiger sharks.

As long as they didn't think of her as a seal, she ought to be relatively safe. But the sooner she got started, the better.

She tested the mouthpiece and got a good flow. The oxygen gauge showed full tanks.

It was time to start swimmng.

She heard a motor in the distance and saw the Coast Guard

cutter bearing down on her location. She considered waiting but then disregarded the thought.

Instead, she turned and submerged herself, descending rapidly before the cutter's propeller blades turned her into shark chum.

The visibility in the northern Atlantic was far worse than it had been in the Philippines. Annja could see maybe thirty feet in front of her. The level of sea life seemed far less, as well, but as she took herself deeper, she could make out more and see a little farther than she had closer to the surface.

On her bearing now, Annja set off at a good clip, figuring that Spier and his team had maybe fifteen minutes on her. She had to cut that down to nothing if she had any hope of defeating them.

She'd keep a lookout for oxygen bubble trails. With five of them swimming, they ought to be relatively easy to spot, provided she could find a way to catch up.

Despite her recent injuries, Annja felt strong as she swam through the ocean. Her breathing felt measured and confident. She willed herself to drive harder, faster, so she could cut down the distance.

She saw the wreck of an old fishing trawler lying on its side about fifty feet below her. She had the quickest flash of worry lance through her as she considered whether Spier would have left someone behind to ambush her just in case.

But no, that would have split his forces. And Spier no doubt had some sort of complicated escape plan all worked out. He'd need all his men with him in order to make sure this gambit paid off. Plus, he'd never believe she could have outsmarted him.

Annja swam on. She saw a dark shape glide past her some distance away and was sure it was a shark. But it paid her no attention and Annja calmed down her breathing and heart rate. It wouldn't do her any good to get freaked out now.

She'd burn through her oxygen in no time and then she'd really be in trouble.

Besides, she had her sword, and if it came to finishing off another shark, she wouldn't hesitate to do it. If she didn't stop Spier and his team, no one would be able to. Worse, if their bomb detonated, then the sea itself might be contaminated. And that would mean more sharks and other sea life would die.

Annja tried broadcasting that message out of her as if she could communicate telepathically with the ocean life. Don't mess with me, she thought over and over. She knew it wouldn't do anything but it gave her something to focus on as she swam ever harder.

She could feel the tug of the current on her body, but she ignored it and kept her legs churning behind her. She figured she'd covered a mile pretty quickly. A glance overhead showed no increase in boat traffic. In fact, there were no boats in the area at all.

I wonder if Vic established an exclusion zone? she thought. That would at least rule out the possibility that Spier had another boat.

Annja drove herself forward and altered her course as she checked her position against the coastline. She turned slightly to the right and kept swimming.

Her legs were starting to tire.

The realization that she'd have to ignore the pain and keep going made her breathe harder than she had been.

This isn't good, she decided. She took a moment and pulled up, allowing herself to float in the water, semibuoyant. She closed her eyes and tried drawing on that inner wellspring of strength that she'd drawn on rarely in the past.

She searched inside herself and found the strength necessary to keep driving on. She reminded herself what was at stake and she felt the telltale surge of adrenaline in her bloodstream.

Annja pointed north and started kicking harder.

Her breathing, despite her energetic output, was measured and calm. She knew her muscles needed a ton of oxygen, but she felt no greater pull on her reserves than if she'd been casually diving.

Good, she thought.

A face zipped past her. Annja noticed the whiskers and the freckled face of the harbor seal and grinned. The seal wanted to play apparently.

Annja waved him off. Sorry, little pal, she directed to the seal. I can't stop right now. Some other time, perhaps.

But the seal seemed determined to stay with Annja, zipping out in front of her and then falling behind. She watched its fins and how it jetted itself through the water as if there was nothing holding it back.

Of course, its body was much more streamlined than Annja's. She smiled and thought, Sure, it'd be easy if I looked like you.

They covered the third mile keeping each other company and then the seal abruptly shot off into the darkness.

Annja frowned. I hope that's not a bad omen, she mused.

When the sleek torpedo shape slid past her a moment later, Annja's stomach plummeted. The seal hadn't wanted to play, after all.

It had been using her for cover.

She saw the great white lazily flick its tail once and eyeball her as it slid past. With its mouth open to allow water to flow over its gills, she could see the serrated rows of teeth. Unlike the tiger shark, the great white's teeth were especially designed for sawing through thick seal and whale blubber.

Or divers.

She estimated it ran about fourteen feet long.

A big fish.

Annja felt a twinge of annoyance at the seal for using her

to shield itself from the massive predator. But then again, she thought, I might have done the same thing in its situation.

Annja kept swimming, hoping that the big fish wouldn't take an interest in tasting her.

I don't want to have to kill this thing, she thought.

She knew she could have her sword out and in front of her in a blink, however, as she swam on toward where she figured Spier and his team were heading.

The great white kept swimming around her, keeping its distance by perhaps forty feet. But she could see it wasn't particularly interested in her. She knew that if the shark wasn't searching for food, it would be unlikely to attack her. But she still fought to keep her heart rate and breathing under control.

The shark rolled past her again and she marveled at how it could simply propel itself with a tiny flick of its massive tail fin. She shook her head. Give me three hundred and fifty million years of living down here and I might be able to do that, too, she countered.

Annja kept her speed up, but the great white matched it easily. I may as well be running on a treadmill next to this big guy, she thought.

It wasn't the first time she'd been face-to-face with a great white in the open ocean, but each time felt like the first, she decided.

If only there was some way to use this big guy to her advantage. She wanted to ask it if it'd do her a favor and take a bite of Spier and the boys while she disarmed the bomb.

But of course, how in the world was she going to do that? Unless…

She frowned. No way. That was insane.

And when she'd seen it done before, she'd merely shaken her head and said, "That is absolutely nuts."

But now in the open ocean with this massive predator nearby, Annja found herself thinking over its merits.

And it did have several.

Worse, before reason could prevail, Annja found herself doing exactly the opposite of what her instincts screamed at her.

She swam toward the great white shark.

35

It seemed to Annja that as she swam toward the massive beast that dwarfed her by almost three times, it had the ability to appear almost motionless, when in fact, it was moving at great speed.

Annja, for her part, was forced to swim harder than she had before, a crazy situation since she was trying to actually get closer to something that could kill her with a single bite.

But she drew near to it. For its part, the shark looked exactly like she thought it would when it realized what she might have been up to. It seemed to give her a distinct look as if to say, "Uh…you know what I'm capable of, right?" She couldn't tell if there was a mixture of vague amusement in its eyes or if it was simply trying to size up how many calories it would get from devouring her.

Annja summoned the sword to her right hand and swam closer to the right side of the great white. It kept pace with her and Annja drew parallel to it, aware that if it simply chose to alter its course with a subtle direction change, she'd be seeing the business end of the rows of steak knives that inhabited its mouth.

But the shark didn't change course.

And then Annja reached out with her left hand and grasped the great white's massive dorsal fin.

She felt the instant tug on her, surprised at how much faster the great white moved than she had. It was slowing down to keep pace with her before. But now, unburdened by the puny human's attempt to keep up, the great white seemed to shrug and say, "Okay, hang on."

Annja hung on.

They coursed through the water and Annja let her legs rest, grateful for the reprieve. Of course, there was still a chance the shark would be irritated when Annja finally let go, but she could cover a lot more distance at that moment by hitching a ride.

If that poor seal could see me now, she thought. It would probably be horrified at what I've done. Then she thought about her friend Cole, from whom she'd learned this trick, and was grateful that his passion for sharks had taught her to respect and understand them.

Annja kept her head forward, willing the shark to stay on the northern route direction they'd both been following when she was swimming with it. If it veered away or looked as if it was heading toward open ocean, she would have no choice but to disembark.

She figured they covered two more miles within about five minutes of travel. For its part, the great white seemed utterly unfazed by the passenger it had acquired. Annja could sense the terrific power of the fish; it was supremely designed for hunting and patrolling the oceans as its apex predator. And it was truly an incredible sight to behold, let alone be hitching a ride with.

Annja's heart rate kicked up and she tried hugging the body of the great white a little closer. Ahead of them, she'd spotted the oxygen trails of the five divers she'd come to do battle with. Within minutes she could see the divers themselves.

They were maybe a hundred yards ahead of Annja. And she could see the large dark bag that two of them towed.

The pearl.

Only now, it was a bomb.

What are the odds I can induce this fellow to take a chunk out of Spier? she wondered.

But at that moment, she felt the great white start to change direction.

Annja got the message. Thus endeth the ride.

Reluctantly, she released the massive dorsal fin and allowed herself to bob in the water, her sword ready to handle the shark, if necessary.

The great white continued on its course, not seeming to notice she was no longer attached. She watched for a moment as the great beast swam away.

She turned in the water and looked ahead. The oxygen bubbles drifted up toward the surface and she could see that the five divers were arrayed in a pentagon pattern in the water.

Worse, they all seemed to have spear guns.

She swam ahead, cutting the distance between them. Her legs, rested during the five-minute trip on the shark, came to life and they churned the water behind her.

As she swam, she considered her options of attack. They had no idea she was there.

Take out the bomb first, she decided. If they couldn't use it, then Spier would have to call off the attack on the politicians. Stopping the attack was the primary goal, Annja thought.

Annja watched the two divers towing the bag. They were holding on to its straps.

She could surprise them and cut the straps before they knew she was there.

But what if it exploded when it dropped to the seabed?

Annja had no way of knowing how volatile the pearl would be. Would Spier have rigged it to explode if it was jostled? Or would they leave it on a timer to do its work?

I'll have to take the chance that Spier has it on a timer, she decided. If it could explode that easily, then Spier and his team could have been killed if something went wrong while they swam.

Annja had no doubt that Spier intended to come out of this alive. With his money, he could easily run for office in Germany and win. And with the former chancellor out of the way, Spier would have little opposition to his bigoted views.

And the rest of the world would have a genuine problem on their hands. A revitalized Reichstadt under Spier and his ex-KSK commandos.

Annja had cut the distance down to under twenty feet now. She kept her eyes on the seafloor, aware that men as highly trained in combat as Spier's team would have the ability to sense when someone dangerous was approaching.

She waited until the very last moment, and then she surged forward, reached out with her sword and made two quick cuts. One on each strap.

The reaction was stunned surprise as the pearl suddenly dropped and then disappeared somewhere beneath them.

Annja would have to worry about that later.

The divers turned and Annja saw she faced Heinkel and Mueller. Their facial reactions behind their masks were of surprise followed by rage.

She saw the spear guns come up at almost the same time. She pivoted and cut down, slicing into Mueller's gun first. The spear shot wide as Annja cut the elastic band. She backhanded Mueller in the face with the pommel of the sword and his mask cracked.

She heard the swish and felt the barbed head of Heinkel's spear lance her side, but it only grazed her. Still, she winced in pain and then cut back with the sword, coming down on Heinkel's air hose, slicing it open.

Oxygen immediately flooded the area around them with a swarm of bubbles. Heinkel was forced to ascend or risk drowning.

Mueller, however, had pulled out his diver's knife and now faced Annja, bobbing in the ocean.

Annja closed with him.

He jabbed straight out at her, trying to go for an immediate kill shot at her heart, but Annja brought her elbow inside to block the blow, sliding her own blade between them.

Mueller retreated and then came at her again with an overhead thrust aimed at impaling her head.

Annja allowed a sudden swell of current to lift her to the side and she cut down on Mueller from behind. She watched her blade bite into the oxygen tanks and Mueller shot off into the deep, unable to free himself from the explosion of pressurized oxygen.

She heard a swish and ducked as another spear went over her head.

The surprise, it seemed, was over.

Gottlieb bobbed in the swells about fifty feet away. He was desperately trying to reload another spear to shoot.

Annja swam through the water to reach him.

Another spear shot past her. Farther away, she could make out Hans aiming at her.

Spier had vanished somewhere.

Probably went after the bomb, Annja thought as she continued to churn across the distance between her and Gottlieb.

He managed to get another spear loaded. Annja watched as the gun came up, level with her face.

She was too far away.

The spear shot and Annja brought the sword up. The spear

bounced off the flat of the blade and spun away toward the bottom.

Annja charged toward Gottlieb and he barely had time to raise his arms to ward off her attack. But it was too late. Annja plunged the blade through his wet suit and into his chest.

Gottlieb's mouthpiece flew out as blood exploded from his chest and mouth at the same time.

Annja spun him around and used her feet to anchor her as she pulled her blade free of him. Gottlieb's eyes had already gone black and he drifted away in the current, dead.

Annja had little time to appreciate the win. As she turned back, she felt something impale her leg. She glanced down and saw the horrifying image of a spear jutting out of her thigh.

Had she been on land, Annja might have screamed out in pain. But instead, she gritted her teeth and saw that the spear was nowhere close to her femoral artery. Yeah, it hurt like hell, but it wasn't a fatal wound.

Annja wasn't about to give Hans time to ready another spear, however. Despite the waves of pain flooding her body, she swam right at him, willing her legs to work and get her there as fast as possible.

Hans gave up on the spear gun and drew his own knife. It wasn't a regular diving knife. It had an angle in its blade that aided its cutting ability. Underwater, she wasn't sure what sort of advantage that would give Hans, but she certainly didn't want to find out. Annja had seen that type of blade—a kukri knife like the kind the Nepali Gurkhas use—in action enough times to know it was indeed a formidable weapon.

So, this was how it was going to end, she thought with a frown. From lovers to haters.

Mortal enemies.

Annja held her sword in front of her as Hans eased himself closer to her with gentle kicks.

He's trying to get closer so the sword isn't as effective, Annja realized. She jabbed with the blade and kept him at bay.

Not this time, she thought. I might have liked you once. But that was a lifetime ago.

Hans smiled and then waved at her, trying his best to egg her on. Annja was having none of it. She held her position and waited for him to make his move.

When he did, it was so smooth Annja almost didn't register it. But Hans came at her with a backhanded slash, aimed at slicing her neck wide open.

The leading edge of the blade slashed just millimeters from her. Annja jerked back and then shot her arms out.

Hans recoiled and let the kukri knock the sword off target. Then he cut back again, trying to score a line down the front of Annja's body.

Again the kukri missed by a fractional distance. If they'd been on land, she might have met her match. Hans knew how to use that kukri, and the longer they sparred, the more dangerous it was going to get for her.

Time to end this, she thought.

Hans came in harder now, trying to stab her.

Annja waited until she was certain he'd committed himself and then brought her sword down following his arc. The blade bit into the tops of his arms and she simply let the blade bounce back up into his throat.

She heard the gasp even underwater as the sword cut his throat open.

Hans dropped the kukri and it flashed through the water as it sank.

Blood streamed away from Hans as he drifted away, desperately trying to stem the flow of blood from his neck.

Annja watched him for a moment longer before turning away to locate Spier.

36

She saw a thin trail of oxygen bubbles far off in the distance. Annja raced toward them, aware that the spear jutting out of her leg hurt her far more than she wanted to admit. Plus, the trail of blood that dribbled from it was of concern, as well. She might have hitched a ride with a great white a few minutes before, but blood in the water meant it'd likely be back to see just what the deal was.

Fortunately, it had a lot of potential meals to choose from, not just Annja. Heinkel, Mueller, Gottlieb and Hans were all out there somewhere, surrounded by lots of blood. The odds seemed decent that if the great white was going to attack anyone, it would opt for them first.

Annja saw a flash of movement.

Spier was swimming about a hundred yards away from her. In his arms, she saw something large and round.

The pearl.

He'd managed to locate it even after Annja sent it sprawling to the seabed. She frowned. He was determined to see this thing exploded one way or another.

I guess that rules out talking him into surrendering, she thought.

Annja swam faster, fighting the lancing pain in her leg. Sooner or later, she was going to have to remove the spear, but there was no time at the moment. Fortunately, it had gone in at the top part of her quadriceps muscle. She just had to be careful she didn't catch the leg on anything and make the wound a lot worse.

She kept the sword in her hands, unaware if Spier had any weapons he could throw her way when she drew closer to him.

But Spier seemed oblivious to her presence. Perhaps he thought that his men would have been more than a match for the television-host-cum-archaeologist, or maybe he went even further, thinking that there was no way a mere woman could defeat four highly trained commandos.

Whatever the case, Spier showed no sign that he even knew she was around and seemed intent to deliver the pearl to the area roughly one hundred yards offshore.

Annja felt the seabed rising sharply as they got closer to the coastline. Part of her grew worried that if the snipers hidden in the bluffs above spotted them offshore, they'd fire down on them. She'd have to remain underwater the entire time.

This didn't seem to bother Spier, who had found what he was looking for. He approached a rocky outcropping on the stony seabed. Spier slowed and allowed the pearl to come to rest nestled in a shallow grove that seemed almost made for receiving it.

He made a few final adjustments and then started to swim away.

Then he saw Annja.

His eyes went from her face to the spear jutting out of her leg. Annja saw the pleasure in his eyes as he regarded the thing that was causing her an extreme amount of pain.

Annja steeled herself. He'll attack me now, she thought. I've got to be ready.

But Spier, who seemed to have made an entire life out of defying convention, turned and swam off toward deeper water.

Annja frowned. The choice was plain—either try to disarm the pearl or go after Spier.

But she couldn't do both.

She took one final look at Spier as his fins drove him farther away and then made her decision.

Annja dove deeper to get to the rocky outcropping, but even as she closed in on it, she could see the digital readout swiftly counting back down from two minutes.

Annja examined the housing, which Spier had apparently built to encase the pearl itself. She tried to recall what she knew about nuclear detonation, but quickly shrugged that train of thought off and concentrated instead on how she could disconnect the wires from the bomb itself.

She saw a number of colored wires going to and from the different parts of the casement, but nothing seemed to be connected directly to the pearl.

Annja's fingers felt as thick as sausages as she tried to make sense of the assembly. It was almost seamless metal surrounding the pearl itself. Even in the cool waters of the Atlantic, Annja could feel the heat the pearl gave off.

Incredible power, she realized.

She decided it was time to act, no matter what. She grabbed the red wire and yanked it out away from the pearl.

Annja waited to see what would happen.

The digital readout continued.

Annja's heart raced and she sucked oxygen faster than she should have dared.

There were five wires left. Any one of them might set the bomb off. Or they might disarm the bomb.

Which one?

She'd been in front of bombs before. She knew trust and confidence were the only things that would get her out of this alive.

She felt the sword in her right hand.

She brought the blade up and watched the digital readout continue to spiral down toward zero.

It has to be now, she thought.

There's not enough time to try to work this out logically. Disarm it and then let the experts come in and recover the device.

The clock shot down.

Thirty seconds.

Annja felt herself sucking too much oxygen. She felt dizzy, like she was going to pass out.

She brought the sword up and positioned the blade under the wires. She pressed the steel of its blade against them all.

She held her breath and cut.

THE DIGITAL READOUT FROZE at three seconds.

Annja almost collapsed into the midst of the ocean.

Her sword dropped to the seafloor, coming to rest on the sand and smooth rocks.

She felt her shoulders droop and she slowed her breathing to keep herself from blacking out.

She'd done it.

The pearl, its shiny black surface, lay resting still in its enclosure, but there was no detonation. And the German chancellor was safe.

Annja looked closely at the pearl and she could see her reflection in it. She looked like she'd aged ten years over the past day.

She certainly felt like that was the case. But in the end, things had worked out. But what to do about the pearl?

Where would it go now? Who would take possession of it? If this was some new type of nuclear material that originated in nature, did that really belong to anyone? Would it make people go crazy over this stuff again? Regular nuclear weapons were bad enough, Annja thought. And the world had come close to the brink of nuclear annihilation too many times before to ever make such an object as the pearl a safe thing to possess.

After all, Spier had gone hunting for it to take over his homeland and then perhaps the entire planet.

How could it ever rest in any one government's hands without attracting jealousy, rage and indignation from others?

Annja picked up her sword and used the blade to pry apart the enclosure that surrounded it.

The metal and plastic bits came apart easily enough and then the pearl lolled over into the sand.

Annja found herself strangely attracted to it. Despite its power, she no longer felt sick from being so close to it. Perhaps the seawater nullified its radioactive components? She had no idea. Nor did she really want to find out. If it wasn't affecting her any longer, that was good.

Annja released her sword and reached for the pearl.

She caught an unusual reflection in it and turned just as a knife blade cut through the water where she'd been a split second before.

Annja rolled in the water and came to face the threat behind her.

Heinkel and Mueller had found her. They still wore their weight belts but they'd shucked their oxygen tanks.

And they came at her too quickly to retrieve her sword.

Mueller attacked from the right and Heinkel the left. They tried to trap her between them, cutting and jabbing with their knives.

Annja pivoted in the water and evaded the blows, but then she felt the most agonizing sensation.

She glanced down and saw that Heinkel had grabbed the

spear still jutting out of her leg and had wrenched it around inside her thigh.

Annja felt the wound growing and saw more blood spilling into the water. She wanted to scream. Sweat broke out under her mask.

Annja chopped down on Heinkel's hand and broke his contact with the spear.

But that gave Mueller the opening he needed and he drove in, plunging the knife in between Annja's ribs.

Annja sucked air and water and screeched despite the mouthpiece.

More blood poured into the water.

Annja smashed an elbow into Mueller's face and he pulled away. She'd broken his nose.

Annja willed the sword back into her hands.

The blade appeared between Mueller and Heinkel.

Their expressions changed and Annja could see the looks of fear.

But fear wasn't enough to stop men like this.

They both drove in again at her. Slashing and hacking with their knives.

Annja was injured and the water around them became a fuzzy mix of salt water and blood.

She did her best to block their attacks, but she was growing dizzy from fatigue and the loss of blood.

She brought the sword up and swung out at Mueller, who was driving in toward her face again.

She caught him on the underside of his arms, biting into his flesh. He grimaced and fought to get to the surface. How he and Heinkel had managed to hold their breath for so long amazed her.

Mueller was swimming away but Heinkel was still with her.

He came in so hard that Annja felt herself forced back from his onslaught. The flashing steel of his blade bit at her again and again and Annja had only a moment to bring the sword blade up as Heinkel tried to drag her down toward the seabed.

Annja felt her strength slipping. She sucked on her mouthpiece and tried to flush her muscles with the badly needed oxygen.

And in that split second, she found her last bit of strength. She stabbed Heinkel in the stomach, cutting back and forth, tearing him open.

Heinkel clutched at his stomach, and then he was rolling over, drifting up and away.

Annja saw a flash shoot through the bloody water and realized that the great white shark had returned.

Or maybe, she thought on the fringe of consciousness, it was a different great white on patrol.

Either way, Heinkel's body disappeared in a split second as the shark devoured him.

Annja succumbed to the weightless sensation of drifting and falling into the abyss.

37

Annja awoke surrounded by white light.

But she wasn't in the water.

She tried to shift and found that she was unable to move. A searing pain bit into her side.

"Easy, Annja. Don't go tearing those stitches out now."

She opened her eyes and blinked repeatedly as she tried to adjust to her bright surroundings. "I'm guessing this isn't heaven."

She heard laughter. "Hardly. But it might be as close as people like you and me ever get to it."

She turned her head and saw Vic lying in a bed next to her. His face was bandaged and she saw a lot of tubes going into his body. "Man, do I look as bad as you do?" she asked.

He chuckled. "I'm not going to answer that question, Annja. It might mean I don't get another chance to take you out for a meal."

"Uh, I thought that was my line," another voice said.

Annja smiled as she recognized it. "Hello, George."

"She still remembers me. I suppose that's a good thing."

Annja shook her head. "What the hell happened?" She glanced at Vic again. "I thought you were killed when they stormed the hotel."

Vic patted his side. "They fished three slugs out of me. Eating solid food might be a problem for a while. But I'll manage. I'm a survivor. Sorta like you, Annja."

George peered closer at her. "What the hell were you doing thinking you could take them all on like that?"

Annja tried to shrug but it hurt too much. "No choice. There wasn't any time left. And I thought that if Vic was dead, the guy they put in charge probably wouldn't believe me. I had to do it myself."

George glanced at Vic. "Damned stubborn woman."

Vic nodded. "And thank God she is. Otherwise, none of us would probably be here right now."

Annja closed her eyes. She saw flashing images of the last few moments when she thought she was dying in the ocean. "How did they find me?"

She heard Vic's voice explaining things. "The Coast Guard put some patrols on the water once they found the wreck of the boat you'd been on. They skirted the coast for a while, and then they saw a commotion in the surf ahead of them. They tracked you down to just offshore of the chancellor's place."

George's voice continued the story. "Coast Guard says there were sharks in the water. Did you see any?"

Annja smiled. "You could say that."

"You could have been killed."

"Yeah, well, sharks were sort of the least of my worries about that time. I had to stop Spier and his men. They were occupying more of my attention than the sharks were."

"You were very lucky, Annja," Vic said.

"We all were," Annja said. "Did they find Spier?"

"No."

Annja frowned. "I could have stopped him, but I had to

disarm the pearl. I chose the pearl. I had to let Spier go." She sighed.

"You did the right thing, Annja," George said. "If that thing had gone off, there's no telling what sort of damage it would have caused."

"Did they find the bodies of Spier's men?"

"Yeah. What's left of them. Those sharks did a fair number on them before letting the pieces go."

Annja nodded. "I guess they didn't much care for the taste of scum."

"I guess not."

Annja felt her side. "How bad am I wounded?" She opened her eyes and looked at Vic. "Don't sugarcoat it, either."

"You almost lost your spleen. If the knife had gone in a few millimeters farther south, you'd be prone to infection for the rest of your life." Vic shrugged. "Otherwise, they patched up your thigh, cleaned the wound, which wasn't bad to begin with thanks to the salt water. You probably feel a helluva lot worse than you actually are, if that helps any."

"Not really," Annja said. "So the chancellor is safe?"

"Completely. She left the island this morning, as a matter of fact. Word is you'll get a commendation."

Annja sniffed. "Nice of her to stop by and offer it herself."

Vic laughed. "Yeah, well, don't count on a politician ever stopping by in person to say thank-you. People like us exist to serve, Annja. Just the way it is."

"Easy for you to say," Annja said. "You're used to that kind of crap. Me? I don't save politicians' lives every day." She shrugged. "Don't think I'll make a habit of it, either."

"Good plan," Vic said.

Annja looked down to the foot of the bed. George's face showed epic amounts of concern. "How long until I can get the hell out of here? I'm allergic to hospitals," she said.

"A week," George said. "And don't you dare try to leave any sooner. Or else I'll get mad."

Annja smiled. "I wouldn't want that."

George waved. "I'll see you in a few hours. Get some sleep."

She watched him walk out of the door and then glanced back at Vic. "So, we're roomies?"

"Yep."

"How'd you work that?"

"Advantages of being in charge and wounded," Vic said. "It's amazing what people will do when you're still alive after being shot three times."

Annja sighed. "Did they recover the pearl?"

Vic cleared his throat. "Funny you should mention that. No. They didn't. They sent a bunch of divers down there, but they never found anything resembling the pearl."

"That's not good."

Vic shrugged. "Nothing we can do about it from here, Annja. Trust me. It was all I could do to stay put while they dug that lead out of me when I knew you were still out there on your own."

"What happened to Roux?"

Vic frowned. "Uh, I don't know."

"What's that supposed to mean?"

"Just what I said. When we went to interrogate Gottlieb, he and George were left behind. George tells me that Roux suddenly said he had to go to the bathroom. The guy got up, walked out and just disappeared."

Annja sighed. "I'm not surprised." She glanced at her bedside table. A fresh vase of flowers sat there. "You got me flowers?"

Vic shook his head. "Not from me, sorry."

Annja saw a card next to the vase. She reached for it and picked it up.

"Glad you made it in one piece—R."

"Who's it from?" Vic asked.

Annja looked at the note one last time and then crumpled it up. "No one."

IT TURNED OUT to be a full week that Annja needed for recovery. She felt like she could have gone home earlier, but George was having none of it. He'd practically stood guard outside her room and took charge of visitors—who could see her and who couldn't. He'd already run off one of Annja's colleagues from *Chasing History's Monsters*. Annja had finally convinced him that he couldn't keep her sheltered forever.

"I'll be going home soon, George. I need to get back to my life."

"Just remember that you've got one," George said. "And I still intend to collect on our agreement."

"All right," Annja said.

Vic left a day before Annja. When he'd finished packing his bags, he came over and sat next to her on the bed. "It was wonderful seeing you again, Annja."

"You, too."

Vic smiled. "If you ever manage to get George to stop paying attention to you, I'd like a chance to take you out to dinner myself."

"Would you, now?"

"Yes. I would."

Annja nodded. "I'll keep it in mind. Try not to get yourself killed for the wrong politician. You're a good man, Vic. You don't deserve to be expendable just because of someone else's agenda."

Vic nudged her. "Neither do you, Annja. We might work for different people, but the game's pretty much the same."

Annja sighed. "You won't get an argument out of me on that one."

Vic stood and grabbed his bag. "You take care of yourself. I'll drop you an email with all my contact information. Don't make me come after you for that date, all right?"

Annja smiled. "Likewise."

And then he was gone. Back to the shadow world he inhabited. Annja saw a lot of similarities between her world and his. But at least Vic knew who he worked for better than Annja did.

George showed up a few minutes later and Annja knew he'd been good enough to give her and Vic a few moments alone to say goodbye. George might have a mad crush on her, but he was always polite and respectful. Plus, Vic had told her all about how George had assumed command when Vic had been shot.

"He's got some real good leadership qualities there," he'd told her. "That guy's destined for greater things than he knows."

"Just don't get him killed," Annja said.

The next day George helped her pack her bags. "You happy to be going home?"

Annja nodded. "I don't like hospitals. The sooner I can get out, the better."

"Been in a lot of them, have you?"

Annja smiled. "More times than I care to recollect. For me, the best care comes from a nice bath back at my loft in Brooklyn. There's no place like home, you know?"

"Yeah."

Annja zipped up her bag. "I'm booked on a flight in a couple of hours. Where are you headed?"

"Back to D.C.," George said. "I used some vacation staying here to make sure you were okay."

"You did?"

He shrugged. "I wanted to be here in case you needed anything."

Annja smiled at him. "Tell me something, George."

"Anything."

"What have I done to deserve such nice treatment from you? I've constantly rebuffed your advances, and yet you're still so good to me. Why?"

George was quiet for a moment. "Why not? We all need someone, Annja. What good is life if you go through it alone and cold and empty inside? I don't call that much of a life at all. And trust me, I ought to know. I've spent so much time with my machines that I forgot how to interact with people."

"Seems to me you're doing a great job."

George shrugged. "It's been a struggle. But you know what? You inspired me to keep going. You don't let anyone's expectations keep you from living a life that most people simply wouldn't have the courage to face."

Annja hefted her bag, aware of the dull ache in her leg. "Thanks, George. I really mean that."

George eyed her. "Dinner. Don't forget, okay? I won't bother you with it now, but once you fully recuperate…"

"I won't forget," Annja said. She leaned in and kissed him on the cheek. "I promise."

They walked out of the hospital together.

38

It took a few hours for Annja to get home from Martha's Vineyard. The flight from the island to the small airport in Westchester County was rife with turbulence. Annja had spent the majority of the flight thinking how incredibly ironic it would be to come through encounters with sharks, a spear in her leg and multiple knife wounds only to have the plane she was in plummet to the earth on her way home from the hospital.

Fortunately, it stayed aloft, but Annja was thrilled to get off the puddle jumper. She grabbed her bags and walked to the small terminal. At the entrance, she saw a black car waiting and a driver holding a placard with her name on it.

"That's me," she said to the youngish driver holding the card. "Who sent the car?"

The driver took her bags. "Your friends at the television show," he said. "There's a bottle of champagne on ice in the backseat, if you'd like to spend the drive getting comfortable."

Annja smiled. "Thanks, but I think I'll wait until I'm off my medication."

He nodded. "Looks like you had a pretty bad run-in with a train."

"You should see the train," Annja said. "But yeah, let's just say I'm going to be glad to get home."

He stowed her bags in the trunk and then opened the door for her. "Well, just let me do the driving and I'll have you home in no time."

"Thanks." Annja ducked inside and slid into the leather seats. The cushioning felt great against her flight-rattled spine. In the foot well, she spotted the bucket of ice with the champagne sticking out of it. Annja reached and lifted the bottle halfway out. It looked delicious.

And expensive.

"This is a pretty hefty bottle of champagne," Annja said. "A 1995 Krug?"

"Clos du Mesnil," the driver said. "One of only about thirteen thousand bottles produced that year according to the guy at the store."

"You bought this?"

The driver shrugged. "I was told to make sure you had an expensive bottle to drink at your leisure. I did as I was told."

Annja looked at the bottle. She knew about the Clos du Mesnil champagne. It was what was known as Blanc de Blanc, coming exclusively from a tiny four-and-a-half-acre walled vineyard that was exclusively chardonnay.

"Well, I will definitely have a nice time with this once I'm better. Thanks for choosing it."

The driver shrugged. "Just doing my job. But thank you."

Annja leaned back in the seat and let the rhythm of the car relax her.

She was on several pain medications and had immediately discarded some strong stuff due to its effects on her stomach. But the others she kept. And it did take the edge off, but Annja was always wary of taking too many pills. She'd found they dulled her senses and the last thing she needed in her line of work was dull senses.

No thanks.

The driver steered them onto the highway and the engine kicked into a higher gear. The constant hum of the engine put Annja into a drowsy mood.

Before she knew it, she was fast asleep.

"Miss?"

Annja stirred. She took a breath and realized the car had stopped. Glancing out the window, she saw her building.

Home.

"Sorry, it's been a long trip."

The driver nodded. "No problem. Glad you were able to rest some on the way." He held the door as she stepped out.

"Thanks."

The driver leaned inside the car and came out with the bottle of Krug. "Don't forget the good stuff, Miss."

Annja smiled. "You're a helluva driver, pal. Thanks."

He touched his hat. "My pleasure. Your bags are right over there on the stoop."

The driver got back in the car. Within seconds, he was gone.

Annja stood on the front steps of her building and looked up and down the street. "Damn, it's nice to be back here."

She picked up her bags, unlocked the front door and walked inside.

She desperately wanted a hot bath.

Inside her loft she put the champagne in the refrigerator. "Got to keep that baby cold," she said to herself.

She picked up the stereo remote and hit it once. She'd programmed it to always play on shuffle unless she specified otherwise. Instantly, the sound of Cole Porter streamed out of her speakers.

"Nice," she said quietly.

Annja dumped her bags in her bedroom and then padded into the bathroom to switch on the faucet. She added a sprinkle of lavender bath salts to the water and started to get undressed.

Cole Porter was replaced by Dexter Gordon and Annja nodded approvingly. If the shuffle kept up like this, it would be a good night indeed.

On a whim, she switched her computer on and logged in to check her email. As promised, Vic had sent her his contact information. George had also sent her a note wishing her well.

She saw one farther down from the staff at *Chasing History's Monsters*. She opened it. Dear Annja—Hope your flight was good. Love from all!

Annja smiled. She decided to call to thank them for their care and concern.

She heard the voice of Jenny Stuart, who had just joined as a production assistant.

"Oh, my God, Annja, it's you! How are you?"

"I'm fine, thanks."

"We were so worried when we heard that you'd gotten hurt. Are you all right now?"

"I will be with a bit of rest. So no globetrotting for a while, I'm afraid."

"Everyone's crowding around the phone. Can I put you on speaker?"

"Sure."

Annja heard the click and then a chorus of voices started speaking. Amid the hellos, she heard all her friends from the show. Annja felt a swelling in her throat and realized she should get off the phone or risk crying in front of them all.

"I just wanted to say thanks for getting me the car service and the wonderful bottle of champagne. It meant the world to me."

There was a sudden silence.

"Hello?" Annja said.

"Uh, Annja?" It was Doug Morrell, her producer. "We didn't get you a car service. Or champagne, for that matter. Our budgets would never permit that."

Annja frowned. "You didn't?"

"No. We wanted to do something like that, of course, but you know how things work."

"Let me call you back," Annja said. She hung up and then checked the emails from Vic and George. Maybe one of them had arranged the car service and the ridiculously expensive bottle of champagne.

But neither email said anything about it.

Annja thought about calling them and then shrugged it off.

Roux.

He'd disappeared without saying goodbye aside from the flowers at the hospital. And that champagne was certainly in keeping with his style. She smiled. She wasn't happy that he'd ducked out on her, but the champagne was certainly nice.

Annja sunk into the bath and the scent of lavender surrounded her. She could feel her muscles relaxing as the heat opened them up. Tonight's agenda was set, she decided. After the bath, she'd order some Chinese food from the delivery joint down the street. Sometimes a plate of chicken fried rice and boneless spareribs was just what the doctor ordered.

And then she planned to sleep for days.

She slid deeper into the water until it was just up under her nostrils.

Dexter Gordon changed over to Earle Hagen's "Harlem Nocturne." Another appropriate tune, Annja decided, especially given that she was back in the great town of New York City.

After a good soak in the tub, she decided that if she stayed in any longer, she would undoubtedly fall sound asleep. And drowning in the tub was a pretty silly way to die after all the diving she'd been doing lately.

Annja toweled off, threw a second towel around her hair and walked into her bedroom. After choosing a pair of sweatpants and a clean T-shirt, Annja dried her hair and let it fall about her shoulders.

She walked into her kitchen and found the plastic folder where she kept all her take-out menus. Opening the Chinese restaurant one, she ran her finger down the page examining the appetizers.

Annja reached for the phone as the stereo abruptly switched over to Wagner. The music was too serious.

That wasn't really what she was in the mood for, she decided. She padded into the living room and looked for the remote control.

Joachim Spier sat on her couch. The bottle of champagne was open in front of him. He held a glass in one hand.

He had a silenced pistol in the other.

"I have to admit I'm offended that you chose not to open the bottle in the car," Spier said. "I rather hoped you'd be quite drunk by the time you got back here."

"Sorry to ruin your plans," Annja said. "Too many pills in my system to deal with alcohol right now."

Spier nodded. "I figured there would be, but I was unsure whether you were one of those people who doesn't mind mixing a little booze with their medications." He shrugged. "Apparently you listen to some of your doctors."

"Some of them, yes."

"Dr. Tiko would be offended if he knew how you treat American doctors with more respect than Filipino ones."

Annja shook her head. "I treat them all with just as much respect as they require to do their jobs. But don't think I'm a fan of any of them. Their nationality doesn't matter to me in the slightest."

Spier took a sip of the champagne. "Are you aware of how much this bottle cost me?"

"Probably about a cool grand," Annja said. "It's quite a good bottle."

Spier eyed her. "You know your champagne?"

"The driver and I discussed it on the ride back from the airport. He did as you asked apparently."

"That car company caters to wealthy clients so their drivers are certainly a cut above the usual riffraff that staff livery services. I knew they'd get it right."

Annja stood there wondering what would happen next. "And what is it that I can do for you, Herr Spier? Shouldn't you be hiding under a rock somewhere? Last I heard there was an international manhunt on for you."

Spier shrugged. "Is there? You know, it's rather amusing how much anonymity money can buy you. I can go where I want provided I pave the path with enough bribes and favors."

"Lucky you. Now answer my question."

Spier sipped the champagne and then put the glass down. "You ruined my plans, Annja. And you killed my men."

"I heard a few sharks helped out in that regard."

Spier frowned. "A dishonorable way for them to die. But enough about them. It's time you and I had ourselves a talk."

39

"We've got nothing to talk about, Spier. You should probably leave before I kill you."

Spier pointed at Annja's armchair. "Really, Annja, you should sit down and have some of this amazing champagne. It would be a terrible shame for us to waste this now that I've gone ahead and opened up the bottle."

"Yeah, thanks for the offer. How rude of you to help yourself without asking me."

Spier shrugged. "Well, really, I gave it to you so I felt I could be forward and open it. I even got an extra glass for you."

Annja noticed the empty flute on the table. She sat across from Spier. He leaned forward and poured her some.

When he was done, he lifted his glass and toasted her. "Here's to you and your persistence, Annja. You are quite literally something of a marvel to me and I respect your qualities immensely."

Annja lifted her glass halfway and took a sip. The champagne tasted incredible. She put it back down. "That's quite nice."

"Indeed," Spier said. "And it is a worthy drink for a woman as accomplished as you."

"What would you have gotten me if I hadn't managed to disarm the pearl?"

"If it had detonated?" Spier smiled. "I doubt we would be having this conversation."

Annja nodded. "True, you'd be too busy what with being sworn in as the new German chancellor and all."

Spier laughed. "That would be rushing the natural order of things, I fear. But yes, eventually that position would have been mine."

"You don't seem particularly upset about the fact that I ruined your plans."

Spier took another sip. "You know, Annja, you don't get to be as old as I am without realizing that time is a fickle thing. As many plans as you set up and hope to implement, the universe tends to have its own schedule. So while I was initially enraged at your interference, I have to say that I have relaxed quite a bit."

"That champagne helps, I suppose."

"Oh, indeed," Spier said. "And you know what they say about a good drink, don't you?"

"No. What?"

"That it can often lead to tremendous inspiration. Exactly why so many of the world's most talented authors indulged as much as they did. Hemingway was a notorious drinker."

"So you've been inspired? Is that it? I can expect you to go home and write a book now?"

Spier shook his head. "Oh, my heavens, no. I'm not nearly gifted enough to pen a novel, I fear."

"No?"

"I'm destined for other things," Spier said. "Ruling a country called Germany, namely."

"I'd love to know how you intend to do that," Annja said. "Especially when your homeland won't even welcome you back now."

Spier waved his hand. "It's a trifle of a matter. Once I have the necessary implement back in my possession, everything will fall into place, I have no doubt."

"And what is that?"

"The pearl, of course."

Annja frowned. Vic told her that the divers hadn't found it. Annja had wondered if Spier had managed to come back and grab it. And yet he was here now telling her that he didn't have it.

"That's where you come in, Annja," Spier said. "You're going to help me get it back."

"I don't have it."

Spier frowned. "I warn you, Annja, that as much as I'm willing to let our bygones be bygones, I won't tolerate silly games. I know you disarmed the pearl and then all hell broke loose. But you are most definitely going to tell me where it is. Otherwise, I'll be forced to kill you."

"You'll kill me, anyway."

Spier shook his head. "Believe it or not, I actually relish the notion of leaving you alive. There are so few interesting people in the world these days. You are certainly one of a select few. Regardless of the fact that you bested me, I am willing to leave you be. Unless you make it absolutely necessary for me to kill you."

Annja sipped her champagne. "Sorry, Joachim, but I don't know where the pearl is."

"You're lying."

Annja shook her head. "Nope. When I woke up in the hospital that was one of the first things I asked about. My friends said they'd sent divers down there to retrieve it. But no one found it."

She could see the range of emotions run across Spier's

face as he tried to process the information. Anger won out. "Annja, you're tempting the fates by insisting on such lies. Tell me where they've put it."

"They—and I take that to mean the U.S. government—don't have it. I'm not lying to you, Joachim. I'm being absolutely and totally serious. We don't know where the pearl is."

Spier sat there for another moment and then took a deep sip of champagne. He refilled his glass and gestured to do the same for Annja.

"No, thanks," Annja said. "I'm still working on what I've got here."

"As you wish," Spier said. He drank some more and then set the glass down. He glanced at the pistol in his hand. "You know I could kill you right now, don't you?"

"Sure."

"And yet that holds no fear for you."

"I wouldn't say that," Annja said. "I mean, I don't really feel like dying after everything I've been through. But I can't help you with the pearl. I really can't. So if you're going to kill me, then go ahead and get it done. I'm tired and hungry and was looking forward to some Chinese food tonight."

Spier looked into her eyes and then chewed his lip. "You are telling me the truth, aren't you?"

"Yep."

"Amazing." He grinned. "You know, Annja, I've got to admit that I have become quite…impressed with you. What you're able to do, the things you did in the Philippines and in Martha's Vineyard…I mean, they're simply remarkable. And that sword, of course. I wonder if there's anything you can't do if you put your mind to it."

"I don't know," Annja said.

"What would you say to coming with me?"

Annja raised an eyebrow. "Excuse me?"

Spier leaned forward. "I mean it. Come join me on my

most audacious plan to date. The loss of the pearl is a set-back, for sure, but with you by my side, I would be unstoppable. And we would share in the power and glory of the future of Germany."

"You're kidding me."

Spier shook his head. "I'm absolutely serious. Marry me. Be my bride. I'll see to it that you never want for anything as long as we live."

Annja downed the rest of her champagne. "This has been some crazy week."

"What do you mean?"

"I mean, I've got a computer hacker, a special-operations soldier turned super spy and now a megalomaniac all declaring their interest in me. It's really getting out of hand, I think."

She stood and paced the room.

Spier stood, as well. "Annja, I'm not saying that I'm in love with you right this very moment. But I am certainly fascinated by you. We could be great together."

Annja shook her head. "No, we would be terrible together. You're ancient, Joachim. Not to mention that you are an evil man trying to usurp power for himself and run his country into the ground."

Spier shrugged. "Think of what I could do to my country being the natural genius that I am."

"Modest, too," Annja said. "But no thanks, Joachim. I think I'll take my chances with the cesspool that the dating scene has become."

Spier looked at the pistol in his hand. "I'm not a man who handles rejection well, Annja."

Annja glared at him. Spier had seen what she was capable of. Would he really try to kill her himself? Did he think he could do it?

"You're not going to kill me, Joachim."

"I will if I must."

Annja smiled. "Your men were ready to do it. And they damn near succeeded. But you're not a killer. You're just a facilitator. You hire the killers and then sic them on their targets."

"You're not giving me enough credit, Annja."

"I think I might have given you too much credit actually."

Spier shook his head and then sighed. "So be it."

He raised the pistol and started to thumb the hammer back.

So be it indeed, Annja thought. She was already moving, running and leaping across the space between them, summoning the sword as she did. The steel blade flashed and there was a sharp clang as it cut through the gun Spier held.

Pieces of the pistol clattered away as Spier suddenly vaulted himself over the back of the couch. He regained his footing and smiled at Annja.

"Maybe it's better this way."

Annja shook her head. How was an eighty-year-old able to vault like that?

Spier smiled. "Let's finish this in style, shall we?"

He raced for the stairs leading to the roof, and as he ran toward them, he grabbed a replica polearm that Annja had in her loft.

Annja ran after him, but again Spier's vitality proved incredible. By the time Annja reached the door to the roof, Spier was nowhere to be seen.

An early-evening breeze whipped around her. Annja held up the sword, aware that at any moment some kid with his video phone would no doubt capture the fight and post it to YouTube.

Spier attacked from out of nowhere and Annja felt her feet swept out from under her as he brought the end of the polearm across the backs of her ankles.

Annja landed hard and had to roll because Spier was already trying to spear her with the business end of the weapon.

She felt the gravel and grit bite into her back. She was pretty sure she felt a few stitches tear, as well.

Spier kept up his attack and drove Annja across the roof of her building. "You should have joined with me, Annja. We could have been amazing together. The world would have feared us."

Annja came up in a semicrouch, eyeing Spier. The sword in her hand shimmered in the fading sunlight. "Not a chance."

Spier unleashed a scream and raced right at Annja.

Annja sidestepped the attack and cut down on the polearm. Her blade chopped it in two but then Spier spun the piece in his hand up into her face.

Annja felt it strike her hard and she saw stars for a moment.

"I was a master of European martial arts," Spier said. "It was a long time ago, of course, but some things you don't forget."

Spier attacked her again and again and Annja felt her strength waning under the weight of her past injuries, the medication and the champagne. But she knew that Spier wouldn't stop.

She rolled across the roof and came up on one knee.

Spier sensed her weakness. "I'm sorry it has to end this way, Annja."

He brought the polearm up high overhead and slashed down at her.

Annja rolled again and came up under the arc of his attack, stabbing straight up and in with her sword.

The blade slid into Spier's body and the old man simply slid down the blade until his last breath escaped his lungs.

Annja dropped the blade and let him fall.

Spier's lifeless body lay in a widening pool of blood. Annja stood over him, looking down at his corpse. It was unbelievable that he was finally dead.

She raced downstairs and immediately called Vic.

"Annja? What's wrong?"

"Spier was here."

"Are you serious? Jesus Christ. What did he want?"

"He wanted to marry me."

"What? What did you say?"

"I killed him," Annja said. "His body is on my roof at this very moment. I think you'd better come over and clean things up, if you get my drift."

"I'll have people there shortly."

Annja hung up the phone and then dropped down on the couch where Spier had just been sitting. The bottle of champagne still bubbled in front of her.

Annja drank it while she waited for Vic's people to show up.

epilogue

Two weeks later, Annja sat on the dock by the dive master's shack at Club Noah. She was watching a single sloop carrying one person make its way toward the shore. The balmy breezes blew warm air over her skin. The sunset she'd come to know and love repeated its daily fireworks display. And the turquoise waters of the South China Sea lapped at her feet.

The sloop's motor churned a white frothy wake behind the boat and Annja smiled as the boat drew closer to the dock.

She stood and waited for the person driving it to toss her the rope. When he did, Annja caught it in one hand and tied the sloop to the dock so the coming high tide didn't carry it out to sea.

The man stepped onto the dock. The wet suit he wore made him look like a pear in a strange bag, but he seemed completely unfazed by his appearance and only smiled at Annja as she approached him.

"I wondered when you'd get back," she said.

"It took me a little longer than I thought it would." He nodded at the boat. "Give me a hand with these, would you?"

He handed Annja the set of oxygen tanks and diving gear. Annja carried them up to the dive master's shack. The little man working there accepted them without saying a word. He only smiled when Annja said thank-you.

Back on the path, the man in the wet suit waited for her. Annja walked next to him as another breeze blew the palm fronds nearby. "You don't seem surprised to see me," she said.

The man shrugged. "I knew you'd figure it out eventually."

Annja nodded. "I decided you'd have to bring it back by ship. There was no way something like that could go undetected by an airline after everything that happened."

He nodded. "You guessed right."

Annja shrugged. "The timing made sense. I had to figure in a number of stops along the way. Other ports of call. I knew I had some time to rest up before coming over here."

"But here you are."

Annja smiled. "I have to admit I'm a bit amazed by this. I mean, I'm assuming you gave it back to the Jiao."

He nodded. "It was the only proper thing to do."

"I agree. It's just…" Annja's voice trailed off.

"What?"

"Well, frankly, it's a little out of character for you. I've known you for a long time and you've always struck me as someone who only cares for his own agenda."

Roux smiled. "And what makes you think this isn't in keeping with my agenda?"

"Well, you're being somewhat altruistic here."

"Am I?"

Annja frowned. "Aren't you?"

Roux stopped and looked at her. "Annja, it's true that we've known each other awhile now. But I've been alive a lot longer than you. And the benefit of me being around for so many years is that I tend to have a more wide-reaching perspective than normal people. I don't say that to pretend that I'm better than you—I say that only as a matter of fact."

"All right."

"As such," Roux continued, "it's entirely possible that I might have foreseen this very thing happening. And I decided that I needed to take steps to rectify the situation before something very old and very powerful fell into the wrong hands."

"Much the way you told me that the sword might have led me here."

Roux smiled, his eyes gleaming in the early twilight. "We are both beholden to the same things."

"Sometimes," Annja said. "We haven't always seen eye-to-eye."

"True," Roux said. "But when we do, it is something that borders on deep friendship."

Annja regarded him for a moment. "How did it go when you took it back?"

"The place is a mess, of course. Heinkel certainly made a convincing show of it with his explosives, but the Jiao are a resilient bunch. They'd already made a number of repairs and have been trying to figure out how to power their world."

"So they greeted you like a savior?"

Roux chuckled. "I was afraid of being met with violence, but yes, they were quite relieved. I think they made me an unofficial ambassador or something like that. In any event, it won't matter. They sealed the entry in the cistern. I doubt they'll be having any more visitors. That is probably better than the way things were."

"You really believe they'll be safe that way?"

Roux shrugged. "I have no idea. I could only suggest they do certain things. Apparently there's a bit of a power struggle going on right now. I made sure I conducted my business and then got out of there before one side tried to use me as a pawn in their quest for glory."

"Smart move," Annja said. They started walking again and the main pavilion loomed ahead of them.

"So, what happens now?" Roux asked. "You came all this way to see if you were right about me?"

"I figured you had to have the pearl when Vic told me you'd up and disappeared. That led me to believe that you had to have been following me underwater throughout most of the chase from the boat."

Roux smiled. "It wasn't exactly easy. And that thing you did with the shark—most amazing. Still, I hung around long enough to see you take care of business. And then when Spier swam off, I followed him. He had a bunch of minisubs a few hundred yards away. They were all gassed up and ready to use as their escape method."

"So, you availed yourself of one of them, I take it?"

Roux grinned. "Well, it would have been a waste not to. And me having to lug the pearl back, it just made sense."

"Where in the world did you surface?"

"Newport, Rhode Island, actually," Roux said. "I happen to know a lovely woman there who let me shower and get changed. And then, it was a simple matter to arrange transportation and get on a ship."

"While I was recuperating in a hospital on Martha's Vineyard," Annja said. "And then dealing with Spier showing up at my home—*my home!*—unannounced."

"I sent you flowers," Roux said.

"A poor substitute for actually being there," Annja said with a sigh. "But it all comes out in the wash, huh?"

Roux nodded. "I'm starving. I think I could very probably eat one of those roasted pigs all by myself."

Annja smiled at him. "Is that an invitation?"

"Does it need to be? Why can't two old friends just sit down and have a decent meal together?"

"I never said they couldn't," Annja said. "Just go light on the whiskey tonight, okay?"

Roux feigned shock. "Are you dictating how I should lead my life now?"

"Not exactly."

"Well, good, then." Roux stopped in front of a cabana. "I need to get changed. They tend to frown on wet suits as dinner apparel."

"With good reason," Annja said. "It's a terrible look for dining."

"Is it?"

"There's a similarity to a penguin, I think," Annja said.

"In that case, I shall endeavor to present myself better." Roux headed up the walkway. Annja watched him a moment longer.

"Don't stand me up, Roux. You don't want to see me upset."

Roux laughed. "I've seen you upset, Annja. And I wouldn't dream of standing you up."

"In that case, I'll see you there."

Annja walked on toward the pavilion and turned to watch the sun sinking below the horizon. She could see the first stars coming out in the night sky and felt relaxed.

Genuinely relaxed, she realized.

She walked into the pavilion. As she did so, she met the waiter en route to the small table at the edge of the pavilion overlooking the beach and the crashing surf.

"Good evening, Miss Creed," the waiter said. "Two for dinner tonight?"

Annja smiled. "Yes. How's the *lechón?*"

"Simply incredible, if I do say myself. I dug the pit for it earlier today and the wait has been worth it."

Annja nodded. "That sounds wonderful." She sat down and stopped the waiter just before he left.

"Tell me something—do you have any Krug champagne?"

* * * * *

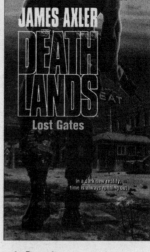

The Executioner®

Don Pendleton's

HAZARD ZONE

Washington becomes ground zero for bioterrorists...

A luxury Jamaican tourist resort turns into a death trap when a vacationing American senator's daughter is murdered. When her body is then used to unleash chemical warfare on the U.S., it's clear this wasn't just a random crime. It was a message—and Mack Bolan intends to respond... even if it means bringing the battle back to Washington.

Available October wherever books are sold.

GOLD EAGLE®